THE H D0790375

"Excellently crafted and lyrically penned, Kristin Landon's *The Hidden Worlds* explores loyalty, politics, intrigue, and desire as two protagonists from divergent worlds find themselves pawns in a game much larger—and much more deadly—than either realizes. Landon's sharp characterization and deft twists and turns of plot keep you hooked. A riveting read. I highly recommend it." —Linnea Sinclair, author of
Hope's Folly

"[A] promising debut novel." —*Sci Fi Weekly*

"With an interesting concept and deftly drawn characters, this is a fantastic science fiction yarn. Landon's created a world with plenty of intrigue and action and high-tech devices while still leaving it accessible for readers new to the genre. There are layers of complexity here, both moral and political, that are sure to give readers plenty to think about."
—*Romantic Times*

"Kristin Landon has written a spectacular sci-fi thriller."
—*The Best Reviews*

"Kristin Landon's novel *The Hidden Worlds* is a space sci-fi with a splash of romance and a dash of politics mixed together to make a very interesting read . . . The story is a great emotional ride." —*Yet Another Book Review Site*

Ace Books by Kristin Landon

THE HIDDEN WORLDS
THE COLD MINDS
THE DARK REACHES

THE DARK REACHES

KRISTIN LANDON

ACE BOOKS, NEW YORK

THE BERKLEY PUBLISHING GROUP
Published by the Penguin Group
Penguin Group (USA) Inc.
375 Hudson Street, New York, New York 10014, USA
Penguin Group (Canada), 90 Eglinton Avenue East, Suite 700, Toronto, Ontario M4P 2Y3, Canada
(a division of Pearson Penguin Canada Inc.)
Penguin Books Ltd., 80 Strand, London WC2R 0RL, England
Penguin Group Ireland, 25 St. Stephen's Green, Dublin 2, Ireland (a division of Penguin Books Ltd.)
Penguin Group (Australia), 250 Camberwell Road, Camberwell, Victoria 3124, Australia
(a division of Pearson Australia Group Pty. Ltd.)
Penguin Books India Pvt. Ltd., 11 Community Centre, Panchsheel Park, New Delhi—110 017, India
Penguin Group (NZ), 67 Apollo Drive, Rosedale, North Shore 0632, New Zealand
(a division of Pearson New Zealand Ltd.)
Penguin Books (South Africa) (Pty.) Ltd., 24 Sturdee Avenue, Rosebank, Johannesburg 2196,
South Africa

Penguin Books Ltd., Registered Offices: 80 Strand, London WC2R 0RL, England

This is a work of fiction. Names, characters, places, and incidents either are the product of the author's imagination or are used fictitiously, and any resemblance to actual persons, living or dead, business establishments, events, or locales is entirely coincidental. The publisher does not have any control over and does not assume any responsibility for author or third-party websites or their content.

THE DARK REACHES

An Ace Book / published by arrangement with the author

PRINTING HISTORY
Ace mass-market edition / July 2009

Copyright © 2009 by Kristin Landon.
Cover art by Craig White.
Cover design by Annette Fiore DeFex.
Interior text design by Laura K. Corless.

ISBN: 978-0-441-01734-8

ACE
Ace Books are published by The Berkley Publishing Group,
a division of Penguin Group (USA) Inc.,
375 Hudson Street, New York, New York 10014.
ACE and the "A" design are trademarks of Penguin Group (USA) Inc.

PRINTED IN THE UNITED STATES OF AMERICA

10 9 8 7 6 5 4 3 2 1

For my family

Once again I thank Anne Sowards, for her patience and guidance; my writing group (Patty Hyatt, Karen Keady, Candy Davis, and Skye Blaine), for their continuing support and honest assessment; my agent, Donald Maass; and finally my family and friends, who were so patient with my absence and absences.

ONE

SANTANDRU: MORAINE

Linnea Kiaho stepped forward under the eyes of the village, her hands tight on the wreath of sea grass and pale yellow crocus flowers. The stark new memorial cairn loomed above her, a shadow against heavy blue-gray clouds, dominating the little square in front of the village church. The cairn's meticulously laid stones and new-white mortar gleamed, wet from the recent rain. Ready for its first Feast of Saint Andrew.

Linnea heard the shuffling and whispering of the villagers filling the square around the pillar. She felt their hard stares on her back. Her heart raced, her breath caught, as the wild impulse flared: to bolt for the skyport at Middlehaven, back to her jumpship, back to the rich, welcoming beauty of otherspace—

Back to her purpose, the work she could do best.

She took a deep breath. *No. Not yet.*

Carefully, with what grace she could muster, Linnea laid her wreath at the foot of the pillar, beneath the old metal plaque that had been moved there from the porch of the church. Beside the old plaque, a new one gleamed, etched with the names of the men who had died more than five standard years ago in the explosion of the village's fishing boat, the *Hope of Moraine*. That disaster had driven Linnea from her village. Driven her to a servant's contract on the decadently luxurious world called Nexus. Twisted her life into a strange new shape.

Linnea made herself look at the old, fogged plaque, searching the ranked columns of names for the one she had always sought as a child. DONIAL PIOTR KIAHO. Da, drowned sixteen years ago. His face had mostly faded from her memory. She bent her head in the ritual gesture of grief, then stepped back to her place in the crowd.

Marra, beside her, was next. Linnea watched as her sister laid her own wreath at the base of the new plaque, flanked by her children Orry and Rosie, whose father had died when the *Hope* was lost. A cold, rising wind ruffled the flowers piled around the cairn, hissing around the hard stone corners of the church, flapping the heavy skirts and shawls of the village women. The dark morning was getting darker. Linnea glanced up the village street toward the ridgetop, to judge the weather coming in from the sea. Strange how black that one cloud was. . . .

Then she saw the flames at the base of the cloud. Smoke. Fire, licking up from behind the long row of houses. Fire at the top of the street. She took a breath to shout. Then saw the others there, watching her. Looking from the fire to her. Keeping silent.

So they knew of it, and still went on with their ceremony. No one had cried the alarm. Which meant—

"Marra," Linnea said, her voice strained and strange, "they're burning Ma's house."

She would not let them see her hurry. She walked, steadily, beside Marra up the steep, muddy street, at the head of a silent crowd of villagers. Near the top of the slope, she stopped. Ahead, clear to see now, was the small house where she and Marra had been born, where they had lived all their lives until the *Hope* was lost.

The house was nearly gone. A column of flame, greasy with the black smoke of burning plastic, blazed against the darkening sky. A few men stood silhouetted against the flames. Watching. Making sure it didn't spread.

Marra caught up to Linnea and stopped beside her, looking aghast at the fire. "Linny," she said, her voice thick with tears. "Why would they do this? No one was even living there."

Linnea did not answer her sister. *You know damn well why.* She started forward again, splashing through the wind-ruffled puddles that filled the ruts in the street. Icy water soaked the thin, city-made shoes she had put on for the memorial ceremony. The men watching the flames did not turn as she approached. Well before she reached the stone fence around the old house, she felt the heat of the flames against her skin. They must have started it with lamp oil—it would never have burned so fiercely on its own.

Linnea turned and faced the crowd of watching villagers. At their head, close behind her—as she had expected—a tall, heavyset man in the long black robe of a priest stood looking past her at the flames, his hands in the pockets of his raincoat. She took a step toward him. "Father Haveloe. Why?"

The priest looked down at her, his broad ruddy face set grimly. "You know why. An infested man entered that house. For all we know, some Cold Minds nanobots are still lurking in there."

Linnea's fists clenched. "The house was cleaned completely," she said. "Marra told me what they did. There was no chance that anything was left." She took a breath. "That house was my sister's property. It was important to her family. She could have sold it for school fees for the children."

From the corner of her eye she saw Marra's chin tremble, saw her clutch Orry closer.

"The house was, of course, the property of Marra's new husband," Father Haveloe said. "Not hers. But in any case, there are higher matters than property rights. The safety of this village is paramount."

"Then why did you wait until now to burn it? Until Marra was here to watch? That was cruel!"

He shook his head slightly, pityingly. "They weren't thinking of Marra."

She said nothing, but his meaning was clear: They had done this because *she* was here. *To put an end to any thought that this village was still my home.*

Linnea took her place at Marra's side again, slid an arm around her sister, and stood silent for a while, watching. Beside her, Marra wept quietly as the home of their childhood collapsed into lopsided ruin. The metal frame of the house creaked and sagged, part melted by the intensity of the flames from the ancient plastic floors and walls and windows. No one had dared to live there in the two years since its contamination.

Linnea looked around at the faces of the men watching the fire. Some she had known all her life. Eddo the medtech—she'd thought him a friend, a sensible man. Beyond him stood an old neighbor, one of the few Moraine fishermen who hadn't been out on the *Hope* when it blew, all those years ago. He gave Linnea a cold glance and turned his back on her.

As she watched the fire, the wind rose, and the black pillar of smoke tilted, diffused, spread. The sky beyond was almost as dark, and spatters of rain began to fall. Marra shook her head and left silently with the children for the shelter of their room down at the guesthouse.

Linnea knew she should go, too. There was nothing more to see. Nothing but the message the burning had been meant to send her.

And there was nowhere to go. So she turned her back on the guesthouse, the church refectory, and breakfast, and walked instead past the fenced yard of her ruined house, up the steep path to the ridgetop overlooking the sea.

At the crest, the wind met her like a wall, and her eyes streamed tears from the force of it. The sea stretched out below her, cold, bleak, and empty, the surf near the shore clotted with yellowish foam. Farther out, a glimmer of pure white through the mist told of heavy breakers offshore. She could hear the rumble of surf, taste the salt on her lips.

She wished Iain were here. He would remind her that he had warned her—yet he would also understand, too well, what losing her old home meant to her. Knowing that it was here, even if not for her, had given her another reason to fight.

But Iain was not here. No, the notorious ex–Line pilot Iain sen Paolo had stayed in Santandru's one city of Middlehaven, declining to exhibit himself to her village.

And maybe that had been wise. She'd heard the inevitable whispers about her Pilot Master lover. One of *those*, one of the aristocratic brotherhood of jump pilots who had controlled travel and communication throughout the Hidden Worlds for six centuries. She shivered in the cold, remembering.

Iain had never been one of the Line, not truly—a great scandal. Even though he was a pilot, with the rare gift that allowed him to guide jumpships through otherspace, he was one of her own humble people by ancestry. A grandson of this backwater world of Santandru. The revelation of that long-held secret had helped put an end to the powerful monopoly of the Pilot Masters, the lords of Nexus.

And, some said, it had broken the will of the best defense still left to humans in the Hidden Worlds. She pushed the thought away and walked north along the ridgetop, picking her way carefully in the steady wind.

Even knowing that Iain was really one of them had made no difference to her people. To them he was what he'd been bred up to be—as corrupt as the world that had reared him.

Linnea's coat, rain gear borrowed from Marra, flapped behind her like a flag snapping in the wind. No, she could understand why Iain had stayed in Middlehaven. He'd be working to prepare their two jumpships for the next leg of their planned loop through the scattered worlds of the Rimini Fading, to inspect the newly trained jumpship patrols assigned to watch out for any hint of Cold Minds ships.

The need to make this trip had grown in Linnea in the months after she and Iain returned from Nexus, from the brief, sad victory the remnants of the Line had won there. That fight had cost what remained of the power of the Line; and the new patrols in the fringe worlds were reporting contacts with what had to be Cold Minds scout ships. She rubbed her hands along her arms, reaching for warmth that was not there. It was only a matter of time until the Cold Minds moved again—until another world fell to them, or was destroyed in order to save it.

But still Iain had agreed that he and Linnea should come here: He knew how desperately she needed to see her home. Because, of course, they traveled first to Santandru, to take Marra and three of her children home from their temporary refuge on Terranova—back to Marra's husband, Asper, a government official in Middlehaven. Linnea had flown Marra and the children out to Moraine together for this memorial ceremony—to lay their wreaths, to see their home village again.

And now she only wanted to be away from here, to travel away with Iain again, travel anywhere. He would be ready to leave. She knew he'd tried to hide his worry about the danger signs from the Cold Minds, his urgent wish for them both to return to their duties; but if this was what she needed first, to give her peace, then with all the great generosity of which he was capable, he wanted her to have it.

Yet Iain hadn't been able to hide his dislike for the bleakness of her world, the unfriendliness of her people toward a former Pilot Master, the bitterness of Santandru's leafless spring. She did not turn to look back at Moraine, but she knew the patches of dirt behind the houses and down toward the bay, knew that potato and cabbage plants were just beginning to straggle, pale green, up from the sodden earth. She knew the houses glistening dark in the rain, low against the slopes beyond, barren gravel rising toward the glacier and the mountains beyond.

Once this place had seemed warm, welcoming. Now she understood how small it was, how worn, how cold and comfortless. Perhaps two years living in the Terranovan capital of Port Marie, vividly sunny and lush with life, had changed her eyes.

Or perhaps it was the people here, once *her* people—turning away, pushing her away, resentful of the gift she had given them. She had been a fool to expect anything else.

Now she did turn, looking down toward the harbor, where the new fishing boat lay snugged against the quay. Marra had told her how glad they were to get the money Linnea had earned on Nexus to replace their fishing boat, how eagerly they'd used it to bring Moraine back to life. But in the end, in the result, proud people hated nothing so much as an obligation. Especially an obligation to an outsider.

She looked down at the rock of the ridgetop, splotched with pale green and orange lichen, but worn bare where generations of women had walked back and forth, watching for the *Hope*, for their husbands and sons returning safe from sea.

No. This place was not her home. And never would be again.

Icy rain stung her face, blurring the view of the village below. She was *not* weeping for this place, these people.

She would not give them even that; she would give them *nothing* more—no power over her mind or over her heart. *Shake it off, shake it off.*

She bent her head. But if this was not her home, where was it? And if these were not her people, who was? Those she happened to love? Those she happened to fight for?

No one?

A hand touched her shoulder, and she jerked with surprise. A looming figure in black—Father Haveloe. "It's foolishness, to be up here when you're not dressed for the weather," he said.

"I don't own any clothes for this weather," she said flatly. "But you're right. I've got to go and pack. It's time to leave, Marra needs to get the children back to school in Middlehaven—"

"The children that remain to her," the priest said. "Marra and I have talked. I'm worried about her, and I feel that I must speak to you."

"Then I'll listen," Linnea said coldly. *For Marra.*

He gave her a dark look. "Your sister is heartbroken that you lured away her oldest son to stay behind on Terranova. To study piloting—and who knows what else."

"He asked Marra's permission, and she gave it to him," Linnea said.

The priest looked sorrowful. "But how much did Marra understand? How much did you tell her?" He shook his head. "Left on Terranova, his mother gone, a boy of fourteen in the hands of the Pilot Masters—"

"He has the gift," Linnea said. "He has the right to learn to use it." *To be one of us, a pilot, maybe to die with us*—Oh, Marra had known.

"And then you come to our world, traveling openly with your Pilot Master lover—"

"I will not," she said, "allow you to speak to me about that."

"I once asked you to marry me," he said mildly.

"And I said no." She dug her hands deeper into the pockets of her borrowed coat and shivered. But she couldn't seek shelter yet. She would outwait him, see which way he went, so she could take a different path.

He showed no sign of turning to go. To make him angry, to drive him off, Linnea said, "They tell me you're going to marry Pirie Stayart, now that she's of age." His head went back, indignation of course, and she pressed on. "She'll make you happy. I never would have." She shook her head. "It's time for me to get back to my work. To my home."

He lifted an eyebrow. "And where," he asked, "is that?"

She looked into his pale eyes, knew he would not understand, but answered honestly anyway. A debt to herself, not him; she had lied to these people when she was younger, when she'd pretended even to herself that she was one of them. *Never again.* "My home is where Iain sen Paolo is. And his, where I am."

"Sad and rootless," Father Haveloe said, "with no future in it." He looked at her searchingly. "I could have made you happy here on Santandru. If you had been willing to try."

She lifted her chin. *I am happy,* she wanted to say, but he would hear the doubt in it; he sensed any hint of weakness, it had always been what he saw best in everyone. "I'll find my own happiness."

He looked at her for a long time. "No," he said at last. "No, I don't think so." His voice was low. "It's not your gift, Linny."

She jerked her gaze away from his, stared out to sea, into the wind and rain. He was wrong, wrong.

He set his big hand on her arm and squeezed gently. "Good-bye."

She could not help herself; she jerked her arm away from his touch. He only shook his head again, gently, sadly, and left her there. She watched him pick his way down the path, waiting stubbornly for him to pass out of sight.

She pulled the coat closer around her. His words had stung like a slap. *No gift for happiness.* Better to say she'd never had the gift of peace. Childhood here, poor and orphaned. Then servitude on Nexus, and torment from Rafael sen Fridric, who marooned her on a world infested by the Cold Minds. Then the war that began last year, salvaging the bitter loss the Pilot Masters had suffered in their attempt to retake Nexus from the Cold Minds. No rest, no home, never standing still.

The only constant was Iain. A man, not a place; not a home. Not enough of a home. She remembered Ma's words, years ago when she was dying: *Only fools depend on feelings.* Linnea'd had a place, here, years ago; and she'd thrown it away. For Marra and her children—because she'd loved them. For something better—the chance of something better—for all of them. It had come to very little in the end.

But not to nothing. Iain was waiting for her in Middlehaven, waiting with the patient warmth he had shown for so long. And then, back in their jumpships, they would return to otherspace—to the freedom, the sense of power Linnea found only there, piloting her ship between the worlds.

She closed her eyes against the failing light, and her heart raced. On the jump from Terranova to Santandru, she had felt the call of otherspace more strongly than ever: a yearning, a need, pulling her onward. And there were flashes, images, of strange, rich beauty—places she had never seen. Images that now filled her dreams—even here.

Those dreams, that beauty were all that still fed her spirit, giving her strength for the fight that would certainly consume her life: against the Cold Minds, endemic now in the Hidden Worlds. Perhaps never to be defeated. Humans had overcome the Cold Minds' first major attack, on Nexus, but the danger to every other one of the Hidden Worlds would never fade. Constant vigilance, constant work, patrols around every world to be maintained and inspected. A long, losing battle of attrition, Linnea foresaw it: falling back and back, surrendering bit by bit what she and Iain had once condemned the Line for refusing to defend. Maybe in one cruel way the Line had been right; maybe the few worlds they had proposed defending would be all that could, in the end, be saved.

If that much.

But Iain was waiting. Otherspace was waiting. That would be enough, for now. She started down the path toward shelter from the rain.

L inny, I was afraid of this from the start," Marra said. "I didn't want to say anything. But I thought something like this might happen. Maybe not this bad, but—"

"You thought they might turn on you, just because of me?" Linnea stood, leaning against the sill of the window in her tiny room in the guesthouse, the plastic pane cold against her back. Though it was past sunset, she had not lit the lamp, not even when Marra knocked and came in. There was nothing here that Linnea wanted to see. The room's air oppressed her, stale and cold, even though she'd set the little heatbox going at midday. The greasy fish stew from supper sat like a lump in her stomach. "Then why didn't you tell me to stay behind in Middlehaven?"

Marra folded her arms across her chest. "I wish now I had. If you hadn't come they—they might have left Ma's house alone."

"I'm sorry for that," Linnea said. "Iain and I will find a way to make it up to you. Pay you."

"No," Marra said, her voice steady. "We—Asper and I don't want any money from you. From *him*." She took a deep breath. "But, Linny, it's my fault, too. I was the one who talked you into coming here for the memorial service. I talked myself into hoping they'd welcome you back."

"Iain knew better," Linnea said bitterly. "He was right to stay in Middlehaven."

"He stayed because I told him to," Marra said.

Linnea's head jerked up.

"I warned him," Marra said. "If they—if the village saw you with him, there would be no chance they would forgive you."

"Forgive—" Linnea stared at her sister. "*Forgive* me for saving this village!"

"Forgive you for *how* you saved it," Marra said. Her voice was harsh, but Linnea knew there was compassion behind the words. Marra did understand; but Marra couldn't, wouldn't try to explain it to anyone else here.

"They accepted my money," Linnea said flatly. "They have no right to judge me. No right at all." She looked down at the worn plastic floor. "I did feel ashamed. At first. But that was—that was this village, thinking and judging inside my head. Father Haveloe, thinking and judging. Not me." She straightened. "I know who I am now, Marra. I know what I want."

Marra sighed. "And what is that, Linny?"

Linnea looked away, into the gathering shadows. *Freedom.* The soaring joy of otherspace, of openness, beauty, possibility. There was danger, yes, but with Iain at her side . . . "Nothing I can explain. I'm sorry." Her hands tightened on the windowsill.

"You *have* changed," Marra said, her voice hard. "I saw that on Terranova. This—life you've found for yourself. You don't care, you don't even understand what you threw away so you could have it."

"Yes, I do," Linnea said. It had taken her half a minute to look the room over when they got in last night: a narrow, sagging bed; a small table and two battered chairs; a basin on a low cupboard; a plastic tank of drinking water; the sharp, salty tang of mildew.

This morning, in the chill gray light, she had read the

handwritten list of rules tacked neatly to the wall. *Please keep a tidy room. Blankets on the shelf. Clean linens in the cupboard. Wash them at the village laundry—see map. Meals in the refectory in the parish hall.* Times for setup, for eating, for cleanup. *Please be present for all three. No liquor. Please attend church on Sundays. Eucharist offered each morning, thirty minutes after dawn. For questions, please see the village priest.* The placard was signed, in neat square printing, FR. HAVELOE.

"I know what I threw away," Linnea said. "And I'd throw it away again."

Marra sank down on Linnea's bed. Its metal springs screeched. "Then you really have moved on," she said, her voice thick with tears. "You and Iain, you took my son from me, my oldest, I'll never see him again. Or if I do, he'll be one of those people. Those *pilots.* Like you."

Linnea knew the next step in the old, familiar dance: She would go and sit beside Marra, hold her, comfort her for the pain of all the mistaken things Marra could not stop believing.

Yet she could not make herself move from the window. *No gift for happiness.* Maybe that was true.

Marra buried her face in her hands. "Linny—" She looked up. "I don't know how to say this."

"Say it anyway." Though she knew.

"It's—it's best you go."

Linnea took a steadying breath. Another. Her chest felt cold, hollow. *Don't let her see.* "All right," she said after a moment. "We can leave in the morning, as soon as the children are ready."

Marra went still, staring down at the floor. Then she said, "I bought tickets for the children and me on the flat-loader two days from now."

Linnea's head went back. "You would pay *money* to spend three days in the back of a 'loader, when I could get you home to Asper in a few hours, for nothing?"

"The flatloader is our way," Marra said, her voice stronger. "The flyer is yours. I have to live on this world, you see." She looked up at Linnea. "These are my people."

"So you don't mean—" Linnea took a breath. *Make her say it.* "You don't mean just, I should leave Moraine. You mean—"

"I want you to leave Santandru," Marra said. "And don't come back. Unless you're bringing my son home to me, to live the life his father would have wanted—don't come back. It's best."

Linnea stared at her. Then dug into the pocket of her tunic, brought out a few coins, slapped them down on the little table. "Give those to the priest," she said. "It ought to be enough to cover the hospitality I've had."

"Linny—"

She pulled the coat she'd borrowed from Marra off the peg, laid it on the bed beside Marra. "There's nothing else of yours I have?"

Marra took a shaking breath, clearly on the verge of tears. "That's all," she said.

Cold black tremors filled the hollow place inside Linnea. But her hands were steady as she stuffed her few possessions into her travel bag. "I'm off, then."

"Tonight! But, Linny, the wind—"

"I'm a pilot," Linnea said. "I know how to handle a flyer in wind." In the deepening dark, Marra's face was a shadow. Through the age-scoured plastic windowpane beyond, Linnea could see that the rain had turned to wet snow. The promise of spring, broken again.

Marra stood up, picked up the coat. "Won't you even say good-bye to the children?"

"Tell them—" Linnea broke off. "Tell them what you like. You will anyway." She held out her hand. "Good-bye, Marra."

Marra hesitated, then took the offered hand. Her rough fingers closed tight over Linnea's. "I didn't mean—I'm only thinking of my children's good. Of your good, Linny." Linnea heard the despair in her voice.

"My life's no concern of yours anymore," Linnea said. Then relented a little. "Look. I'll message sometimes. Through the commnet, so no one will have to know you've heard from me."

"I have no right to ask it," Marra said. Her voice broke. "But—tell me how Donie is. . . . And take care of yourself. Oh, be careful. Be careful. So much has hurt you, I wish you could just come home and be safe."

"But this isn't my home," Linnea said. As if through some stiff barrier, she took a step toward Marra. Kissed her cheek. "Good-bye, Marra."

Outside, coatless in the cold wind, the wet snow, in the blue dimness of almost-night, Linnea let herself shiver. The small landing field where her rented flyer stood was only a couple of hundred meters from the row of attached guesthouses. When she reached the flyer, she moved around it, hurriedly casting off the tie-downs as the little craft rocked in the stiff wind. Finished, she opened the hatch, tossed in her bag, climbed in after. Her hands moved over the board, lighting it, starting the engines warming. There was no one attending the field for her unexpected flight, so she'd have to risk lifting off without field lights— flying bare-eyed, without the intimate links she would have had with her jumpship, the visual interface that could turn night to day. No such thing in this little vessel.

Rising into the sky, sensing and compensating for the pressure of the wind, she kept her hands tight on the controls. Below, the few dim lights of the village sank away into the haze of falling snow, then the flyer shuddered in buffeting wind as she rose into the low clouds. All ties to ground gone. Flying free.

Rootless—No. The feeling of emptiness was freedom, that was all. Freedom at last.

Above the clouds now. The sky overhead, unusually clear

in the bitter wind, showed her the familiar hazy nebulae of the Hidden Worlds. They were calling to her, calling. . . . Her hands moved on the controls, and the flyer leaped forward toward Middlehaven. Toward Iain.

Toward her jumpship, and the freedom for which she had paid . . . everything.

TWO

SANTANDRU: MIDDLEHAVEN

Iain sen Paolo watched from the shelter of the control shed's wall as Linnea's flyer settled onto its pad, its jets sending up puffs of steam from the frozen slush. It was well past midnight and bleakly cold. Wind-driven snow made long slashes of white in the harsh beams of the field lights. His long coat, made for Terranova's mild weather, swirled around him, barely keeping him warm.

His apprehension held him back. He left it to the Middlehaven skyport ground man to secure the little vessel against the wind. Linnea's voice had sounded—strange, remote in her communications with Control. She had sent him no private message. And she was arriving two days earlier than they'd planned.

Iain grimaced and tugged the collar of his coat higher against the cold. On top of whatever her sudden arrival meant, he was not looking forward to telling Linnea the latest news from Terranova.

The hatch of the flyer opened at last, and he saw Linnea

scramble down, her old cloth travel bag slung over her shoulder. She turned and closed the hatch firmly.

So Marra and the children had not returned with her. Now that was a *very* bad sign.

Iain strode forward, into the wind, into the glare of the lights. She looked up, her eyes wide and dark, the wind streaming her black hair out behind her. Then she moved forward to meet him.

He kissed her quickly, then set his arm around her shoulders as they turned toward the control shed. Inside, in the close, wavering heat from an iron stove, he waited near the door as she settled her account for hiring the flyer. She seemed steady enough. Too steady, maybe, counting out the coins to the attendant. And that was another little insult dealt out by this world: hard currency only, for pilots' dealings with the port. *Your credit's no good here.*

Then it was back out into the bitter night, across half the field to the pilots' barracks, the quarters for the squad of young Terranovan pilots who made up Santandru's new orbital patrol. The building was new, made with materials brought in by cargo ship: a linked string of prefabs, laid out and inflated, their double walls of thick plastic filled with spray foam cure-hardened into rigid strength. No time, no money to build anything better.

Iain opened the door and waited while Linnea ducked through, then followed. Inside, the ceilings were low, the angles odd, but at least the thick, insulated walls cut off the howl of the wind.

At this late hour there were no off-duty pilots in the tiny front lounge, but Iain still waited to speak until they had reached the small room they'd been assigned. As soon as he latched the door, Linnea dropped her bag on her bunk. And then she was in his arms.

Her strong hold on him, her stubborn silence, made his heart turn over. He stroked her damp, wind-tangled hair. "Tell me."

Her face, turned away, was half-buried against his shoulder. "You were right," she said, her voice low and hard.

"They told you to leave," Iain said.

"No mistake about that," Linnea said. She took a breath, and another, while Iain waited patiently. Then, in a rush, she said, "But I didn't think that Marra would—" She broke off, and her arms tightened around him.

Marra, too, then. "Oh, no," he said. "Linnea. I'm so sorry."

She did not weep, of course; she wept far too rarely. But it was another four breaths, five, before she could speak again. "I want to leave tomorrow morning. Go on to our next stop. Get back to what we came out here to do."

Carefully, Iain released her, guided her to her bunk, sat down beside her. "About that," he said.

In the weak light of the little lantern, her face was stiff with distress, her dark eyes wild, trapped. "Iain, don't tell me we can't. I need—I need to get back to my ship. I need to move on. Get away from here."

"I see that," he said. "I'll get us clearance to leave tomorrow. But we can't go on with the trip we planned. I'm sorry. We're needed on Terranova."

He saw her expression shut down. "No. Please. We left Zhen and Torin and the new board in charge of training, and the Line was beginning to cooperate with setting the patrols. Surely together they can handle—"

"There have been five new Cold Minds incursions," he said. "Five that we know of."

He saw her frown as she absorbed that. "How bad?"

"One death," Iain said. "A ship found drifting in-system off Prairie, with a dead pilot—infested. He'd killed himself." Then he added quickly, "Not one you trained."

She said nothing.

"And an unmanned scouting probe vanished in the Terranova system—expensive, and too close to home. The Line Council has set a higher level of alert in the Terranova system. Zhen says it's straining our resources, keeping us from sending reinforcements out to the fringe worlds on schedule."

"I told you the Line would do that at the first sign of danger to Terranova," Linnea said, sounding irritated.

"And there's another matter," Iain said. "They refused your petition." He took her hand. "Torin sent a detailed report on the results of the debate. There will be no expedition to Nexus. The Pilot Masters say that the matter of what we discovered there last year is closed. They're angry, Linnea. The Honored Voice himself says you are not to present such a request again."

She shook her head. "How can they bury this?" she said. "How can they ignore what we found out about those Cold Minds pilots? We need new weapons, new defenses to help us in this fight. Or we'll lose. We'll *lose*, Iain. I know you understand that as well as I do, I see it in your face every day."

"But those poor maimed people—" Iain took a breath and made himself choose different words. "Those pilots. What is it you think we could have learned from them? They're gone, they're burned." He hated the memory of the mute, mutilated, permanently installed human pilots of the Cold Minds ships they had investigated on Nexus, after the grim, costly Line victory there.

"We might have been able to recover some genetic material from the burn pile," Linnea said. "We might have been able to learn how we are related. Who they are. We could guess where they came from."

"They can't be our brothers," Iain said, without thinking.

"We'll never know, now," Linnea said. "The Line has put them out of reach." She shook her head. "And I thought we killed them and burned them out of mercy." She lifted her chin. "But I see now. The Line doesn't want evidence of the truth. It would mean facing the fact that they failed at Earth. That they left living humans behind."

"We know that we did," Iain said. "We had no choice, Linnea. We—assumed they all died soon after, that none of them could possibly have survived." He looked down at his hands. "And they didn't survive. Not as humans."

"You saw the markings on their bodies," Linnea said. "Those tattoos. Flowers. Decorations. They *were* human."

Iain looked away, remembering: a chain of daisies around a wrist, a brightly banded snake twining up an ankle. Faded signs of a previous life that—Linnea was right—must have been at least partly spent in freedom. But as the pilots were, catatonic, eyeless, deeply and permanently linked to their ships—"We couldn't have done anything to help them, Linnea."

"Iain," she said, her voice unsteady, "you know what we're facing. Years, decades, of fighting the Cold Minds, we have to expect that—but centuries? Look at me. Answer me honestly. If we don't defeat the Cold Minds soon—do you think that, fifty years from now, any human will still be alive and free in the Hidden Worlds?"

He looked steadily down into her eyes, concealing the ache in his heart. "No."

"Then the fact that there are free humans still living in Earth's system is vital," she said. "Don't you see? Six hundred years after the fall of Earth, and they are still alive, still—some of them—free. We need to understand how they've done it."

Iain sighed. "But we can't, Linnea. Earth is too far. You know that." He spoke as gently as he could. "Any exploration mission to Earth would take far too long. Years would pass here. It would be decades before we got an answer. And for what? How could a pilot even find a few human survivors hiding in an entire solar system? And what could he learn from them if he did?"

"The human thing to do," she said stubbornly, "is to try anyway. Not to give up. Not to let a Line Council ruling stop us. We never have before."

Of course she would say that. "Please," he said. "Let it go. We have battles to fight right here in the Hidden Worlds. Torin says Hakon sen Efrem is whispering that you and the other non-Line pilots want the Line's move to Terranova to fail. You don't want them to rebuild their power."

She stood up. "He's right about the power."

"And it's let him do a lot of damage since you and I left Terranova." Iain rose and faced her. "We have to get back there and work to undo it."

"I wish you'd joined me in the petition," she said. "They respect you."

And not me. He heard the words as if she had spoken them. And, of course, she was right, about the older Council members anyway; despite her deeds on Nexus, Linnea Kiaho was still only a woman, only an outsider. But—

"You know why I couldn't," he said. "I can't spend my political capital on a—a side issue, Linnea."

"It is not," she said coldly, "a side issue. Not to me. Not to anyone who truly thinks it through."

Iain looked soberly into her angry eyes. No, it was not a side issue. If even a few fugitive humans still survived in the shadow of Earth, now the center and fortress of the Cold Minds—it should be impossible, and yet they'd both seen the evidence that it was true. Linnea was right: Understanding how humans had survived under those conditions could be vital.

But the Hidden Worlds were fighting their own war, right here, right now. How could Linnea, how could anyone waste time, energy, resources, on so slender a possibility, so dangerous a journey?

"We'll talk about it at home," Iain said. "Please. Let's go home. Marra is safe now. You're free to move on."

"I'm ready to move on," she said, her voice tight. "I'm

sick of being groundside. I can't rest. I want—I want to be
out in the stars, in otherspace." She looked at him squarely.
"Away from people judging me. From politics. From seeing
everything from seven points of view. It's the only freedom
I've got left. I need it so much, sometimes, sometimes I
think—" She broke off, and he saw that her eyes were
bright with tears.

"Linnea." He pulled her gently against him. "Tell me."

She was rigid in his embrace. After a long time, she
said, in a choked voice, "I'm having—dreams."

The back of his neck prickled. "Dreams about—"

"About otherspace," she said. "I dream about it all the
time." Her voice was distant, slow. "Every night. I dream
about what I see in otherspace—pictures, images, places
I've never been. And all I want in the dream is to get there.
I wake up crying, I want so much to be there. It—it calls to
me. Somewhere out there is my home." Her voice changed,
tightened again. "But I don't know where it is."

She could not go on. He stood there holding her, his
hand absently caressing her hair, but he stared off into the
shadows across the room, his heart beating slowly with
dread. This happened sometimes, to young, new pilots.
Othermind, the Line called it—that, and blunter names. He
felt cold, remembering. Othermind could end a career,
ground a pilot forever.

But Iain had thought Linnea was past the risk. Too well
trained, too experienced. Otherspace overwhelmed the
mind and senses, its beauty undeniable; he loved it himself,
missed it when he had been groundside too long. But this
mindless yearning—He hid his face in her hair.

This happened sometimes.

This was madness.

Linnea shivered in the cold, still morning air. Santandru's
distant, pale sun, masked by a thin haze, hung low over

the snowy eastern hills. Its light did not warm her as she walked around her ship again, her booted feet crunching in frozen slush. Once again she checked that all fueling and power connections had been properly released, all supply ports were sealed, the skin seamless as it should be. Ready for launch.

She still did not feel completely one with this ship. Iain had urged her to accept it, new from the yards, when the chance came, and she hadn't resisted. The old ship Iain had stolen for her had suffered damage on Nexus that left it better suited to short training jumps in local space; it could no longer land or take off safely in planetary gravity.

This jumpship was a beauty, a long narrow knife blade of gleaming gray metal with none of the usual marks of age or wear from many atmosphere landings. Its smooth skin was unbroken by ports; when Linnea piloted in normal space, she "saw" with the eyes embedded invisibly in that skin, not through any window.

And in otherspace, of course, she could not see at all. Not in the same way. She had only the inner sight, entirely within her mind—the experience no pilot could describe in words, even to another pilot.

She brushed her hand along the chilly metal, seeing the blurred reflection of her own face, dark against the white glare of the hazy sky. This ship had a range far beyond her old one. It could carry three passengers safely on a long jump, swaddled in its state-of-the-art passenger shells, and it had supply and recycling capabilities to match. Even though it was larger than the expensive Line linker ship that had been Iain's since boyhood, it was almost as fast and maneuverable. Torin had been justifiably pleased with the ship, the first of a new model come fresh off the yards on Terranova, and he had presented it to her with obvious pride.

And yet the ship still felt like a new winter coat—a little stiff, a little strange.

But it would take her where she needed to go.

She had persuaded Iain to make one stop on the way back to Terranova, to check on the patrols at the little farming world of Paradais. That would give her two more jumps, not just one, before it all ended—before she and Iain were tied down again to Terranova orbit and the political wrangling groundside in Port Marie.

Two more jumps. Two more chances to open herself to otherspace, to let herself listen.

"Good morning, Pilot," Iain said behind her. "Ship status?"

She turned and forced a smile. "I could leave this moment."

He did not answer her smile. "I've scheduled us with the portmaster," he said, "for launch at noon."

She looked at him for a moment, and clenched her jaw to keep from shivering again in the still, icy air. "That's hours yet. Why the delay?"

"Let's go aboard," he said.

"You don't need to check my boards, you know," she said, flushing.

"It's not that. There's something I don't want to discuss in the barracks."

She turned and set her palm on the slightly duller oval of metal beside the hatch. The cold from the metal bit into her skin, but she felt the faint vibration as the hatch dilated in response to its pilot's touch.

Inside, through the tiny lock, the narrow passenger compartment was warm, silent, brightly lit. Three empty passenger shells hung closely stacked against the far bulkhead. Storage lockers crowded the rest of the space. But Iain had already moved through the door to the pilot's compartment. It was comfortable, almost roomy for one person, with a tiny refresher compartment and a workstation and chair for use in port if the pilot chose to live aboard. Silently, Iain gestured Linnea into the chair.

She sat with a feeling of dread. He leaned against the bulkhead opposite and folded his arms. The dark piloting shell loomed in the center of the space, a barrier between them, half-hiding him.

"I'm worried about you," he said. His voice was quiet, but she saw how rigidly he held his folded arms. Control with Iain, always control. Especially when he was afraid. "It's these dreams."

"Everyone has dreams," she said.

"Tell me that they have only been troubling you since you came to Santandru," he said. "Tell me that your urge to get back to otherspace, back to the jump, only came when you knew you had to leave here."

He was inviting her to lie to him. What could frighten him so much? "But that's not how it is," she said. "This has been coming over me since the jump from Nexus. It got worse when I had to make that run to the yards on Kattayar and back. Worse yet on the way here."

"Worse," he said. His eyes were dark, unreadable. He looked down at his booted feet. "This can be—a difficulty. A danger, with new pilots."

"You mean other pilots have these dreams?"

"Some," he said reluctantly. "Images from otherspace, things they remember there, that come back to them in their dreams."

"Iain, these aren't anything I *remember*," she said. "I've never seen them before. A canyon, red rock, bigger than any in the Hidden Worlds. A jungle that goes on all the way to the horizon. There's nothing like that here."

"You may think you've never seen those images," Iain said. His voice was tight. "But you have, you must have. Your mind supplies them out of your memories, to explain what you experience in otherspace. The emotion you talked about, too—that's a response to the strangeness, when it threatens to be overwhelming. It's a sign that you're—you're letting too much in. You're too open."

Make him say it. "What are you afraid of, Iain?"

"Sometimes," Iain said reluctantly, "pilots like that—they jump to otherspace and—never come back."

She got to her feet. "You think I'm weak. That I'm going to fail. After all this time." She let him hear the anger in her voice.

"I know your strength," he said with obvious pain. "More than I ever would have believed, in the beginning. I trust you, Linnea." He took a breath. "But you're not well. You may need—rest."

The breath left her body. *Rest.* He meant not piloting. Maybe never piloting again. Panic caught at her throat, and she breathed carefully, mastered it.

She set her hand on the piloting shell. He must not see the fear that filled her mind at the thought she might be grounded, cut off forever from otherspace, beyond the reach of—of whatever it was that spoke to her there. *Tell him what he needs to hear.* "Iain, what can I do? How can I show you that I'm all right?"

"You and I will review some of the techniques Line pilots learn, for lessening the impact of otherspace." The patient compassion in his voice only frightened her more. He was speaking to her as he would speak to a child. Or to a person with a deadly illness. "I went over them with you in training, but obviously not well enough."

She remembered that part of the training. "You want me to deliberately close myself off from otherspace," she said. "Blind myself to everything but my course, the timing of the jump. Is that it?"

"Otherspace is too much," Iain said. "Too much for anyone. You don't look directly at the sun."

She smiled stiffly. "I can't say that came up very often, growing up here."

The worry in his face did not ease. *Keep pushing.* She went to him, set her hands on his arms. "Iain. I'll be all right. It's just—worry over Marra, over coming back to

Santandru, that's all. But we'll review those techniques if you want, and I'll try to learn them."

At last his tense expression eased, and he set his hands on her waist. "And you'll use them," he said, giving her a gentle shake. "Promise me."

Her heart gave a thump. "I will try."

He looked down at her searchingly, then seemed to realize that this was the only promise he would get. He leaned down and kissed her, and she tried to make the kiss another promise.

Because she was not sure, not sure at all, that she *wanted* to close herself off from the experience of otherspace.

Or that she even could.

THREE

SANTANDRU NEARSPACE

As Linnea guided her ship out to jump radius, with Iain's ship pacing her own, she let herself look back at Santandru. Through the close neural connection to her ship, she saw her home world slowly receding, a thin sunlit crescent of blue and gray and white. Even the ship's sharp "eyes" showed her no visible lights on the nightside of the planet: The tiny fishing villages were lit by fading power plants, or only by oil.

That was her world. And she might never see it again.

With an effort, Linnea turned her eyes and her thoughts away, remembering Iain's words this morning: *Do nothing that makes you feel emotion. You must always be calm when you face otherspace.*

Linnea's mouth twitched in a bitter smile. She knew Iain had not followed that rule last year, when they finally made their escape from the contaminated ruins of Nexus. He'd tried to hide his grief, then and in the long months since. *Don't feel—always safer not to feel.* The custom of the Line, the custom his father had taught him. That she'd hoped she was finally beginning to break through.

She'd tried that way of living for a while—she'd thought it would numb her to the pain of memory, of what she had suffered in Rafael's hands. But, in the end, only Rafael's death had let her do that. That and time.

And her happiness with Iain.

She checked her distance from Iain's ship—steady, of course; they'd flown together so often. She must do this exactly right: She must prove to Iain that she was capable of piloting safely. Or, thinking to protect her, he would take away the last freedom that mattered to her: the freedom to use her piloting skills to fight the Cold Minds. Instead, she would become something else he had to protect. A burden. Useless.

Iain's voice spoke in her ear, relayed from his own ship but sounding as close as if he lay beside her in her piloting shell. "Radius achieved. Are you ready for jump?"

"Ready," she said.

"Focused? The way I taught you?"

Shut down, he means. "Yes," she said, her voice tight.

She heard his quiet sigh—knew he was forcing himself not to say more, not to make it worse. "The mark is Paradais," he said, "minimum radius plus twenty thousand, nightside. Pilot, have you the mark?"

"I have it," she said, visualizing it. She had never been to Paradais, but her shipmind stored multiple images of all standard jump points, and she had studied this one last night.

"Calm," he said. "Remember that, Linnea."

She did not answer.

After a moment, he said, "Engaging jump. Follow in five," and the green-circled mark of his ship vanished from her sight.

Linnea caught her breath.

Five.
Four.
Three.
Two.
One.

Her mind *flexed*, and the universe vanished. Her body vanished. For the first moments, in the utter absence of sensory input, she felt the usual prickle of panic. But she knew it would pass. She reached out in her mind and found the input from her ship, the shipmind an insentient but comforting presence, ready to respond if she "spoke" to it. Iain was beyond her reach now, of course; there could be no communication between ships in otherspace.

Be passive, Iain had said that morning. *Let otherspace come to you. Don't seek it.*

But she could not help seeking it. She stilled her mind, knowing that the body she could not feel would calm as well. It was like straining to hear a faint skirl of music carried on a night wind. Like the brushing touch of silk. Like the cool damp breeze before dawn.

And then otherspace was around her, enfolding her as she sailed through it, filling her mind and her senses and her heart. She stretched herself out, farther, farther, reaching for the beauty, for the soaring sense of freedom. Beyond anyone's reach. Joyous. Alone—

Wait.

Not alone. . . .

A ghost-touch seemed to slide along the back of her neck. A physical sensation that she should not, could not feel.

But this had happened before.

With it came, again, that sense of an *other.* Another mind—out here. Not Iain, not the familiar, beloved presence she knew from jumps where they had been linked in the same ship. This was the faint, unfamiliar edge of a mind

she had never known. Except here, once, twice before—
sharp, questing. She knew what was coming, and braced her
mind for it.

This time it came as a wash of emotion—the fear of loss,
a longing for—something. Hope?

Longing and command. Wordless, but the meaning was
there:

Come to us.

Come to us, find us, we are here.

We are still here.

Then her inner sight filled again with an image like the
others that burdened her dreams. This was a new one, a still
image of a waterfall of incredible size and height, plunging
in a deep wide U into a misty blue abyss. A big yellow sun
hung low on the horizon beyond, rising or setting, touching
the mist of the waterfall to a veil of gold. She felt again the
knot of another mind's grief in her heart. *Lost to us forever,* the other mind said. Clearer now. *Gone into the
cold. . . . They're killing us. We need you. Hurry. Come.
Come now.*

No. Linnea pulled back into herself, in terror. *No.* She
was nowhere near Paradais yet, with long days to go even
in the jump; but the call had never been this strong before.
As she struggled to focus and quiet her mind, more images
bloomed and flickered in her inner sight: blue mountains
impossibly tall. Then a rocky coastline, with bright water
shading light blue to blue-green to indigo.

Then a broad tan desert covered with tall plants with
thick, curved branches.

Then ice, ice like home on Santandru—but burning
white in hard, pure sunlight. Not like home. Not like any
place she had ever seen.

No. She reached out unthinking, calling for Iain, seeking the familiar, seeking safety.

The wordless call again, carrying meaning somehow:
Come. You must come now. Soon it will be too late.

Yearning.
Direction.

A jump point, forming in her mind, a strange one: a world faintly banded in cold blue-green, no white at all; a globe of mist, half-lit by a dim sun she could not see. It was not any world she knew—a gas giant hanging alone among cold stars, bare in blackness, frigid, dark. . . .

Here, here. Nearer, louder, triumphant now—

No! Desperate, blind, alone, Linnea flexed her mind again.

Dropped out of otherspace.

Silence flooded her mind, as the clouded glory of the stars of the Hidden Worlds flooded her ship's eyes. She seemed to be hanging motionless among the silent stars and nebulae. Too far away from anything for any motion to be visible.

Alone in the dark of her piloting shell, she took a hissing breath and swore. A stupid trainee's mistake. She had panicked. And now it would take her half a day, more, to recalculate her present position, find the correct reinsertion vector for Paradais, make her way on along the hyperdesic to safety.

And it would take her more time than that to think of what to tell Iain. How to tell him.

How to tell him, in a way that would not make him certain she was mad, that now otherspace was speaking to her.

She took a breath, trying to slow the pounding of her heart. Someone was speaking to her in otherspace. Someone had summoned her. A human mind had summoned her.

Summoned her—it *had* to be—to Earth.

PARADAIS NEARSPACE

Iain sen Paolo stretched out his limbs again in sequence, in the familiar routine used by pilots confined too long in their shells: to ease his stiff muscles and, he hoped, clear his mind. His fingertips brushed against the smooth inner walls of his own shell. Weariness fogged his brain, swirled queasily in his stomach.

Two days he had spent here, in his ship orbiting the small, bright world of Paradais—ever since he had emerged from otherspace to find no sign of Linnea. No sign then or since. She had not appeared at the rendezvous.

Again fear prickled along his skin. Again he took a calming breath, forced his mind back to hope—a stone he had worn nearly smooth in these two days.

She will come, his mind told him, stubborn, disciplined as always; it was only his body, only his heart that feared. He would overcome it as he always had.

Once more he assessed the space around the ship. He was linked in; its eyes were his, and through them he could see in all directions. He turned his attention out-orbit, then in-orbit, scanning the bright limb of Paradais, thick clouds swirling over shining ocean. Then around to nightside, where the lights of a few small cities glowed.

His ship's systems would spot Linnea's jumpship before Iain could, but still he searched. Still, again, he saw only the familiar stars, the veils and folds of surrounding nebulae bleached pale by the nearness and brightness of Paradais. This world had little orbital traffic, and nothing was moving now. Only his own ship. Paradais had no orbital port where he might have waited in greater comfort, still within quick reach of Linnea when she appeared.

The voice of Paradais groundside spoke in his ear again. "Pilot sen Paolo? You didn't respond."

Iain sorted through his mind for the words that he had last heard. They still wanted him to land, eat, rest. The commander of the Paradais orbital patrol thought he'd been up here too long.

Best remind her who was senior. "It is not your decision, Ground," he said. "I will remain in orbit."

There was a pause. He knew she would not give up. She had responsibilities, and if anything happened to him, she would certainly have trouble with Terranova Central.

Her voice when she spoke was cool, measured. "If— when Pilot Kiaho arrives, our patrol ship can reach her just as quickly as your own ship could, and we can help her just as efficiently."

"I must be there as well," he said, and took a breath of the sour air inside his shell, released it slowly. Brought an image into his mind, the flame of a candle, a quiet tongue of light in a dark, still place. *Focus.*

"Sleep at least, Pilot sen Paolo," the woman's voice urged him. "You can sleep. Your ship will wake you if there is any change in the situation."

"I note your advice with thanks," he said, and broke the connection.

Though he could not see the dark interior of his shell while his vision was linked to the "eyes" on the hull, he could smell his own stale sweat. All the time in otherspace on the jump from Santandru, and the days in orbit. . . . The ship, as always, continued to sustain him with fluids and nutrition— and stimulants, until the shipmind had begun refusing his demands a few hours ago—but the shells weren't designed to be used for long periods in normal space, where the pilot could sense his surroundings.

Yet only in here, linked in, could he share his ship's eyes. Only in here would he be able to instantly spot and instantly assess any incoming ship.

Which would be Linnea's. Logic said it would be. Must be. He closed his eyes just for a moment, to focus, to think— drifted. Drifted. . . .

A windy beach, in a vast, flat, empty landscape under a gray sky. He saw Linnea—he knew it was Linnea: a dark figure far away, so far he could not call to her, but he sensed her restless spirit, the stubborn courage he loved. She stood gazing out to sea, her back to him.

Then he saw her begin to walk toward the water—white surf that foamed and churned in eerie silence. He must reach her, touch her—stop her. . . . He saw a wave break around her ankles, far ahead. But he could not run. His feet dragged in the sand. She was moving away, moving deeper—he was losing her. He could not catch her. He would have to follow.

Follow Linnea—

Iain jerked awake, the quiet new-signal alarm chiming in his ear. He forced his mind to alertness, scanned the sky. There, out-orbit, right at the chosen emergence point, he saw it: the orange ring the shipmind placed to mark an unidentified ship, too distant to see but visible to the ship's sensing systems. Then the ring flicked green, flagged with familiar call numbers.

Linnea's ship. He caught his breath.

And then he let his shoulders sag, let himself feel how tired he was—dizzy with relief. That was Linnea's voice, giving her name and call sign to Ground, requesting permission to land. He heard the weariness under the routine words.

He opened the private link between their ships. "Linnea. It's Iain. I'm in orbit. Are you all right?"

Another burst of communication interrupted before she answered, this time from Paradais Ground—assigning Linnea a landing site, speaking words of formal welcome. He heard exhaustion echoing his own in the flatness of Linnea's response. But she was following procedure. So far.

"Linnea," he said again on the private frequency. His voice was unsteady. What had happened? He would not ask her yet—he wanted to see her, see her eyes. Judge her condition. Know the truth, whatever it might be.

Again she did not answer him. He dug down into the anger that had built over the past hours and days, used its strength to make his voice cool and even. "Pilot," he said, senior to junior. "Report." If that new, insufficiently tested ship had given her trouble, he would—

Now she answered. "I'll explain groundside." Which was no answer at all. And still he heard that sinking exhaustion in her voice.

Before he could respond, the vector codes attached to her ship's symbol shifted, flickered to new values, and he realized that she was beginning her landing sequence. Which effectively cut him off from speaking to her; one did not interrupt a pilot during a maneuver, no matter how routine.

"Groundside, then," he said tightly, and broke the connection.

I ain settled his ship into its landing cradle at his assigned site beside Linnea's. It was night at the skyport, but the high yellowish field lights burned bright. He saw Linnea's ship steaming faintly as drizzle struck its hot skin. Then he cut off his connection to his ship, removed the sensory leads with careful urgency, disconnected himself from the support systems in the shell. For these few moments he could not see outside, could not see her ship. As he pulled a black coverall over his sweaty, aching body, he realized that his hands were shaking, his breath coming hard.

Fear flamed into anger. She'd had no right to do this, no right to risk herself. Her life did not belong only to her. It hadn't for years.

Dressed, booted, Iain dilated the hatch and climbed out onto the hard field. The warm mist fogged the lights, gave an eerie yellowish cast to the dark, shining pavement, the two or three off-duty patrol ships locked down and empty. He started toward Linnea's ship. His legs felt rubbery after the long jump, the many hours waiting in orbit, but he forced himself to walk steadily. Two ground crewmen were already helping Linnea's ship link to fueling lines, ground power, but no one had tried to open the hatch; it was not done, a pilot's ship was his domain. Her domain.

Never mind that. Without speaking to the crew, Iain slapped his hand onto the control plate next to the hatch, tapped out a pilot instructor's emergency override code. The hatch dilated, and Iain blinked as light spilled out. Without another thought or word of formal request he boarded and passed through into the piloting compartment.

She was there. She stood staring at him, clutching the coverall she had been about to put on. Her dark hair twined around her shoulders, matted and oily, as was to be expected after a jump. Her eyes were wide, dark. "Iain," she said.

In two strides he reached her, but stopped short of embracing her. He set his hands on her shoulders, looked hard into her face. "Are you all right?" Again he heard the raggedness in his voice, heard his own fear for her.

She looked away. He slid his arms around her, drew her closer. "Tell me."

She dropped the coverall, set her clenched fists on his chest. He felt the tension in her bare, slender shoulders ease slightly, but still she kept her eyes down, on her hands. "There was—I felt—" She broke off, and swayed against him. He caught her, steadying her.

Then she pushed away from him, picked up her dark blue coverall, and stepped into it. He saw her hands fumble with the front seal but did not reach out to help her. Covered, she ran her fingers through her hair and stared up at him. "How quickly can we refuel?"

Iain blinked at her. "We'll settle that after we've both rested, had some real food and a good night's sleep—"

"I don't need any of that," she said. She turned and leaned over her ship's status board, studying the readouts. "Just full fuel tanks, full supplies—"

"We're heading home," Iain said. "You don't need full supplies now."

She turned her head, and he saw the opaque reserve in her eyes. "Just in case."

Iain set one hand on the bulkhead, let it shore up his exhaustion. "Linnea—it was worse this time, wasn't it?"

"Better," she said distantly. "Clearer. I even—Iain. I saw a jump point. He, they, showed me a jump point."

Iain could not speak at first. Then he took a breath and said, "Let's go find our quarters." He took another breath, to keep his voice from showing his fear for her, or the grief for what he knew he must do. "We both need rest."

"I only want—"

"If you love me," he said, and he knew she could hear the edge of fear in his voice, "please—come and rest."

She looked at him for a long time, considering, and the band of ice tightened around his heart. But then she shut down the board with a sharp wave of her hand, straightened, came to him.

She came to him.

As he took her into his arms, his throat aching, he wondered if it would be the last time.

NEPTUNE PENUMBRAL SPACE
EARTH SYSTEM

Esayeh moaned. Always so hard to wake, to return, always so hard. He turned over and over, blind, knowing he was twisting the piloting leads plugged into his skull behind his left ear.

No matter. This time he'd done it: clear, definite contact.

Through the sparks of his joy his mind sent him a wandering melody, and he sang it, the words clear in his mind: *Out of the deep have I called unto thee—*

Familiar hands caught him, *her* hands, as they were always ready to do; her dry voice, Pilang's voice, the beloved friend of years and wandering: "Blasphemy, Esayeh?" Her hands pulled his rotation to a stop, uncovered his eyes, and he blinked hard in the dimness, all music fled.

"I did it," he said. "Connection. Connection, Pilang!"

"Oh, no doubt." She was unlinking him, *snap, snap, snap,* from the piloting plugs.

"No," he said, against the rising weariness; after all her patience, patience of years, he wanted her to see, to share this moment. "I made contact. I reached another pilot's mind. A pilot from the Hidden Worlds, Pilang."

Now she floated with her back to him, pretending to fumble with folding the leads into storage. She would not let him see her face, but he knew. She did not believe him. "I did it," he said stubbornly. "The first rope across the chasm. The way is opening."

She was silent for a while. "And you believe that now they will come? Just because of this—connection?"

"Now, at least, there's hope of it," he said. He caught her ankle, made her spin to face him. "Someone has to try," he said to the brightness of the tears in her eyes. "Or—"

She closed her eyes. Nodded. A bright tear floated free.

"Hope," he whispered, to her, to himself.

To all of their people.

FOUR

PARADAIS GROUNDSIDE

For the next two days, in the pilots' quarters at the sleepy little skyport, Linnea carefully did as Iain suggested in everything: resting, eating the good fresh food, sleeping long hours. She knew he asked it only for her sake, to help her, to keep her safe.

That only made it worse.

He'd locked down her ship the first night, she discovered. The following morning, Iain had left for a meeting with the patrol's commander and had insisted she stay in their quarters and rest. As soon as he was well away, she'd slipped out of the quarters building and onto the field, made her way through the sharp shadows of the bright Paradais sun to her ship's berth.

And she'd found what she feared: a lock-patch, keyed to Iain's hand of course, slapped down over the access pad. It blocked her own palm, even refused the instructor's tap-code she knew as well as Iain did.

She clenched her fists, set them against the hatch, and swore. This was her ship. *Her* ship!

And, being Iain, he'd let her discover for herself what he had done. He was afraid to hurt her—at least when he could see it happen.

Linnea sighed. She was just as afraid to hurt him. Since their talk after she'd arrived, she had said nothing more about otherspace. His fear for her was plain, and painful. But still, thoughts of otherspace rarely left her mind, and she knew that he must guess that.

She leaned her forehead against the hatch and closed her eyes. As he knew her mind, she knew his. If she forced Iain to name his fear openly, he'd be locked into the one course of action that would seem right to him: to take her back to Terranova as a failed pilot, to live out her life groundside or, at best, as his passenger. She would never have another moment of freedom in otherspace.

She lifted her head. *That must not happen.* She had heard the call. No one else had heard it, or even believed it was real. No one else could answer it.

The sense she got from that other mind, the other pilot—the sense of rightness, of completing something important—whatever was behind that could save them all. Even, she was sure, the one who had called to her.

And there was no one else to answer.

The second afternoon, after telling Iain she would rest, she stood motionless at the small window in their quarters, looking unseeing out at the clump of tall, silvery-leafed eucalyptus trees that sheltered the patrol leader's office shed. Thinking hard. If she left Iain behind, if she jumped as far as Earth . . . then, when she returned, *if* she returned, years would have passed for him, many more than for her. There was no reason he would wait for her, or even remember her kindly—a woman who had betrayed his trust, abandoned him, and abandoned what he saw as her duty.

But only Linnea could carry out this task. If Iain did not

believe her, did not understand, then no one would. And he had made it clear that he did not.

Heartsore, she made her decision. One from which there would be no turning back.

On the second night she lay awake long after Iain had drifted to sleep. Finally, restless, she slid out carefully from his embrace. He did not seem to wake. She sat in the dark, watching him sleep. Now that she knew she was going to try to leave, sadness weighed her down, an ache too deep for tears. In the weak yellow light from the nearby field, Iain slept on, his long black hair loose silk on his pillow, spilling over one brown shoulder, the strong lines of his face softened into peace.

She would not let herself count over the few years they had had. She pushed away the thought that this was cowardice, that she owed Iain a farewell. Because the moment he understood her intent, he would call port security and have her confined for her own sake. To protect her, he would disable her ship—spin down the jump engine. Maybe he would even let it unbalance, shattering the fine calibrations that kept its energies controlled when it was operating. The containment interlocks would crush it into nothing, irretrievable, never to be repaired.

Maybe he had already done it. She looked down at him, considering.

No. Iain had honor. He would not kill her ship without telling her.

It doesn't matter anymore.

She climbed back in beside him, curled against him, and held herself still until sleep took her.

In the morning, Iain was gone—an early meeting in the town, she remembered him mentioning it in passing. She rose, washed quickly, and dressed in her dark gray pilot's tunic and trousers—finely woven fabric, the most formal she owned. Fitting for a last voyage. Then pulled from under their bed the travel bag she had packed in secret last night.

She let herself out silently, willing herself not to look back at the empty room. She would see him again—someday.

She would hold to that hope.

Out on the field, in the blue-gray stillness before dawn, she made herself walk at a normal pace along the little row of ships. The one technician she passed looked at her without apparent surprise or interest, then bent back to her work on one of the patrol ships' fueling lines.

Linnea's heart gave a thump as she reached Iain's ship, stopped in front of its hatch. She had access, of course; and she was sure she could reach orbit even in a ship not specifically fitted to her. Orbit, and radius, and one short jump. Direction would not matter, after all; the jump would just be to put her beyond Iain's reach. Then, when she had laboriously made the ship her own, she would jump again. Jump, and listen. Wait for word.

She touched the cool, smooth metal of the ship's skin. This was Iain's ship, his own since his first year as a trainee in boyhood; and now she was stealing it from him.

But she was betraying so much else that mattered even more. Years of his trust, his love. His belief in her good faith. Against that, this theft would hardly weigh in the balance. She forced down a wave of guilt and raised her hand to the access pad next to the hatch.

And Iain's voice behind her said, "Linnea."

She froze. Then turned slowly to face him.

He was dressed as she was, in dark gray tunic and trousers: not quite the attire of a Pilot Master, but a sign of pride and serious intent. He stood formally upright, his hands clasped behind his back.

When she saw the leashed pain in his dark eyes, she could barely speak. "I'm sorry," she whispered.

"Sorry, for planning to steal my ship?" He did not move toward her, and his expression, firmly controlled, did not change. "But, Linnea, you can't steal it."

"You locked it down?"

He shook his head, patience clear in his eyes. "No. You can't steal it because—because, Linnea, all that I have is yours." His mouth quirked. "Not that it's much."

Now the tears came, burning in her eyes, in the back of her throat. Beyond the shadows where they stood, the first light of the sun touched the top of the clump of eucalyptus at the edge of the field. "I had to try, Iain," she said. "I couldn't give up."

"No," he said gently. "You never could." He touched his ship, and the hatch dilated. "Let's go in. There's something I want you to see."

She climbed in after him, and stood watching in his cramped piloting compartment as he woke the commscreen, sorted through files, and finally called up an image: a world hanging in the blackness of space, in half-phase, the continents strange to her and yet familiar, known from so many pictures and stories. Earth. Earth long ago, when it still lived.

She looked at him in puzzlement. Still he was watching her with that deep, considering gaze. "Linnea." He clasped his hands behind his back, as if to keep himself from touching her. "Tell me. Why is this so important? I know you hope to learn something, find a new weapon to use against the Cold Minds—but it's more than that, isn't it? What is it that makes you so determined to try this journey, alone, in a ship you don't know?"

She stood for a moment, fighting for calm. Pulling the words up, the thoughts she'd hidden from him for so long for his own pride's sake. "Remember those children we found when we went back to Nexus," she said. "Pilots' sons, left behind when their fathers escaped or died. Left alone. Forgotten."

He looked away for a moment, took a deep breath. "I remember them."

She chose her words carefully. She had to make him

understand. "They waited more than a year, without any hope, with the Cold Minds hunting them down, imprisoning them. Remember how afraid they were. Hiding like, like rats. And the boys the Cold Minds did catch—do you remember what we found?"

She saw the memory in his eyes. She knew how it had scarred his dreams. He nodded.

"But, Iain." Her voice shook. "These people—*our* people, just as much as those boys were—they've waited for six hundred years."

He was silent for a while. Then he sighed. "What if I join you in another petition to the Council? If we propose a properly supported expedition, men with experience and credentials—"

"They won't listen," she said. "The Line doesn't want to know. If there are humans alive in that system, that means some were left behind who could have been saved. Who waited, and hoped, for nothing. Who are still waiting."

"It was too dangerous," Iain said, an edge of anger in his voice. "After more than forty years of the rescue, the risk of losing ships was rising. And we needed those ships here, among the Worlds. If anyone was left behind, it was not done deliberately. And they could have followed."

She faced him. "Could they? Did they have jumpships of their own? Pilots of their own?"

"They must have," Iain said. "But maybe not enough will. Or enough skill."

"Or—they didn't know where we went."

"You mean that my fathers kept the secret from them." His dark eyes sparked with anger. At the Line, or at her?

She set her hands on his arms. "The Line used their disciplines, the ones you tried to teach me, to blind themselves. Don't you see why? They were closing the door behind them, Iain—closing it and locking it."

"But the Line never forgot Earth," Iain said.

"They never forgot their *dream* of Earth," she said bitterly, remembering shards of sapphire in a ruined chamber, the dripping of dark water, blackness and rot. "They never forgot Earth the way it was in the old stories. In their minds, they failed no one, abandoned no one. But the truth—" She looked up at him. "Someone wants me to find the truth. Someone in Earth's system."

"It's too far," he said, openly angry now. "Even a ship like yours can't sustain you over a jump that long."

"It will," she said with a confidence she did not feel. "It's new, it's powerful. Fully stocked, it should last. And you know I can make an efficient jump. I'm a good pilot, Iain."

He was silent. Assessing her madness, deciding on a course of action? Then he said, "I brought you in here for a reason. I want you to tell me your dreams. Describe one of the images you saw."

She blinked at him impatiently—then called up the memories. The most vivid was the red canyon, kilometers deep, with snow dusting the walls and ledges and the vast pillars of rock rising from its floor, fresh snow falling on the far rim.

Before she had half described it, he said, "Is this what you saw?"

She looked at the commscreen, and her breath leaked away. "That's . . . that's exactly the image I saw, Iain."

"And you have never seen it before?" His voice was calm.

"No," she said firmly. "Never."

"It was called the Grand Canyon," Iain said. "In a place named Arizona. Another?"

One by one she described them; one by one he called up the images, and they were the same: the ones she had dreamed.

Places she had never seen.

Now they were looking at each other, and she felt the same fear she saw in his eyes. "What are these, Iain?"

He sighed. "These are images we—men of the Line use

in some of our private meditations, to focus our minds on Earth. They're part of a collection that our ancestors brought from the Earth system. They've been—part of the inmost secrets of the Line for all these years. Sacred, you know that word? You could not ever have seen them, not growing up on Santandru. We don't share them. We don't publish them. They're—part of the Sorrowing. Which we also don't discuss."

She was silent for a while, looking at him. Then she said, "So they're real places? Places on Earth?"

He was silent.

Time to press. "Iain. Do you believe me now?"

She saw how that hurt him, but did not regret it. But he shook it off. "This jump point you mentioned," he said. "What did you see?"

She described it for him: the blue-green gas giant. The blackness of space, bitter and bare without the Hidden Worlds' comforting nebulae. The sense of cold and isolation, far from the warmth of the sun.

And as she described it she saw his eyes change, saw pain fade, replaced by questioning.

"There is no planet like that in the Hidden Worlds," Linnea said. "I know it. I searched through the atlases for every system. There is no sky like that anywhere. And the world—it wasn't Earth, but—"

"There is a world like that in Earth's system," he said quietly, and touched the commscreen again.

The world she had seen hung there, cold blue against infinite emptiness. A different image, in full phase, but the same world.

Unspeakable relief flooded her. *So that, too, is real. He sees that it is real.*

"I have to try this, Iain," she said, her throat tight with tears. "I know the way. I can bring those people hope." She looked up into his face, dark in the dim light of his ship, willing him to understand. To believe her. "And they can

give hope to our people. Do you see? They've survived in
the shadow of the Cold Minds. Defended themselves, somehow. Think what that might mean for us, for our people."
She swallowed hard. "This is more important than one ship,
one life."

He was silent for a long moment. Then he reached out
and took her hand. "One life—or two."

Of course she would be breaking his life as well, in leaving him. She felt a tear slide down her cheek and took his
hand in both of hers. "I have to try," she said again, thinly.

"I do see," he said, and took a breath. She waited for his
words: words of return to Terranova, confinement, the end
of her freedom, all for her good. But then he said, "You
can't go alone." As she stared up at him in shock, he set his
hand gently on her cheek. "I won't *let* you go alone. Did
you think I would?"

She could not speak.

"I can't follow you through otherspace in my own ship,"
he said. "So I'll travel in yours."

She stood there frozen, realization a cold trickle down
the back of her neck. When she found breath she said, "Are
you sure?"

"Yes," he said. "I know you, Linnea. I know what makes
you judge the way you do. And I've seen it: You judge
rightly. So I'll follow." He raised her hand in his and kissed
it, soberly, formally. "Take us to Earth."

SEVEN DAYS LATER

I ain sen Paolo lay, tense, immobilized, in the darkness of
his passenger shell—running through the prelaunch
checklist in his mind just as Linnea, in the piloting shell,
was doing in reality.

As a courtesy, she had linked him in to all of the ship's
displays, even though his shell could have no control

capability. Using those links, he could have followed her
progress directly. But he knew—oh, how well he knew—
how Linnea hated the feeling of anyone watching over her
shoulder. Even the man who loved her, whom she'd learned,
it seemed, to trust. So he was with her only in thought.

His internal sight showed him the wide, bare landing
field around the ship—the ground crew withdrawn to
safety, red warning lights set into the pavement spinning to
mark the danger zone. Sharp purple shadows stretched far
across the sunset field toward the edge of the trees. Iain had
spent almost no time on Paradais, in his career as a Pilot
Master, and he regretted that now. He wondered if either of
them would ever come here again.

The week of preparation had been intensely busy. Linnea had insisted, and Iain agreed, that they would prepare
thoroughly for the jump, all supplies at maximum; Iain
passed it off to Paradais Ground as part of the shakedown
run for Linnea's new ship. They had the ground tech crew
check every system in the ship, and Iain tested them as
well. They added extra air-recycling and water-purifying
capacity by having the units built into two of the three passenger shells, under Iain's close supervision—though it
drained what remained of his offworld letter of credit almost to nothing. He would travel in the third shell, now
half-hidden by reserve storage for food and oxygen.

Of course Paradais Ground suspected that something
strange was up. But the habit of obedience to Line orders
still persisted; even though they knew Iain was not, offi-
cially, Line, they knew he and Linnea had power on Terranova, knew that their world's protection from the Cold
Minds depended on the pilots Iain and Linnea were, partly,
in charge of training.

Iain's left arm and shoulder ached coldly where the
connections for food, fluids, and drugs had just snaked into
place. At Iain's insistence, three days ago the best clinic on
Paradais had thoroughly examined him and Linnea, in-

cluding, of course, the traditional pilot-competence examinations for mental stability. There was no sign of trouble in Linnea's results, physical or mental.

But she had taken these tests before, and she'd read hundreds of trainee tests—she knew the answers the examiners looked for.

He shook himself. *No.* He'd told her he trusted her. He would not make that assurance a lie by doubting her now.

Ten minutes to launch. Linnea should have been finished already—perhaps she was running through the checklist twice. But Iain did not dare speak and interrupt her concentration. Instead, he ticked over the other issues in his mind.

Supplies were a problem with no good answer. The intravenous nutrients that would support them during a long jump were only part of the need. Even after they reached their destination, it might take days or weeks in realspace to find human habitation and new sources of food, water, and oxygen. And would the people they found give them these things simply because they needed them?

In the end he and Linnea had stocked the ship with medical supplies, technical and cultural libraries, anything of small mass and high value that they might be able to trade for what they needed. Assuming they were allowed to dock in the first place.

Iain had privately considered the possibility that they would find no welcome among the humans in Earth's system—that they would have to return immediately to the Hidden Worlds. He'd packed away a stunrod and neural fuser for each of them, saying nothing to Linnea. If they had to return, they would get the supplies they needed—however it had to be done.

Linnea had left it to Iain to compose the official, formally worded message for Terranova: taking leave from their positions, saying nothing of their intentions, but making clear that they would not be returning or communicating for several years at least. Iain knew that this alone would stir suspicions within the Line, given Linnea's highly public interest in the issue of human survivors in Earth's system.

But if the Line could not be *certain* of Iain's meaning, of Linnea's intentions, he knew that they would take no action. Iain's old opponent, Hakon sen Efrem, with his ever-growing influence with the Line Council, would certainly be able to persuade them to let the matter drop; Iain's and Linnea's absence would clear the field for him, after all. The Council would publish a message of mourning for Iain sen Paolo and Linnea Kiaho, and that would be the end of it.

It was Linnea who'd written the brief personal message to their friends Torin and Zhen. Iain had read it: It was warmly affectionate and entirely cryptic. Torin and Zhen would grieve together, and wonder; yet it could not be helped. If hotheaded, overconfident Zhen guessed what they were attempting, she would undoubtedly try to follow them, even though she had no destination point, and even though her piloting skill, her gift, was not as strong as Linnea's. Her husband, Torin, would never be able to prevent her.

Better leave it a mystery, Iain had agreed—perhaps to be solved someday, perhaps not. But, still, he'd given orders at the skyport here for his ship to be returned to Terranova and placed in Zhen's care. That he'd chosen to abandon his beloved ship would probably frighten Zhen and Torin more than anything else about this; but they would not be sure why he had done it. And they would never be sure where he and Linnea had gone.

Iain's regret was an ache that did not fade. Maybe he would reclaim his ship someday—maybe he and Linnea would see their friends, their home on Terranova again. Maybe.

Iain turned his head restlessly. If Linnea had sent a parting message to her sister Marra, he did not know of it. He'd spared Linnea the pain of asking.

Five minutes. Waiting there in his shell, Iain allowed himself to grieve, silently, for what he might never see again: not only their friends, not only the home he and Linnea had begun to make on Terranova; but the Line. His former brotherhood of Pilot Masters. Last year he'd refused their offer to be reinstated to the Line as the full heir of his father. In honor, it had been the only choice he could have made. But regret at that refusal was still a secret grief, one he hoped Linnea had never guessed.

By comparison to the ordered, deeply traditional Line, the new pilots he and Linnea had helped to train seemed less disciplined, raw. They could pilot, they could fight; but they had no binding tradition, no honor beyond the individual. It had comforted Iain to deal with the Line at Council meetings, or to work with former brothers as training instructors. He shared with them an unspoken language that he had learned in childhood and still loved, but that no one now close to him could understand. Not even Linnea. Soon he would be far from anyone who knew it.

At last Linnea's voice spoke in his ear, giving her name and her ship's call sign to Paradais Ground. "Checklist complete. We're ready for scheduled launch. Destination radius plus ninety, down-orbit."

"Acknowledged," the deep voice of the duty controller said. "Launch when ready. Travel safely, Pilot Kiaho."

"Thank you, Ground," Linnea said. Her voice sounded steady. They had been careful to rest as much as they could, the past few days, and in that quiet time alone together the physical bond between them had deepened further. They had never been so close, she had never been so openly loving, as in those few days. And now it was all to be put at risk.

But he heard no doubt in Linnea's voice. This was what she wanted. What she must have: to travel so far, he had thought in his bitterness, that her homelessness no longer mattered even to her.

Launch. They had chosen a conventional trajectory, conservative of fuel—not Linnea's style at all, or even his own, but they must waste nothing. So it seemed to take forever to reach jump radius, time when Iain could do nothing, could not even speak to Linnea. Then she chose to make the first jump at once.

The initial jump was a short one, to a point just beyond the edge of the Paradais system; it took barely an instant in otherspace, the merest flicker of nothingness. Arrived, they floated in silence, surrounded by the pale, starry folds of the clouds of gas and dust that had concealed the Hidden Worlds for so long. Through their joint neural link to the ship, Iain felt Linnea's presence clearly. In otherspace, this link would make it possible for him to communicate with her, if she allowed it; or at the least to let her sense his presence.

Finally, she spoke, through their connection. "I'm ready, Iain."

He had to ask, once more: "You're sure of this?"

"As sure as I can be." He sensed no fear in her, saw no agitation in her physical readouts.

"I'll be with you," he said. On so long a jump they would both probably spend much of the time drugged into unconsciousness; even in the jump, where much less time passed than in the outer world, they would be helpless in otherspace for weeks, maybe months, and only drugs brought sleep to a mind there. "Reach out to me if you need me."

"I will," she said after a pause. Then, "Iain, I love you."

The words she would never say. "And I love you," he said, feeling tears sting his eyes. He took a last breath in normal space, feeling the air move into his lungs, feeling the softness of the shell around his body. Any second now—

Flick.

First came the familiar time of blindness, deafness,

isolation, when nothing could penetrate. It took longer, he remembered, to reach through to otherspace when one was flying as a passenger rather than as pilot. He had not jumped as Linnea's passenger since the last of her training runs, more than three years earlier.

So, when otherspace found him, and he stretched out his distorted senses to touch it, he gasped. He had never experienced this sense of headlong flight. Flight under tight direction, masterful control. Flight toward . . . no destination he could sense or understand. He did not have the mark. That was in her mind, not his. He was flying blind.

But flying blind in the company of a pilot such as he had never known. He did not dare to reach out to her, not in these early moments of the jump; an error now would force her to abort the jump, shake her confidence for the next attempt.

And yet he felt oddly sure that her confidence never *could* be shaken. This, more than he had ever guessed or imagined, was Linnea's rightful world. He hadn't known. He had never known.

He abandoned himself to the flow of it, to the strange shape of a jump he had never made before, of a hyperdesic whose sharp line vanished beyond the horizon of his mind. He felt himself and Linnea sinking deeper into otherspace, beginning the long journey between all that he knew and Earth. Earth, the home of their enemies; the dark center of the system where, Linnea believed, a few humans lingered in concealment.

Humans who might have a weapon the Line lacked. Humans who deserved the hope of rescue.

Now, here, with nothing else to distract his mind, Iain knew that he was afraid. He had been afraid from the moment he agreed to this journey, afraid for Linnea even more than for himself.

What would they find? How human would they really

be—people who had lived in hiding, so near to such danger, for centuries? And if Linnea's certainty was false, if there was no weapon—would they survive the return? *Fear*—

Then reassurance. Words formed in his mind—Linnea's voice, her presence behind them: a sharp flame of intention and courage, hope warm as silk against his skin, a ghost-memory of her warm hand sliding down his back. The taste of her mouth in memory—in memory only. Perhaps never again.

Her words, her presence. *The way is open.*

Go, then, he urged. And sensed, in reply, a low laugh of delight.

Down and down. Faster and faster. But joy, all joy. Her exultation filled him. It was as if he could feel his physical body again, as if it tingled and shook.

He was in Linnea's hands. He was in her governance. And there was nowhere, nowhere else he wished to be.

FIVE

Heat, and dark, and a rhythmic whistling. Linnea tried to turn, to escape the sound, to sink back into unconsciousness. But she could not move. Strapped, tied, pierced, she could not move. She felt heat, and a stabbing ache in her chest, and the trickle of sweat between her breasts. Floating. No gravity. She could not see. She could hear only the whistling sound.

She held her breath to listen, and the sound stopped. She breathed again, heard the whistling of air into infected lungs. Felt the crackle as she breathed. Far from anywhere, and disoriented, and sick—

Dully, she understood. They had arrived. They had arrived somewhere.

But where?

She reached out in her mind, trying to sense Iain's presence. Nothing. No link at all, to anything.

A surge of panic sped her breathing, made her cough. "Ship," she croaked.

Silence.

"Ship. Link in."

A fragment of response flickered through the link from the shipmind, muttering of overloads, depletions, disaster.

"Eyes," she said, and coughed again, pain ripping her chest.

And she saw.

At first only utter blackness sparked with stars—strange, cold stars, no soft veil of nebulae. She turned her vision. There: a star brighter than all the others, bright enough that it was masked. The primary. The sun—the sun of Earth? She swung the ship's eyes farther.

A blue world swam into view—in half-phase, the bright side lit only wanly. Not the blue of a living world; the harsh cyanic blue of a cold gas giant.

The jump point.

They had made it.

She called again through the link to Iain, but again no answer came. He must be unconscious.

He *must* be unconscious.

And she was torn. Only her link to the ship gave her a clear view outside it and exact control over its systems. But the link kept her immobilized inside this shell. To check on Iain, to see him with her own eyes, know what had happened, would blind her to everything else and leave them powerless.

But she had to know. If he was still alive, she could think, she could plan. If he was not—

She pulled back, willed the neural connections to withdraw. Again the ship muttered, confused words about *necessary maintenance* and *warning*. She struggled with weak hands to finish disconnecting herself from the ship's support.

Then—the ship lurched, and something heavy clanked against the hull.

No time to reestablish control connections. Linnea tore

loose the last tubes, pushed the shell open, launched herself to the external control board. When she slapped it awake, most of its lights burned amber and red. The proximity-alarm light blinked purple, but there was no sound. Burned-out, broken, power too low. Her ship lurched again, and she pulled herself into the chair at the panel, strapped herself in. Through the fog of fever, she woke the viewscreens, tried to get a look at what had taken hold of her ship, but it was too near: Some views were blocked completely, others showed nothing but stars.

She heard the scrape of metal on metal, to the rear of the ship, in the passenger compartment. Panic clawed at her throat. Someone, or something, was trying to force the hatch.

She hit the release for the restraining straps, floated up to a locker, and fumbled inside for the stunrod she had hidden there. Then launched herself into the rear compartment, where Iain's shell hung silent and sealed, its readout lights a wild mix of green, amber, red, no time to interpret them. She caught herself and looked at the air-lock hatch. The light above it glowed green, indicating pressure on the other side, outside the ship. There should not have been. Someone had attached a docking tube. Someone was trying to cycle her ship's lock from outside, trying to come in. If they persisted, they might damage her ship, even disable it—

Gripping the stunrod, she slapped the control that dilated the outer hatch, then the inner one.

A bulky shape floated there in the lock, humanlike, encased in a black vacuum suit. A mirrored visor hid its face, its eyes. Through the fever a chill shook her as she understood, again, the risk they had taken: If this was an infested human, if these were the Cold Minds, then she and Iain were dead. She had killed them both.

A voice spoke, distorted and harsh, from a speaker on the suit. She could not quite understand the words—rapid, slurred, differently shaped. The voice spoke again. Then she realized there was another suited shape behind the first one, and each of them held a weapon, a gun, aimed at her.

She let go of the stunrod, let it float out of her hand. "I am Linnea Kiaho," she said. "From the Hidden Worlds. You sent for me."

An interrogative, one she almost understood. A suited hand swept a gesture including her from head to toe, and she realized how she must look: naked, filthy, hollow-eyed. "Yes," she said firmly. "You sent for us. We came because you called."

"'We'?" the voice said. The mirrored visor turned toward Iain's shell, lit and obviously in use.

She controlled nothing here; she could not protect Iain, she could not even protect herself. If these people would not help them, neither she nor Iain would live much longer.

She nudged herself toward Iain's closed shell, took hold there, slowly lifted the lid.

The breath drained out of her. He lay there—breathing, alive. For a moment she forgot the suited figures behind her, forgot the danger in the overwhelming relief that he had survived. The black interface mask covered his face. Gently, she peeled it away, feeling the heat of fever beating from his skin.

A suited hand gripped the rim of the coffinlike shell, and the gleaming visor looked down at Iain. He lay with his eyes closed, his black braid floating gently just above his shoulder. His ribs showed clearly, but his breathing sounded normal. But still he was unconscious, even after the programmed dose of postjump stimulants—not a good sign.

Sick as Linnea was, she had to think, and fight, for both of them. She took a breath to speak again.

Armored hands gripped her arms, pulled her away. The other person took hold of the braid, jerked Iain into a sitting position, and she cried out, "No! The shiplinks, don't pull them out, you'll hurt him!"

"One of *them*," the voice said, the tone deep, ugly. The other one said nothing, but the grip on Linnea's arms tightened.

The reflective visor turned toward her. The voice spoke one more time, one finger jabbing at Iain. "Out," it said clearly. "Now."

With fumbling hands Linnea disconnected Iain from the linkages that had joined him to the ship, kept him alive. He seemed deeply unconscious, floating loosely as she tugged him around to reach the links and tubing. As soon as he was free, the suited man pushed her aside and bound Iain's wrists, then his ankles with wire twisted tight. The helmeted head swung around to face her again. Spoke again, clearly and slowly. "This pilot will be sorry he came."

"But we're—" She fought to speak clearly. "We're the ones you sent for."

For the first time the figure holding her spoke, the voice deep and distorted. "We sent for no one."

"In otherspace," Linnea said, dizzy and sick. "I heard you. You sent me the jump point. That's how we came here."

"Not possible," the man said stubbornly. "No one sent for you. Maybe a trick, maybe the Cold Minds." He tugged Linnea forward. "Move."

Linnea closed her eyes, helpless in the man's strong grip. No answers here, no answers yet.

But she would find them.

Their captors manhandled them through a chilly boarding tube and a cramped air-lock into the docked ship. Linnea's grip on awareness was wavering as her thirst and fever increased. The lock cycled, and her thoughts revolved uselessly: Who were these people? Not infested, she kept assuring herself—but how could she know?

Their captors slung them into a small metal compartment, barely two meters in any direction. This was like no
ship Linnea had ever seen: the crudely finished metal plates
that formed the bulkheads were joined by roughly welded
seams, and the hatch was merely a swinging metal plug
with a hand-wheel in the center. Nothing like the refined,
beautifully machined Line ships Linnea had known.

The suited men backed out through the hatch and pulled
it closed. The wheel turned with a screech, then latches
clanked shut outside.

Clutching Iain's slack body against her with one arm,
hanging on to a metal loop with the other, she looked
around the bare, dirty compartment. Its old gray paint was
scraped and scuffed in the way of a ship used to carry
cargo. Faint light gleamed from a recessed panel covered
with yellowed plastic. There were no acceleration couches,
no padding of any kind. And she realized, with a jolt of
fear, that this ship would be moving at any moment.

Which way would be "down"? She looked around, made
a frantic guess based on the positions of the light and
hatch—tugged Iain with her into a corner, where she braced
them both in place as best she could, pressing her bare
back, her bare feet against the metal. Then waited, her
heart beating hard.

But the acceleration, when it came, was gentle,
prolonged—nothing like the quick fiery maneuvers of a
well-handled Line ship. And she'd guessed right: They
were lying against the bulkhead that was "down." The compartment was cold, the metal rough against her bare skin,
but she could do nothing about that but endure it.

And wait. Someone would help them soon. Otherwise,
these people would simply have killed them.

During the acceleration, Iain stirred and muttered but
did not open his eyes. She held him close against her, feeling his quick, feverish heartbeat against her own. After an

indefinite time, the acceleration stopped abruptly, and they began to drift away from the bulkhead.

Then she recognized the whistle of atmosphere along the skin of the ship and the steadily increasing tug that meant deceleration. *No*—She tightened her hold on Iain and closed her eyes. They could not hope to survive a landing without any padding whatsoever.

But again the changes in motion were strangely gentle, and the thin scream of wind against the skin of the ship never built to the roar of a landing through heavy atmosphere. After a long time, the ship settled, the engines cutting off, leaving an echoing silence. Gravity, real gravity, held them gently to the deck—so gently that the hard metal was almost comfortable, except for the cold.

Linnea eased Iain to the floor and untwisted the wire from his wrists and ankles. It hadn't cut in, thank God. Then she gathered him close again and fought to order her thoughts. The descent through atmosphere meant that this was a planet or moon, not a station. Thin atmosphere, light gee—it must be a moon. Not that green gas giant from her vision, of course—probably one of its satellites.

Maybe the one who had called to her was here, on this moon. She felt a twinge of hope.

She heard, distantly, the receding clank of suited footsteps, then the heavy clanking slam of a hatch. The lights dimmed, and the faint hiss of circulating air stopped.

Then came silence, silence so deep she could hear only her rasping breath, and Iain's. Nothing else. Without life support, without heat, how long could they last?

In her arms, Iain stirred again, still feverish. They both needed fluids, electrolytes, food, warmth. Surely their captors wouldn't leave them to die in this cold compartment after they'd traveled so far. She'd told them she was from the Hidden Worlds. Surely that would get someone's attention, and help and relief would come.

And someone with answers. Someone *had* sent that summoning call. Why else would she and Iain have dared such a voyage—sliding past all the long, cold dark, the hard vacuum and radiation, tunneling instead through the intricate beauty of otherspace, the endless depths. . . .

Second Pilot Timmon Abrakam, commander of Gold Wing Triton and chief of the Night Guard, stared at his commscreen in disbelief. Patrol Pilot Smid, his voice carefully respectful, said, "It's more impressive up close, sir."

"Look at those lines," Timmon said reverently. "Look at the *size* of it. I've never seen a ship like that. Never even dreamed of one."

"No, sir," Smid said.

"And the pilot—alive, you say?"

"Held for testing, sir," Smid said. "Two of them, a man and a woman."

Timmon pulled thoughtfully at his chin. "If they're clean, put them in isolation. And—message First Pilot Kimura. He's got to see this."

"He's at the Residence, sir, with Madame, and he specifically ordered—"

"For this," Timmon said, "he will want to be waked. You may tell him the responsibility is mine, Pilot Smid."

Smid bowed and left, leaving Timmon alone to contemplate the mystery. A ship from nowhere.

So was this the first happy result of the grand new strategy the First Pilot had been hinting at?

Or was this the first sign that, like all the other grand new strategies, it had failed?

An endless time later, Linnea jerked awake, instantly afraid, as the hatch of their compartment clanged open.

She flung her arm over her eyes to shield them from the
harsh light playing over the compartment—someone's hand-
light. Beside her, Iain made a rusty sound of protest.

Two people entered—the same, different, she could not
tell—sealed inside anti-infective barriers, their faces again
invisible behind gleaming reflective visors. But this time
one of them carried a medkit, the red cross shape clear
and familiar. Relief washed over her, then vanished when
the figure opened the case and pulled out a syringe—a
syringe with a *needle* on it, like something from an old
simspace historical tale.

One of them gripped her arm in a gloved hand while the
other tied on a tourniquet, jabbed her with the needle, drew
blood. "Are you testing me for infestation?" she asked. But
neither of them troubled to answer or even to give any sign
they had heard her. They drew an identical sample from
Iain and vanished again. The hatch banged shut.

She slept some more, and endured the times of waking
with Iain increasingly restless. His eyes opened, once, but
he looked at her with frightened incomprehension and did
not answer when she spoke to him. Her fear for him grew.
She could feel herself getting weaker, dizzy with it, and he
must be weakening, too.

She woke from a dream of the shadows in the corners
growing, leaning over her, to find herself in motion. Hands
gripping her arms and legs, carrying her headlong, somewhere. She heard muffled voices, but she could not understand.

They passed out of the ship into a high, wide, cold space.
Thin, bitter air, lights sliding past overhead, smells of
metal, paint, chemicals. Faces looking down at her, hard to
see, dim light. "Iain," she croaked, and a female voice
said something indistinct, in a peremptory tone. The lights
stopped moving past, stayed still. Now she was lying on a
table, no, a bed, soft enough for a bed, and warm water

trickled along the skin of her arm. Then pain stabbed the back of her hand. "Iain," she muttered again, starting to cry. Her eyes were too dry for tears.

Someone said "Quiet"—her own voice, Iain's? The leaning shadows joined, flowed, rose all around her bed, and she sank under the surface into silence.

DEEPSIDER OUTPOST *STAR RIVER MEETING*

Esayeh burst into Pilang's sleep cubby, startling her awake—caught her hands in his as he floated against her sleeping sack, kissed her on the forehead. "He came," he said, joy making his voice tremble. "Twelve hours ago. A beautiful ship, like nothing I've ever seen, I saw the images through Thaddeus's telescreen—he came!"

She rubbed her eyes with the heel of her hand. "Wait. Who?"

"The pilot! The one from the Hidden Worlds!"

"From the Hidden—" She stared Esayeh in the face. "Is he here? Now?"

"Well—" He looked away. Not deepsider courtesy, but Tritoner evasion—she knew it of old.

"Then it can wait until I wake up," she said.

His face fell. "I thought you'd be pleased. This is important, Pilang."

She sighed and ran her hands along his shoulders. "All right, then. Tell me about it. Did you even see him?"

"No. The ship jumped in too close to Triton—damn the timing, a day either way, and they'd have been out of range, I could have gotten there first. The orbital monitors spotted the ship. And the patrol picked it up—and whoever was aboard."

Pilang wriggled out of her sleeping sack, floated to where she had left her work clothes, started pulling them on. "So your mysterious Hidden Worlds pilot is now on

Triton," she said. "Locked up safe in fifteen layers of guards. And probably lots more comfortable than he would be here—your Madame Tereu wouldn't dishonor herself by showing poor hospitality."

"I'll get him out," Esayeh said.

"You can't even set foot on Triton," she said. "Not outside your ship. They'll arrest you."

"Which is why," he said, "I need someone who can go there freely, someone who won't be suspected—"

Her head went back. "Oh, no," she said. "No, no, *no*."

"I'll send some messages ahead," he said, pleading now. "The way will be set for you—all you have to do is receive the pilot when he comes to you and guide him to the ship."

"No," she said. Esayeh and his wild dreams, his crazy rickety structure of hope, his "bridge between worlds"— she would not be pulled further out on it. "You can't expect this of me. If I do anything against the Tritoner regulations, they'll revoke my visa. I'll lose my right to go there, lose all the trade credits I depend on to keep my circuit clinics alive. No!"

"But if this works—we won't *need* their trade credits anymore. Not ever."

"Wild hopes," she said stubbornly.

"What other kind do we have?" Esayeh floated away from her to the opposite wall, clung there stubbornly, facing her. "If this fails, if the pilot does not appear, I won't ask you to try again. I promise you."

"You promise," she muttered. She pursed her lips, then gave him a fierce look. "One try. Send your messages."

He bounded across the little space to her, caught her up in a hug, kissed her resoundingly. "You are the fountain of my hopes."

"I," Pilang said bleakly, "am a fool."

He laughed, flipped neatly in the air, and launched himself out through the curtain of her cubby.

She looked after him. *I promised myself, no more of this.* . . . Then she caught a glimpse of her face in the bit of mirror. She was smiling. She twisted her face into a fierce scowl and went on getting ready for her day.

SIX

TRITON

Morning, maybe. The chrono on the wall said so, anyway. Linnea knelt beside Iain's bed in their lavish, windowless hospital room—watching him sleep, schooling herself to patience. Since waking, she'd asked everyone who came in here the questions burning in her mind: Where was the pilot who had called her here? Could someone please ask a pilot to come and talk to her? But no one seemed to understand. The middle-aged nurse who was tending them, a tall, austere-looking man, only pursed his lips and shook his head, as if her questions were somehow improper.

Linnea itched for answers, itched to go out looking for them. But she knew she could not risk leaving Iain alone here, helpless—not after the hostility their original captors had shown. They thought he was Line—and clearly that was not a good thing here.

The nurse had been kind enough—professional kindness, dealt out with impersonal efficiency. He'd helped her sponge off the dried sweat and dead skin of the journey, given her clean blue coveralls to put on. To be clean and warm was grace enough for the moment. That and the intravenous fluids that she knew were gradually restoring her strength, and must be helping Iain as well. Their reserves in the jumpship had been so low, she guessed, that the shipmind had dropped the infusion rate well below optimal—keeping them on the bare edge of dehydration but getting them through the jump alive.

And the nurse had given Linnea a comb, with which she'd tidied her damp hair and tucked it behind her ears. She had not tried to do anything with Iain's long black braid; best leave it as it was until it could be washed.

The soft, napped fabric of the coveralls warmed her clean body. A small machine strapped to Iain's arm hummed gently, feeding him fluids, sugar, electrolytes—or so the nurse had told her. She had one on her arm, too, its plastic reservoir bag attached to her waist.

It was not uncomfortable; nothing weighed much here. The gravity pulled far more weakly than even the half-gee pseudograv of an orbital station. And yet this was really a world. A moon called Triton, the nurse had told her when she woke. At first Linnea had struggled to understand him and to make herself understood; people talked differently here. But it was getting easier. The language was almost the same—it was still what she would call Standard. Some of the sounds were different; that was all.

Their room was spacious, easily containing the two thinly padded beds that were all the gee required. A hanging against one wall was embroidered with wildly plumed, iridescent birds, and against another wall was a long, padded bench covered in shimmering red cloth. There was even a private bath. But the place was still an infirmary: sterile and cold, with a faint tang of plastic and cleaning chemicals in the thin air. These people were caring for them decently, treating them well—a hopeful sign. But no one seemed willing, yet, to give her the answers she needed.

She'd seen only two medical people so far: their nurse, and their doctor, a bony, white-haired woman in a severely cut white tunic and trousers. She'd come in once or twice to briskly assess their condition and give the nurse orders. She had nothing to say to Linnea, did not seem even to hear her questions.

The one time Linnea had tried to open the door and look out into the corridor, she saw a tall man in green leaning against the opposite wall, who straightened, looked hard at her, and said, "No, Miss, please"—clearly ordering her back inside the room. There didn't appear to be any other patients on this hall; she heard no voices. Isolated, under guard—clearly they were still under suspicion.

But Linnea could not ease their captors' fears until she could *talk* to someone. Answer all their questions—then ask hers. She looked down at Iain. If he would only wake, they could plan. If she knew he was going to be all right, she could plan. Until then, the haze of dread clouded her thoughts. She felt only fear for Iain, and the future stretched out blankly before her. Until he woke.

And there was another urgent matter. She had to get to her ship, make sure it was being repaired and replenished as it needed. But so far all her questions about it had been met with stony and apparently indifferent silence.

At least she and Iain were together. She touched Iain's cheek. In the hard light of the lamp above his bed, the bones showed too sharp under his fever-sallow skin. Because he was larger, the decreased infusion had affected him more. "Wake up, you," she muttered, for the tenth time—and caught her breath as his eyelids fluttered. Fluttered again. Opened.

She held her breath and waited. But this time, his eyes stayed open. This time, his gaze settled on her face—and he smiled faintly.

He saw her. He knew her.

Blinking back tears, she kissed his cheek. "Welcome back," she said gently.

"We—made—it," he said with obvious effort.

"We did," she said. "We're safe, so far."

Iain tried to sit up. "Your ship?"

She pushed him down. "They have it. Somewhere out of reach. They won't *tell* me anything! Except that this is a city on Triton."

His eyes widened slightly. "Triton! Moon of—moon of Neptune."

"Whatever that is," Linnea muttered.

He grinned. "We—really did it. Earth."

"Pretty far from Earth, I'm told," she said. "Which is a good thing, remember."

"Yes," he said sleepily. "Out in the dark. Out on the edge. Hidden." He licked his dry lips. "Water?"

"I suppose you can have some," she said. "They left some by the bed." She held the straw of the clear plastic bladder to Iain's lips, and he took a few careful sips.

"No cup," he said.

"Gee's too light," she said. "Only about eight percent, they tell me." Water would have swirled and sloshed out of a cup at the slightest motion, or maybe even crawled up over the rim on its own. *Living here must be strange.*

She cranked the head of Iain's bed up and knelt on the floor again, so he did not have to look up at her. In this gee, kneeling was as comfortable as standing. When he'd emptied the bulb of water, she took it and set it aside. Then, looking down at her hands resting on the side of the bed, she said, "Iain—I'm sorry for this."

"Don't, Linnea," he said, so gently that she looked up into his face. His dark eyes shone clear—the quiet determination that had made her love him in the beginning, that bound her to him even more strongly now. "Just be patient, love. We'll find him. The one who called you." He brushed a thumb along her cheek, a tender gesture.

She managed a smile.

"But until then," he said, "it's enough that we're alive here. That we're both still alive."

It would have to be enough. She rested her head on his chest and closed her eyes. She would take this moment of peace and relief; who could tell how many more they might ever have?

Then her head jerked up as their nurse hurried into the room. He said nothing, but his expression was grim. Moving quickly, he changed the reservoir bag on Iain's IV for a full one. Then he went to work on Linnea's reservoir; she sat down on the edge of her bed, her arms raised to keep out of his way, helpless.

As the nurse leaned closer to secure the full bag to her belt, he whispered in her ear. "Watch for the blue flower." She took a breath to speak, and his hands dug into her arms in warning. "Watch and listen." He straightened. "Being moved to better quarters," he said out loud to Iain. "Both of you. You're to be Madame's guests." He handed Linnea a flimsy printout. "Care for the pump units," he said. "Bad signs to watch for, fevers. You keep that. And"—he caught her eye—"watch."

The door opened, and a stranger entered: a man, tall and dark-skinned, his head shaved smooth, his eyes cold. He carried himself like a man armed with something concealed and deadly. The light-skinned man behind him was the one who had been watching the corridor. The dark one spoke rapidly to the nurse—then scooped Iain up lightly in his arms.

"No!" Panic sharpened Linnea's voice. "He's still very sick. You can't just—"

And the other man picked her up, as easily as picking up a child. She tried to twist free.

"No, Linnea," Iain said. "We have to trust these people." His urgent expression added: *We have no choice.*

She knew he was right: They knew nothing, had no way to escape. Bewildered, she stopped struggling. Tried to make sense of the nurse's words. *Blue flower.* Had she heard that right? Did it mean anything at all? What had he meant, *Listen*—to a flower?

The corridors they passed through were empty—narrow ones first, the hospital, then gradually widening into what must be public spaces. Even there the walls and doors, neatly painted metal or plastic, looked spotless as a surgery under the bright, cold lights. Plants, precisely pruned, their leaves waxy, stood every few meters in orderly arrangements of tubs.

Every door they passed was tightly shut. Standard precautions, Linnea knew, in a station in what was essentially vacuum. And yet, to see no one visibly at work, to hear no voices—surely that was strange. She heard no machinery—no sound but the whisper of air, and the soft footsteps of the men who carried them. The floors were smooth black, a soft polymer that seemed to grip the men's shoes. They rounded a curve in the corridor; the flooring flowed partly up the walls and for a few moments they walked at a slant. *Light weight, same mass.* She was going to have to learn to walk all over again.

On a wall at one major intersection she saw an information board covered with official-looking notices, some of them flashing; next to it a pool of light marked out the flat portrait of a lean, dark-haired woman of middle age, her hands folded on a desk in front of her, her expression impassive. An intersection or two later was another board, another portrait—the same image. It was the only decoration she had seen here; even the walls and doors were painted a uniform light blue-gray.

Linnea struggled to gather her scattered thoughts, calm herself. This could finally be her chance to ask questions that would be answered. To begin to understand what she had let herself and Iain in for. She would need all her wits, all her skill with people, to protect them both.

They passed another man in green standing guard, and entered a different corridor—more spacious, more artfully lit. And the air was definitely warmer. Another guard stood at the end of the passage, in front of a high door made of copper-colored metal. As they stopped in front of him, he raised his wrist to his mouth and muttered something.

The door slid open, and they passed through into warmth and brightness.

A gust of fresh-smelling air ruffled Linnea's hair. She blinked, looking around. Sunlight? That couldn't be sunlight. And she smelled grass—

Their guards set them on their feet just inside the door. "You'll walk from here," the dark-skinned man said. "Madame expects it." Linnea moved to Iain's side, cradled his arm in both of her hands. She looked around, disoriented, a little afraid.

The space was huge by the standards of any station she had ever been on; larger even than a landing bay for a passenger shuttle. She couldn't judge its size; the ground was grassy, rising and falling in little hills. Shrubs and clumps of small trees blocked her view of the space's walls. But the air smelled green, alive. Somewhere birds were singing, though she couldn't see any.

A nudge in her back, and she and Iain started forward along a path that looked like stone. Maybe it was. Iain had his head down, his strength already about gone, she guessed. It was up to Linnea to observe everything. That blue arching ceiling, meters overhead—that was no sky, of course, just artful paint. White clouds glowed here and there, concealing the light sources. A curve in the path brought them to a stone wall, more than man height, and a gate of—wood? She supposed it could really be wood. There were trees here. But how—

The guard spoke rapidly, and a distorted voice answered. The gate swung open. A short stretch of path, symmetrically lined with immaculate white pots of red flowers, led to a door painted glistening red. The door slid aside as they approached it. She could see only shadows beyond. She helped Iain over the porch sill and into the—house? The guards followed; the door slid shut, sealing them all in.

Linnea blinked in dimness. It was a large room—warm, softly lit, carpeted in amber and black. A window at her left must overlook the park—if that was the word—but heavy black curtains had been drawn over it. An arrangement of orange and blood-colored flowers stood on a tall table near the door. On a hearth beneath an open chimney of hammered copper, a stone glowed orange, shimmering with heat.

And from a high, flimsy-looking chair near the hearth, a tall figure rose to face them.

A woman. Clear, direct brown eyes met Linnea's, moved to study Iain. Linnea knew at once that this woman held power. Black hair streaked with gray, pulled tightly back, framed a face that was still handsome. She wore a sleeveless tunic of shining red material that reached to her sandaled feet, skimming her body. Her pale, slender arms were bare even of jewelry.

With a shock Linnea recognized her: This was the woman in the portraits she'd seen in the corridors on the way here.

A woman who might have answers to give. But clearly Linnea would have to be careful.

The woman turned to Iain and spoke, her voice hard. "I am Tereu of family Perrin, First Citizen of the people of Triton. This is my residence."

Iain only looked puzzled. But Linnea understood—she had been learning to hear these people, to understand the words framed in a strange accent, the vowels a different shape, words spoken quick and clipped. After a moment, she said, "He's not used to how you talk here."

"Your name," Tereu said to her.

Linnea eyed her. "Linnea Kiaho."

"I am addressed as Madame," the woman said. "Family Linnea?"

Linnea blinked. "Family Kiaho. Madame."

"I've never heard of either one." Seeming to dismiss Linnea, Tereu turned again to study Iain. The baggy blue coverall hung on his tall, thin frame. The long, frizzled braid hung straight and still down his back as he stood there looking back at Tereu, his eyes watchful. Linnea saw Tereu's hands clench into fists. "You are Line," she said curtly. It was an accusation.

This time, clearly, he understood her. "No," he said, and turned aside to cough. "I am a pilot, as Linnea is. But not Line."

"A Line pilot would lie from fear, of course," Tereu said. "And he would be right to fear, on Triton." She did not move her gaze from his face. "Your name and family?"

"Iain, Madame," he said. "Of family—of the family of Paolo."

"We are not Line pilots, Madame," Linnea said. "We—"

Tereu's hand whipped up, palm out, and Linnea broke off. "I will not be lied to," Tereu said, still speaking to Iain. "You look Line to me, from the old records. And this woman—*she* cannot be a pilot at all."

"Madame, the ship we arrived in is mine," Linnea said quietly. "I was pilot."

Again the hand flashed up, commanding silence. Tereu studied Iain, then frowned, steepling her fingers at her chin.

Then she looked up, waved a hand in a gesture of dismissal, and their guards left them. As the door sealed behind the men, Tereu broke into a warm smile. "I apologize for my discourtesy, but it was necessary for me to judge you for myself before I could welcome you correctly. You have had a long journey, and I'm told you have both been ill. Come and rest by my fire."

She waved her hand toward two chairs like her own, facing hers near the glowing stone. Puzzled by the change in Tereu's manners, Linnea settled carefully into her own chair. She found that it held her more naturally and comfortably than a low chair would have done, with no need to bend herself tight in the middle. The hearth gave off waves of welcome heat. She hoped it would not make Iain sleepy.

Tereu seated herself. A high table made of brushed-silver metal stood at her elbow, with what looked like a spherical black-and-silver pillow resting on it. "Please accept chee," Tereu said—no, "tea." Linnea nodded politely, wondering where the pot was. Then Tereu snapped a small cloth bag onto a plastic disk on the side of the cushion, and squashed the cushion down with her palm. The bag swelled. When it was full, she tugged it free, then leaned forward and passed it to Iain, with a polite inclination of her head. He accepted with the same half bow—to precisely the same degree, Linnea noticed; sick or not, Iain never missed the nuances of status. His Line training, of course. Linnea accepted her own bag of tea with the same nod, then puzzled over it until Tereu pulled a thin silvery straw free of the cloth on her own bag and sipped.

Linnea did the same. The tea was scalding hot and tasted of smoke and salt. She did not let herself react. But not until Iain, too, had sipped at the tea did Tereu speak again. And again her manner changed—the intense urgency returned.

"Forgive me," she said to Iain, "but there are some urgent questions I must ask. First, how you came here from the Hidden Worlds."

Linnea saw the glint of anger in his eyes. "We traveled in Linnea's jumpship," he said. "Madame."

Tereu blinked at him. "So you insist that this is true?" Then she turned for the first time to face Linnea fully. Linnea met her gaze, saw thought stirring there, the elegant brows drawn down into a faint frown. "*You* were pilot," Tereu said, as if marveling. "How can this be?"

"I have the gift, so I was trained," Linnea said steadily.

"A pilot who is a woman," Tereu said. "Not even the deepsiders—" She broke off. "So you have come from the Hidden Worlds. So dangerous a journey," she said, as if marveling. "How far are they?"

Linnea met Tereu's eyes, sipped at her tea. "I cannot say, Madame."

"You mean you *will* not say." Tereu set down her tea, turned back to face Iain, with her fingers laced neatly together. "Your Hidden Worlds are well named, Paolo Iain. Off they went, the last of those great men of the Line, leaving promises. And then silence. We had no ships that could follow so far—we had no one left who could pilot them. No one who knew *where* to follow. We had to teach ourselves to pilot. We had four jumpships left—we lost two, learning. The story is—still painful."

Iain frowned. "I know part of this history," he said. "We learned it as well. But perhaps your people have forgotten that the pilots built as many ships as they could. They made the journey as many times as they could. Your medtechs must have reported to you what that jump did to Linnea and me, in a modern ship. Yet those men in those ancient ships spent their entire lives, for two generations, ferrying people to safety. They saved tens of thousands of people. They founded the Hidden Worlds."

"And ten thousand and more were left behind," Tereu said. "Here in the shadows, living at the edge of the system, like rats in the ruins of a house. You will forgive us if we feel a little resentment."

"We didn't know that anyone had survived here," Linnea said. "And Iain and I rejoice at it."

"We would all rejoice," Tereu said, "if we could be as safe as you in the Hidden Worlds. Hidden away."

Linnea saw Tereu's sharp eyes watching and assessing. Time to hit her with something she did not expect. "We *were* hidden," she said. She saw Iain's expression turn stony, but now she had Tereu's attention.

"The Cold Minds found us, too, Madame," Linnea said. "A few years before we left to come here. We're fighting them, but—you know there can't be any final victory. Not over them."

"I know it well," Tereu said. "That is why I have been wondering—"

A soft chime shook the air, and Tereu stood up. Linnea studied her—the woman's face had gone stiff and sallow. *Fear? Or rage?* "Please excuse me." Tereu turned and left the room through an inner door.

"Perhaps," Iain said quietly, "that was news to her. And not given in the best way." His gaze was calm and level.

"I don't think it was news. That was—something else."

"Remember that we agreed—" He broke off, his eyes on the ceiling.

"Iain." Linnea gripped the metal arms of her chair. "We will get nowhere, we will never be safe, if we lie to these people. And if we lie, that woman will know. She's no fool."

"I don't propose that we lie," Iain said. "I just propose that we give only information that must be given. Because you're right: We will never be safe." Looking hard into Linnea's eyes, he pointed at the ceiling.

After a moment, she nodded. Monitors. Monitors everywhere, probably. *Never safe. Never private. Never alone.*

But still she would ask her questions; still she would learn what she could. They would learn nothing if they stayed on Iain's cautious path.

She took his hand, tried to smile reassuringly. But she saw the watchfulness in his eyes. *He knows me.*

He knows me too well.

• • •

Tereu kept her shoulders straight, her head high, as the soundproof door of her inner office slid shut and sealed behind her. Hiso was waiting for her, as she expected—standing in shadow as he always liked; on a wall-screen behind him, old Neptune glowed in crescent, the old cold bastard, the sign of their exile. And now of their people's end—in three generations, or ten, no one could know; but it was as inevitable as her own individual death.

She locked the door, then touched the control that sealed the room even from her own private surveillance system— sometimes she was sure that Hiso had long had the key of it. "You heard," she said, forcing her voice to steadiness. Her desk screen still showed a view of the room next door, the two strangers sitting silently. She longed to go beyond courtesy with them, to get at the truth of this matter. Yet it could not be done. *Damn custom, and damn hospitality, too.*

First Pilot Kimura Hiso swung to face her. His short iron-gray hair and beard, neat as always, were outward signs of the order and control he prized above all other things, prized most of all in Tereu herself. "Certainly I heard," he said.

"Why did you interrupt me?" Her voice was tight but level.

"I was afraid," Hiso said, "that in your generosity you might say too much."

"Too much?"

"I do not wish them," he said, "to understand us too well. Or—our role in recent events."

"Does it matter?" she asked him acidly. "Here is the great expedition you said would come soon after the invasion struck. Here is the great alliance you promised me. And what have we received? A woman. A sick man. And one single ship."

"A beginning," he said mildly. "They are at war. We could expect little more than this—at first."

"You see hope in these?" Tereu felt the old sick despair rising again in her throat. No great expedition from the Hidden Worlds would descend to destroy the Cold Minds on Earth; there would be no rescue fleet. The bitter thought burned in her mind and heart.

She hoped Hiso could not see it. He *used* weakness. How well she knew it. She summoned her thoughts. "Have there been any more incursions?"

"If there had been," Hiso said, "I would not be here attending on you; I would be out patrolling with my wing. I'm glad I am not. This is more important than you realize."

"Two strangers, one little ship," she said. "I don't believe either one of them."

Hiso smiled. "Yet the woman does have the look of a pilot."

"And what look is that?"

He raised an eyebrow. "A pilot knows." He looked back at the strangers' images on the commscreen. "She is young. They both are. Not as experienced politically—or otherwise—as you and I are. I will use that in dealing with them."

Years ago he had dropped all pretense in private that they were partners, that she was leader. She turned her back on him, sipped water from a bulb, trying to wash away the taste of the vile ceremonial tea.

"I'm sure the man captured your particular attention," Hiso said. "Young, handsome, no doubt a competent pilot. Just what you've liked in the past."

She swung on him. *That was years ago.* "He's Line. Or so he looks to me."

"He is certainly an aristocrat," Hiso said. "Born to wealth and power. And he has a pilot's eyes. He's looked into the deeps. But so has the woman." He eyed Tereu.

"They could not have found their way here without a jump point. Without access to Line records."

"I read the hospital's report," Tereu said impatiently. "The woman has been ill. Fevered. She kept telling some mad story or other—saying she was called here."

" 'Called'?" Hiso's eyes narrowed.

"She's demented. Or else she thinks we're fools," Tereu said. "She's Line, too—by association, anyway. A Line man wouldn't travel with a woman unless she was his."

Hiso smiled coldly. "With you it's always a matter of sex, isn't it? Have you considered that she might be telling the truth? In which case, there's a tale there. An important one."

"You ask her, then," Tereu said, "if you have time for tales." She faced him. "So what have you learned about their ship?"

Hiso made a show of serving himself whiskey, sipping at the straw, sighing with pleasure. She watched him closely. *He isn't sure how much he wants to tell me.*

He set down the tiny bulb, half-slack, and eyed her. "We could examine it only from outside. The ship's hatch is sealed, tight as demon's teeth. I suspect the pilot is the only one who can admit us. But the measurements and readings we've been able to make remotely are—enticing. Power levels that it's hard to believe."

"Can't you cut your way in?"

"No," Hiso said, his voice regretful. "Not without risking damage we can't repair." He smiled. "But—perhaps she'll choose, in time, to admit me. That's one advantage of dealing with a woman pilot."

"Always a matter of sex with you, too, is it not?" Tereu returned his smile, anger flaring behind the rigid mask of her control. "Or power. Aren't they the same? You told me once . . . What else have you learned?"

"The ship is larger than any we have, and will be faster

in realspace. And—" He looked down at his whiskey. "Based on our examination, it is armed."

"Armed with what?" she demanded.

"Missiles of some kind," he said. "Well shielded, but—fission weapons, most likely. But small, smaller than any we can build. That ship could be formidable, in our hands."

"But what use is one ship?" she said. "They're fighting the Cold Minds themselves. Their people clearly don't intend to save us or reinforce us. We are alone. Facing the end, alone."

"We've always been alone, Perrin Tereu." He caressed her shoulder. "Nothing has changed. We'll survive as we always have. The way we've found for ourselves, that has saved us for centuries, is as right as it always has been."

She felt her fists clench, but she did not allow the deep, bitter anger to show in her face. "Yes. As right as it has always been."

Hiso drained the last of the whiskey and set down the bulb. "And beyond that—" He glanced at the image from the other room. "We can still profit from our guests. And from their ship. If I commanded such a ship, at the head of the Triton pilots—" He looked steadily into her eyes. "No one could anticipate me. No one could stop me. No one at all."

"Not even the deepsiders," she said slowly. "Not even—" After all these years, she still could not keep the little break of bitterness from her voice. "Not even Esayeh."

"Not, at last, even Esayeh," Hiso said, and smiled into her eyes. "Now, I fear, I have an appointment. And you must go back to your guests. Make them welcome. Make them happy." He kissed her cheek. "That is your best gift, my love."

She nodded, trying to smile, to hide her racing thoughts. She could not let him use this gift only for his own advantage, to consolidate his power—not at this time of danger for her people. *There will be no end to it. He sees this ship as a key. And keys belong in the First Citizen's hands.*

As the private door closed behind Hiso, her smile faded.

Perhaps there was still hope.

Perhaps, against all odds—against Hiso himself—she could still save her people.

SEVEN

In the private bath of Tereu's guest quarters, Linnea dried
herself off after her shower, luxuriating in the feeling of
complete cleanness, the softness of the rug against her bare
feet, the deep, complete warmth that relaxed her body,
muscle and bone. She hoped Iain felt as good as she did today. He still showed some signs of their long ordeal in otherspace.

They'd had two days of quiet rest in this comfortable
suite, part of Tereu's residence. Then, this morning, they'd
received a handwritten note from Tereu, inviting them to
join her in the reception parlor where they'd first spoken
together. Inviting them to meet, as Tereu put it, a man of
importance.

That sounded promising to Linnea: an end to these im-
posed days of rest and recovery in a suite that was surely
monitored, where she and Iain could discuss their situation
elliptically or not at all. Enough.

Linnea combed her damp hair smooth. She and Iain

understood each other, with no need for words: Finding
Linnea's ship, regaining control of it, was vital. That ship
was their hope of freedom and, eventually, return home to
the Hidden Worlds. From what Linnea had been able to
gather, no ship in this system would be capable of so long
a jump.

Yet these two days had been good. Needed. Apparently
following unalterable custom, Tereu had left the two of
them to rest, alone and undisturbed except for a medical
attendant, who checked them in the mornings and eve-
nings. A silent servingman brought them simple but exqui-
site meals: fresh fruits and vegetables, beautifully cooked
fish, small loaves of soft bread. Linnea watched for a blue
flower, or the image of one; but none appeared in their
rooms, on their meal trays, or anywhere else. Here in
Tereu's house, Linnea guessed, they were well protected
from anyone who might try to get a message to them. And
it was clear that the nurse, at least, thought that Tereu
would wish to prevent it.

But yesterday afternoon the medical attendant had removed their IVs and pronounced them recovered—and
now, today, Linnea could hope for answers, from Tereu or
from this "man of importance." Linnea stretched luxuri-
ously, enjoying the feeling of freedom, and picked up a
white robe from the back of a chair. The soft, light material caressed her shoulders as she put it on.

Linnea left her bath and passed into the softly lit bedroom beyond. The familiar scent of coffee met her—a tray
stood on the table with a shining thermal container and a
beautiful arrangement of sliced fruit and bread.

But something else caught her attention. She grinned.

Iain sat naked on the edge of their bed, trying to comb
some oil through his long, damp hair. She stood for a moment in the shadows, studying him. His unhealthy thinness
would pass, but despite it she still liked the strong line of
his body, the way the muscles moved under his skin, the

poised angle of his head, his intent focus as he tried to work the comb through the end of the long black hank in his hand.

"Let me," she said softly.

He looked up, and his eyes lit at the sight of her. "That's not your job. Not anymore."

"I always liked this part of it," she said, taking the comb from his hand and sinking down beside him. "And so did you." She pushed at his shoulder. "Turn your back so I can work. And sit straight. No, don't turn your head."

"But I like to look at you," he said.

She tugged at his hair. "No arguments, Pilot."

Her practiced hands worked the comb firmly but gently through his hair, spreading the thin, scentless oil. When she had combed the tangles to smooth black silk from the crown of his head to the ends, she set the comb aside. But instead of gathering the hair up to braid it, she pushed it aside—kissed the side of his neck, the warm strong pulse there, tasting the clean, familiar scent of his skin.

He arched his back. "We'll be late for our meeting," he muttered. *Eyes watching,* she knew he was thinking.

"Then we'll be late." *Let them watch.* It didn't matter. How many more days of peace would she and Iain ever have together? Each one could be the last.

She smiled, climbed lightly onto Iain's lap facing him, kissed his ear, and laughed, deep in her throat, at the way his breath caught, and the sudden strength of his hold on her, his hands sliding down to grip her hips. "Remind me how this works," she said.

"You just have to—" His breath caught again, and he bit his lower lip. "Oh. You remember."

It was easy in the light gravity to wrap her legs around his body, easy to fit herself against him and kiss him as he began to move inside her. "You remember, too," she said on a gasping breath, and then for a long time there were no words.

• • •

They were indeed late. But as Linnea and Iain entered Tereu's reception parlor, Tereu and her companion, a gray-haired, upright man with a neatly trimmed beard, showed no concern; they turned, smiling, from the hearth to greet their guests.

Tereu said, "Pilot sen Paolo, Pilot Kiaho, I am honored to present to you my consort and the First Pilot for Triton, Kimura Hiso." She turned to Hiso and set her right hand on his arm, a precise and formal gesture, and continued. "Hiso, please welcome the pilot sen Paolo Iain and the pilot Kiaho Linnea."

"You delight me as always, Perrin Tereu," Hiso said. He turned to Linnea. "As does the prospect of acquaintance with so intrepid a pair of pilots."

Smooth words. But sharp eyes. Linnea nodded politely. She did not need to glance at Iain to sense that he shared her wariness. Sparring with this man for information would be no easy game. Linnea had seen already that the rules and protocols binding this world to order were easily a match for the rules and protocols of the Line.

Familiar territory for Iain. But for her, a battlefield, and a dangerous one.

She watched as Hiso studied them both, his glance flicking over their fine borrowed clothes. The long black sleeveless dress Tereu had provided for Linnea clung to her body in a way that made her nervous, after years of living and working in rough coveralls or sensible tunics and trousers, years of never thinking about how she looked as long as she was clean. Judging from Hiso's smile, Linnea's appearance pleased him; perhaps an advantage, though of a sort she had little experience in using. That had been a lesson from Nexus—one she'd deliberately forgotten long ago.

Tereu waved Iain and Linnea into chairs and served tea before speaking of business. This time the tea was mildly warm, milky, and sweet. Hiso refused a chair and drank his tea standing. No doubt, in this world of tall, long-boned people, he sought what advantage he could. He kept his focus on Linnea. "So," he said. "Tereu and I are all eagerness to hear what you can tell us of the Hidden Worlds. Did they prosper after their founding?"

Last night she and Iain had settled, in whispered words that would have made little sense to an outsider, exactly how much they would say this morning. "They prospered for the most part," Linnea said. "Most are self-sufficient; some are net exporters. But some worlds have struggled to survive."

Hiso tilted his head, his expression politely regretful. "The war?"

"An older problem than that," Linnea said. "Poverty of resources. . . . The Cold Minds have done serious harm to few of our worlds as yet."

"But they have to some," Tereu said. It was not a question. At Linnea's glance, she added dryly, "We have some familiarity with their methods."

"We have suffered some losses, yes." Two worlds— Nexus contaminated beyond recovery, and before that, Freija destroyed utterly. Linnea did not fully understand Iain's insistence that these disasters not be mentioned, but she kept to the plan. "Losses of property and people."

"You've lost people to the Cold Minds?" Hiso asked, his voice full of quiet sympathy. "To infestation? Or were they killed?"

"Both," Iain said. Linnea sensed the disquiet he was struggling to hide. "We're fighting a defensive war, against infiltration. We don't know where the Cold Minds will turn up next."

"But you appear to have defended yourself effectively, if you're still fighting after several years," Hiso said with a bleak smile. "Earth fell in forty-seven days, between the first open rising and the last clean ship to launch."

"I know," Iain said quietly. "We haven't forgotten."

"We've been lucky," Linnea said. "We're mobilizing, finding and training new pilots, building ships as fast as we can, while we can."

Hiso looked at her with frank admiration, and she flushed. "I understand," Hiso said. "You've set orbital patrols, no doubt? And of course you would destroy any unauthorized ship that reaches ground." He sipped his tea. "It will work for a while, until the Cold Minds' numbers increase."

"I would be interested in understanding your own defensive measures," Iain said. "Whether perhaps you could offer any suggestions, any new tactics. . . ."

Hiso set down his tea, and Linnea saw his mouth tighten. When he looked up at Iain, his eyes were strangely bright. Tears? He said, "We do as you have done. I lead a flight of three wings—forty-two jumpships and numerous conventional orbital vessels. We fly orbital patrols. We fight. Some of us die. Some die who should not." His voice was husky. "But the thought of our people sustains our courage. As I'm sure it does your own."

Linnea caught Iain's eye, then looked away. She knew he was sharing her thought: This could not be all of the truth; a force like that could not hold off the full power of the Cold Minds for six days, let alone six centuries.

But judging from Hiso's polished words, and his easy bid for sympathy, they would not startle any new information from him, at least not yet. He was giving with one hand and withholding with the other—as anyone would do, early in a game like this one.

"The key, of course," Hiso said, "is to keep them from gaining a foothold in-system. Too late for us, of course, but fortunately, there's little to tempt them to come out this far. You have—how many entire systems to defend?"

Linnea ignored his question. "You're right, of course— our main objective is to prevent them from planting a base anywhere and easily increasing their numbers."

Hiso hesitated, then said, "Of course." He cleared his throat. "It delights me that this effort has met with enough success to permit the Hidden Worlds to send a ship and two pilots far from your war, all the way to ours. To charm us with your company."

"We are equally delighted, of course," Iain said calmly.

Hiso shrugged with one shoulder. "May I ask—why have you come? Pilot Kiaho, from the reports I have been given by my orbital patrolmen, your words when you first arrived were—confused."

Linnea looked down at her pouch of tea, then up into Hiso's eyes. She and Iain had agreed last night that their mission must appear to be official, sanctioned by the government of the Hidden Worlds. This would give Iain and Linnea some level of immunity, assuming the customs here were anything like those of Earth or the Hidden Worlds. Iain had not wanted to tell their hosts anything else at all.

But Linnea's determination had not changed: She must tell the truth about what had first called them here. "We came because you called me," she said quietly. "Someone here did. A pilot, because it was in otherspace that I sensed it. Again and again, on many jumps, stronger every time. No words, but images of Earth as it once was. And a feeling that time was running out."

She saw Hiso and Tereu exchange a glance. Hiso coughed and said, "Sometimes, during training or even after, younger jump pilots begin to receive . . . emotional impressions while in otherspace. And it soon becomes evident that these are related to—weaknesses in the mind of the pilot. I'm sorry to be blunt."

"I know that," Linnea said firmly. "I've trained more than a hundred young pilots myself. This was different. I received an image of a jump point—a real one. That image brought us here." She described it: Neptune, the stars.

Hiso laced his fingers together, shook his head. "If anyone less distinguished, less courageous had told me this tale—if I did not already know that you had in fact achieved this journey—well, I would call it very strange."

He hints that I'm lying. "And yet we arrived. A dream, a hallucination, could not have brought us here safely."

"Did the Line preserve no records of the jump points for Earth?"

The answer to this would have to come from Iain. But he said only, "I was young when the Line exiled me. There are inner secrets of the Line that hadn't yet been revealed to me. If those records existed, I never knew it."

Linnea took a breath. "First Pilot Kimura—"

"Hiso, please," Hiso said with a brief smile.

"Do you know who summoned me? And how?"

She saw Hiso and Tereu exchange an opaque glance. Then Hiso said, "No. We know nothing about this. It has never been possible to communicate through otherspace. From one ship to another!"

"And yet—" Iain said. He turned both hands palm up.

Hiso nodded impatiently. "And yet, here you are. We must find the pilot who sent you the jump point—find out who has developed this capability."

"Some one of your own pilots," Iain said.

"I suspect not," Hiso said frankly. "There are—other inhabited places in the Earth system. A few jump pilots who are not under my command. Perhaps it was one of them. Tereu has—connections with some of those people, and I will request that she pursue that question."

Linnea had no trouble guessing Hiso's thoughts: *If this is real, it's a weapon.* And he would want it for his own pilots. Controlled, refined, made to carry words or commands, it would give an advantage against the Cold Minds; multiple ships could maneuver together in otherspace, perhaps, or carry out a coordinated attack—things that had never been possible before. She guessed from Iain's troubled expression that this realization was just now coming to him. He had resisted the idea that such communication was even possible for so long that he'd never thought it through.

Well, she had. "I believe that we would all benefit from an exchange of ideas," she said. "A discussion of tactics that have served us both." She kept her voice neutral, her expression noncommittal, but she watched Hiso carefully. "We've had some success in our skirmishes with the Cold Minds. And you—your people have survived in this system for a very long time."

Linnea saw Hiso's face smooth out under bland self-control. "You may not yet grasp our great distance from the sun, Pilot Kiaho. There's little energy here for the Cold Minds to exploit; the solar flux is a thousandth of what it is at Earth. We have no resources the Cold Minds can't obtain more easily in the warm inner worlds—which they utterly control."

Linnea studied Hiso. *There is definitely something you don't want to tell us, my brother pilot.*

But she took her cue from Iain's restraint. *Don't push. Not yet.* For a wild moment she considered asking Tereu about blue flowers. But no, she would dance this dance, follow Iain's lead; these people were much more his than hers. She smiled pleasantly at Hiso. "Iain and I look forward to learning more about your achievements here."

She was watching, and she saw Hiso's bland mask slip, revealing a flicker of anger, gone almost at once. And at the same moment, beyond Hiso, she saw that Tereu, too, was watching him—and her eyes showed a deep wariness.

Linnea smiled at Hiso. *So you are dangerous.*

Well, brother, so am I.

After Hiso had departed with another exchange of courtesies and assurances, two of Tereu's staff of scholars—a man and a woman, both gray-haired and black-clad—conducted Iain and Linnea on what was to be a brief tour of the Triton outpost. Tereu waved them all off with a smile; apparently she had no intention of leaving her comfortable seclusion to continue as their guide and host. After the first few minutes with the scholars, Linnea began to understand why.

They went on foot—trailed at a distance by two of Tereu's men—through the little park that surrounded the residence, then along a high-arched main corridor. This one was walled with gleaming polished metal, lined with the ever-present stunted trees in pots, set meticulously every ten meters along each wall.

"This is spacious," Iain said.

"The city has grown over the centuries," the woman, Cleopa, said with clear pride. "Do you know, Pilot sen Paolo—one can walk three kilometers without ever passing through the same corridor twice?"

Iain shook his head as if in amazement.

"There are slideways," Cleopa said, "and a few dedicated shafts with shuttle cars; but in general, you see, our design encourages regular exercise."

"And yet no one seems to be out walking," Linnea said. This was a radial corridor, leading straight out from Tereu's residence at the center of the city, and Linnea could see far ahead: The wide corridor was empty. She'd lived on orbital stations. There, people were everywhere, pursuing their work, their leisure, their business, the corridors always crowded. Yet here the four of them walked in a shell of emptiness. Much like the one in which Tereu lived, Linnea reflected—in her small, perfect residence in its domed circle of garden. "Is there any public gathering place we could visit?" Linnea asked. "Maybe a market?"

"Oh, I'm sorry, Pilot Kiaho." The gray-haired man who had called himself Scholar Natan smiled thinly. "There are no scheduled gatherings for sport today, and as for markets—we distribute goods rationally here, you see. We have no need to buy and sell among ourselves."

"No, not among ourselves," Cleopa said. She had fallen into step beside Linnea. "But there is always the deepsiders' market—"

"Which is not open today," Natan said repressively. There was an awkward silence. They all kept walking.

"What are deepsiders?" Iain asked.

"Deepsiders are people who live and work in space," Natan said, with a twist of contempt in his voice that made Iain lift an eyebrow. "A diminishing population, without the vigor of Tritoner stock. We allow them to trade with us, when one of their carrier ships is in. But that does not happen to be the case today."

"But it will be tomorrow," Cleopa said, with a glance at Linnea.

"Deepsiders are of no interest," Natan said, repressive again. "You must have something similar in the Hidden Worlds. People who wander from asteroid to asteroid, mining." Linnea wondered at the hostility in his voice. "They scavenge what they can to sell to us, and they manufacture in zero gee what we cannot here on the surface. They're not like us," he said vigorously. "They live in chaotic, smelly habitats, they move randomly from place to place—and their social customs are shocking."

Linnea's eyes met Iain's. "They sound interesting," Linnea said, and looked away from Iain's grin. "A different culture. And I understand that they, too, have jump pilots."

"They do," Cleopa said, with an unfriendly glance at Natan. "A few jumpships, in constant use. You must understand—they live in widely scattered places. It takes years for one of their ore carriers from the Trojan asteroids to reach our orbit. Rocks have the patience for such a journey. But people do not."

"Perhaps the Hidden Worlds never had any need for deepsiders," Natan said. He sniffed. "You don't have to *trade* for water and ammonia and nitrogen. You don't have to *buy* metal, just dig where you stand! Dig here on Triton, and it's ice for hundreds of meters down."

"Deepsiders interest me," Linnea said, catching Cleopa's eye. *Deepsiders, and deepsider pilots.* "Iain and I would like very much to meet some of them. Perhaps we could visit their market tomorrow?"

"I'm afraid it would be too difficult to arrange for your safety on such short notice," Natan said.

"But we've come so far," Linnea murmured, allowing regret to inform her tone. And at that moment she caught a glimmer of humor in Cleopa's eyes. "It seems a shame." She ignored Iain's exasperated expression.

"Perhaps *I* can arrange it," Cleopa said. "After all, Triton is extremely safe. You were telling Madame Tereu only last week, Scholar Natan, how you rejoiced at the fact that a child might walk alone from the refinery quarter to the Palace of Sport . . . ?"

Natan reddened. "There is no need for our guests to visit the actual market. If you are curious about deepsiders, Pilot Kiaho, we can provide educational recordings that—"

"Scholar Natan," Cleopa said blandly, "you'll give our guests the impression that we have something to hide." She slid her arm through his. "I know *you* can arrange this. I know you wouldn't wish to disappoint *these* guests."

Linnea caught Iain's wondering glance, but they both kept silent. *Deepsiders.* Linnea had stumbled onto something important. But she could not yet guess what.

Natan stared at his colleague for a moment. Then nodded with obvious reluctance. "If our guests insist, and if Madame Tereu agrees, I'll do my best to arrange the visit."

They had reached their first destination, which turned out to be a school. In a vividly lit assembly hall, walled in pale green tile and gray metal, perhaps a hundred children knelt, waiting in neat rows on the black plastic floor—girls in clean gray dresses, boys in black trousers and neatly fitting white shirts. The children rose gracefully to their feet, all at once, as Linnea, Iain, and the scholars entered.

A row of pretty, exquisitely tidy little girls stepped forward and sang a welcome song whose words Linnea could not quite follow: words about warmth, and shielding, and the ever-bright light of watchfulness—whatever that meant. A large picture of Tereu, more cheerful than the official portraits in the corridors, smiled down on them all from one wall.

A thin, nervous boy made a speech, his words coming so rapidly that Linnea was helpless to follow them. Then there was another song, about how the minstrel boy to the war had gone, and how his songs were made for the pure and free. And the visit was over.

"There were almost as many teachers as students," Iain remarked, as they left the school corridor.

"We don't have very many children," Cleopa said, with a note of sadness in her voice. "The radiation here—it's more than is quite—safe." She glanced at Linnea. "Have you had any children yet?"

"We're at war," Linnea said steadily. "So that is a decision I'm not free to make." This was not a matter she'd ever yet chosen to speak of; certainly not with strangers.

"You *choose* not to have children," Natan said, with a puzzled glance at Iain, who showed no expression. "Interesting. Do you see, among our people—we never refuse the gift, if it comes to us. So many couples are sterile."

"Can't you match fertile people?" Iain asked. "At least to produce children?"

Natan looked shocked. "That's deepsider thinking." He shook his head. "We would lose too much. Social order. The bond of family. The foundation of our strength." He stopped, with obvious relief, in front of a series of sliding metal doors. "The shuttle to the industrial section." He touched a metal door in front of them. It slid aside, revealing the car, without seats but lined with metal bars reaching from floor to ceiling.

Linnea stood close to Iain as the car started up. As she'd suspected, the acceleration of its motion was so much greater than the weak gravity that she had to brace her feet against the bar as well as gripping it with her hands. As the car careened around a curve, Iain's arm slid around her waist and steadied her, and she leaned gratefully into his warm strength. No one else seemed to feel the cold as she did.

Natan was droning on about nitrogen geysers, the local stability of the crust. "We mine water, and extract ammonia; and there's a region a few kilometers away where we've blasted away the frozen nitrogen and are mining organics, mostly short-chain." Natan lifted his chin. "It's reduced our dependency on the deepsiders—we are no longer forced to buy what they mine out of the eccentric chondrites."

"By which my colleague means asteroids," Cleopa said to Linnea. "Asteroids with carbon in them. Scholar Natan talks like that all the time, I fear." As she was speaking, the car came to a slow, gentle halt, and the door slid open. "Here we are."

The high, cold spaces of the industrial section, smelling faintly of ammonia, were a complicated maze of pipes and storage tanks and pumps, big sealed propane burners, chemical processing. Men in sealed suits and respirators glided past on small carts, anonymous behind plastic visors. "You built all this after Earth fell?" Iain marveled.

"Much of it was already here," Cleopa said.

Natan gave her a cold glance, then turned to Linnea. "The deepsiders had been out here for years already, you see, setting up an immense project to collect helium-3 from Neptune's atmosphere and ship it back to Earth as fuel for the vast fusion plants they were starting to build, right at the end of—before the Cold Minds. A glorious time in

Earth's history, one that—" He caught Cleopa's eye and hurried on. "Well, there was no need for the fuel once Earth was lost; and our ancestors needed shelter. The abandoned project left plenty of material and equipment for us all, here on Triton and in Neptune's orbit."

"And so we pushed the deepsiders off Triton," Cleopa said.

"It was a reasonable division of resources," Natan said. "Deepsiders prefer space; we prefer gravity. Deepsiders complain when they come here, you know. Eight percent gee, and they complain."

"I have a deepsider cousin who comes here often," Cleopa said. "She rarely complains."

Natan moved away abruptly to stand beside Iain, who was looking through a viewing window at an array of tanks and pipes that meant nothing to Linnea. Cleopa lingered beside her.

"Natan thinks I should be more ashamed of my cousin." Cleopa said with a grin. "My cousin says it's not the gee that bothers her—it's everything moving in the same direction when she lets go of it."

"I look forward to meeting some deepsiders for myself," Linnea said, smiling back at her.

"Let me give you my cousin's name and family code— in case you should need it," Cleopa said. She pulled a notebook out of one of the capacious pockets of her robe, scribbled a few words on the corner of a page, tore it off, and pressed it into Linnea's hand." "Keep that safe," she said in a low voice. "Look at it later."

Linnea blinked at her, but it was too late for questions; Natan and Iain had turned away from whatever it was that had fascinated Iain. Linnea slipped the scrap of paper into her own pocket and smiled her thanks to Cleopa.

"I think," Natan said as he reached the two women, "that this has been a long enough day for our two guests. Madame Tereu will be concerned if it should prove we've overtired them. I suggest that we return to the city at once."

"As you instruct, of course, Scholar Natan," Cleopa said calmly. She did not look at Linnea.

And Linnea did not look at Iain. She kept her hand in her pocket, her fingers on the scrap of paper that might be her first clue to the answers she sought.

EIGHT

Iain hid his sigh of relief as the door of their quarters closed behind them, leaving him alone with Linnea. He'd seen her suppressed excitement, the slight tension in her expression, after her short private conversation with Cleopa. Now, at last, he could ask her what had caused it.

In the red "sunset" light streaming in through the window, she stood with her back to him, looking down at something in her hand. Without speaking he walked over to her and looked down as well.

A note on a scrap of paper—was that it? Linnea turned her hand slightly, and he could make out the scribbled words: *Market tomorrow alone FAINT.*

He looked into her eyes and saw only eagerness there. *Alone.* This must be another sign: like the blue flower that they still had not seen, that he hoped they would never see. She could be so incautious when she was sure of herself. Had she even considered that it was one of Tereu's people who had given her this paper? One of Tereu's people who wanted her to go to the market tomorrow, and mark herself out for—what?

He kissed her forehead. "I'm tired. Aren't you?"

"Not really," Linnea said. He saw the question in her eyes.

"I think you should stay here tomorrow and rest." He tried not to put any particular urgency in the words.

But from her quick glance, he saw that she understood him. He saw her hand tighten, crumpling the bit of paper, and she dropped it into her pocket again. "Don't come along, then, if you're tired."

"It's you I'm thinking of," he said, as gently as he could.

She lifted her chin. "Iain, you know that all I want, all I've wanted since we came here, is—the chance to learn."

He took her in his arms. "Today we learned about ammonia purification. Will nothing satisfy you?"

She smiled, but the faint spark of anger underlying it was as plain to him as a flame in a dark room. She set her fists on his chest—the old distancing gesture. "Iain. Please. You've always trusted me to judge what's best for me."

"But I always worry when you take risks," he said. "Which means I'm always worried." He knew she would see past the lightness in his words.

"I do what I have to," she said quietly. "You know that, Iain. And you know you have no right to stop me."

"No right!" *Unfair.*

Her head went back. "No right," she said, and pushed away from him.

At that moment Iain knew, bitterly, that once again he had gone too far in his need to protect her. Once again she would prove her independence by putting herself in danger. And there was nothing, nothing at all, that he could do to stop her.

·　　·　　·

Half an hour before dawn, Hiso stood in Tereu's bed-chamber, straightening and smoothing his clothing before one of her many tall mirrors. Through the window at his left, the watery gray light of earliest morning lit the pale flowers of the walled private garden outside. Tereu lay smiling behind him, curled naked on the thin, soft padding of her bed, sleepy from their lovemaking. Always she liked getting this proof of her power over him; never had she understood that to him it meant nothing.

Tereu had never understood power. Or its price. Or the tools it required to maintain it and increase it. He turned his head, studying himself in the mirror. "What do you have planned for our guests today? Specifically Kiaho."

"She's off on another tour later this morning," Tereu said lazily.

Hiso looked down at her in annoyance. "I told you that I need a private word with her, as soon as possible."

Tereu got to her feet and touched a commscreen. "Then you're in luck. She's already gone to the breakfast room. Early for her—they must keep luxurious hours in those Hidden Worlds."

Hiso turned and looked down at Tereu. "This is more important than you appear to understand. That ship of hers. The engines alone—" He leaned toward the mirror and smoothed his beard carefully. "There should be complete plans, complete technical specifications on board. Do you have any idea what they might mean to our efforts here?"

"That's your department," she said. "You pilots, all of you together. You, and Kiaho, and that man of hers."

Again Hiso studied her in the mirror. "Then you admit that he's interesting."

"I wouldn't know," Tereu said, an edge in her voice. "He almost never speaks. . . . Tell me, Hiso. Once you've gotten inside Kiaho's ship—do you even need her any-more?"

Hiso looked at her in the mirror, wondering again at her lack of subtlety. Without the complex linkage of family that had allowed her to inherit her high position, she would have been a lesser bureaucrat at most—not even a wife and mother; her body had failed at that. *Denying him sons. . . .* "These are early days," Hiso said. "She and the man together are a force we need to understand, before we dare break it. The bond between them—they are not married in our sense, of that I'm sure, but there is something deep and dangerous there."

"Romantic nonsense," Tereu said. "The woman is nothing, aside from her piloting skill. But the man—he's Line, Line by training if nothing else. He must know the meaning of service to humanity. *He'll* understand our need."

"But the ship, apparently, is hers." Hiso turned and faced her. The lines on her face, the shadows under her eyes were plain to see in the bare, cruel light of morning. "And—consider, my dear. They're both outsiders." He folded his arms and looked down at her. "He might serve, they might both serve—until they understood the basis of our power here."

She sat up straight, realization clear on her face. "And what we've paid to remain who we are." He heard again the low, bitter note in her voice, the note he hated; the note that had crept into her voice in the empty years after her final miscarriage.

He let his anger show, to wake her to her cowardice. "Are you becoming weak? Now?"

Her eyes widened a little, even as she gave him a mechanical smile. "You keep me strong, Hiso. You keep us all strong."

"Remember it," he said curtly, and left her there.

In Tereu's richly decorated breakfast room, by the light of a gas fire, Linnea waited impatiently for the hour when she could make her promised expedition to the deepsider market—when at last she might meet, face-to-face, someone who would finally answer her questions. Standing at the sealed window, sipping at a pouch full of coffee, she watched the slow rising of the artificial light over the park. There was almost nothing real about it but the living plants themselves; the birdsong was played from speakers in the trees, Tereu had said. . . . But Linnea had already sensed the reverence in which this small green space was held; those who had been selected to tend it moved and spoke like priests, and the flowers they brought Tereu were offered and accepted with precise ceremony.

The park was false, the shadow of a shadow of real nature; but these people could not know that. No living human in the Earth system had ever set foot on a world with open air, open skies—none of them had ever walked freely under the sun. Not for generations. She could not help but pity them.

She sipped once more at the bitter, fragrant coffee, and looked out again at the symmetrical ranks of rosebushes—stalked globes of red or white blossoms, their beds bordered meticulously by pale pink, fleshy-stemmed flowers whose names she did not know. She'd touched one yesterday, when no one was looking; but the leaves were hairy, and the whole plant had a strange, pungent smell that lingered on her fingertips.

Behind her in the breakfast room, someone coughed. Her shoulders tightened. She arranged a welcoming smile, then turned.

Kimura Hiso, perfectly groomed and smiling, bowed to her. "Pilot Kiaho."

"Pilot Kimura," she murmured. "May I serve you some coffee?"

"Thank you, no," he said. "The servant told me you were here. I was hoping for a word before you leave."

"Of course," she said. They sat down opposite each other

on soft pink chairs near the window, on each side of a small table on which was set a bowl of pink and white flowers that smelled faintly of cloves. Through the glass of the window Linnea could hear the faint buzz of clippers at the far side of the garden, no doubt perfecting the angle of a hedge.

"What I have to say concerns your ship," Hiso said.

"I was hoping to hear of it at last," Linnea said.

Hiso's raised eyebrow registered the reproach in her voice. "We have it safe at our skyport. But we've not been able to check its systems. It will not open to us."

"No," Linnea said. "It will not. It requires my touch." She would not mention, to this man, the Line override codes Iain knew, with which he could always gain access in her absence. "And I believe it isn't, in any case, compatible with your interlink technology? Or so Iain said."

"You're correct," Hiso said. "Our ships are old technology, compared to yours. See—" He lifted the hair behind his left ear, and Linnea saw with fascination the permanent, implanted plugs for ship leads, small buttons of hard black plastic set in his skin and, presumably, the skull beneath.

"So the neural connections are internal?" she said, trying to keep the fascinated revulsion out of her voice. "Permanently installed in your brain?"

"Yes. And thus subject to damage," Hiso said. "Old technology, as I said; dangerous to install; it does not always function correctly once in place, and it can even do ancillary damage to the pilot's brain over time. That is why we're so few—and that few, so proud."

Like my old enemies, the Line. Linnea bowed her head. "Certainly your pilots run great risks."

"We have maintained our ships for centuries with few resources. Some are failing. We have few, and we can no longer build more."

"Cold Minds jumpships—"

"We tried, long ago," Hiso said. "Always, always the pilots who entered the ships and joined with them became infested, had to be killed. We stopped attempting it centuries ago."

"Yet the Cold Minds' own pilots are not infested," Linnea said.

"We know it," Hiso said. "But that must be the Cold Minds' doing. *We* cannot protect ourselves. *We* cannot use their ships."

"And there's no neighboring system you could hope to escape to?"

Hiso laughed. "Why do you think your own people went so far?"

Linnea caught her breath. "So you know where we went."

A momentary hesitation. "I saw you both after you arrived here. You were nearly dead. Wherever you came from, it was far from here. No." He shook his head. "We know all the nearby systems, every sunlike star—data from early explorations with the first jumpships. There are no suitable worlds in any of those systems. Nowhere humans could live and walk on a free surface, breathe free air. Nowhere better than here. So this is our home." He looked at her and took a breath—*swallowing his pride,* Linnea thought—and said, "Will you help us?"

She clasped her hands behind her back. "How?"

Hiso hesitated. "We would be most grateful to learn more about the advances in technology your people have made since leaving this system. To study those advances directly—within your ship."

The thought of this cold, relentless man prying about inside her jumpship made Linnea shudder. She suppressed it. *Stall him. Depending on what happens in the market today, none of this may matter.*

"I don't like the sound of it," she said. "The ship's systems are delicate—liquid circuits, carefully contained.

You would have to allow us to supervise the work very closely and to stop it at any point. And even then—"

He looked her straight in the eye. "I don't wish to be blunt. But you force me to it. You are not in a position of strength here. And we have a great deal at stake. If we need to proceed without your approval, then we will."

"Unless I help you," she said, "you cannot open that ship without destroying its systems. That's the flat truth."

"If we might still learn something that gives us an advantage against the Cold Minds," Hiso said, "I will take that chance."

"You'd be a fool, then," Linnea said coldly. "If our technology gave us any such advantage, we would have driven them from the Hidden Worlds. We didn't—we couldn't." She let those words sink in, then said, "It's you who seem to have an advantage we do not. After six centuries, you're still alive."

He gave an angry shrug. "We have nothing that the Cold Minds want."

"But you do," Linnea said. "You're human. They need human pilots."

"And they take them," Hiso said, his voice tight. "In raids. . . . They take children, babies. Kill the rest."

"Have they raided here on Triton?"

He looked away, out the window at the pale "sunlight." "They choose lonely outposts. Deepsiders—our own space outposts are military or industrial, we do not risk our children in such exposed places." He met her gaze. "Pilot Kiaho. Will you grant us access to your ship?"

She lifted her chin. "I need to consult with Pilot sen Paolo. And I'm inclined at this point to refuse. But it would be of some help if you would answer a question—plainly."

Hiso inclined his head in an attitude of listening politeness.

"Are you certain that you don't know who was sending those images through otherspace?"

His answer was firm. "I've looked into it. It had nothing to do with my pilots. You know that we stopped hoping for help from your people long ago." He shook his head. "We've learned to be strong, to make hard choices. We do not dream like deepsiders, dream of places beyond this one. We only fight—to survive, to keep our children safe. We do—what humans do."

Linnea closed her eyes. The man's pain was obvious; but she knew she did not dare trust his emotion. Or him.

Yet he had her ship, whether or not he could enter it; if he kept it locked up, it was as far from her reach as from his.

She stood up and faced him. "I'll speak to Pilot sen Paolo, then decide," she said. "I can't promise anything more than that."

His voice was warm as he said, "I'm grateful, Pilot Ki-aho. Please send me word of your decision. Telling Perrin Tereu will be sufficient."

She nodded silently and left. As she walked, she slid her fingertips into a pocket, touched the scrap of paper that Cleopa had pressed into her hand when they parted.

Deepsiders. . . . They were part of this puzzle. A step toward the answer she needed. . . .

Soon, maybe, she would know.

In their quarters, Iain listened with disbelief to Linnea's story of her conversation with Kimura Hiso. "No," he said at once when she had finished. "I would no more let him touch your ship than I would let him—"

"Touch me," she said with a sour smile. "I know the feeling." She stood looking down at the carpeted floor, one hand in the pocket of her black dress, a frown creasing her brow. "It's almost time for me to go. But I wanted you to know that this was up, that Hiso might be sniffing around my ship. I think I persuaded him not to try to break in, but you might have a word with Tereu. She seems a little more able to see reason than he is."

"I still think you should stay," Iain said, knowing it would do no good.

"It's only a couple of hours," she said, with a tight smile. "Talk to Tereu. Then I won't worry."

"Come back quickly," Iain said, his voice rough, "and *I* won't."

She came to him, took his hands, kissed him lightly, a quick warm brush of her lips. At the door she turned and looked back at him for a moment, upright, strong, her eyes dark and serious. Iain smiled at her, and she was gone.

He bent his head, stood with his hands clenched into fists, disciplined his breathing. But still, he was afraid.

NINE

At the center of the deepsiders' market, Linnea looked around with impatience and disappointment. Maybe it was the guard in green looming at her elbow. Or maybe it was her fine silk dress, which, today had made clear, marked her as a high-status Tritoner. For whatever reason, no one had tried to speak to her or even met her eyes.

The market, such as it was, stood in a bare, square, high-ceilinged metal space a hundred meters across and ten high, at the junction of four main corridors served by slideways. The chilly air echoed with the hum of voices, sometimes shouting numbers, sometimes words that meant nothing to her. Temporary tables with commscreens set up on them stood scattered throughout the space. From what Linnea could see and hear, what was being bought and sold at this market was contracts for commodities. She saw no blue flowers; there were no flowers at all, just a few of the wan little trees in metal tubs poking up here and there. She should have realized what kind of market it had to be.

Deepsiders were everywhere, easily recognizable in bright, warm clothing made of loose knits or warm napped cloth, bound tight at wrists and ankles. Most of them, oddly, had bare feet. Bright tattoos marked their hands, feet, even some faces: flowers, geometric designs. She knew those. She'd seen their like before—in the Cold Minds ships on Nexus. . . . At the memory of those maimed, comatose bodies, revulsion squirmed in her belly.

The deepsiders clustered around the commscreens carrying on muttered conversations with Tritoners, men mostly—making deals. So much of this grade of short-chain hydrocarbon, she overheard, for so much of this prime ore, or this vacuum-refined metal. She saw a couple of twenty-kilo bags of lentils change hands; that was about the closest this came to the markets she remembered on Terranova, in their home city of Port Marie—markets spilling over with food and flowers and handmade goods, bright with laughter and music. Festival places.

Here the tone was serious, almost grim, aside from the bright colors the deepsiders wore. All trades seemed to be barter, or sometimes slips of bright metal that must be markers. There was no credit system, she guessed—not with people scattered so widely, life so dangerous.

She wished Cleopa had been able to come; the young, blandly handsome guard Tereu had dispatched with her was of no use in answering questions. He wore a comm in his ear and kept his eyes on the crowd; he'd made it clear that she was not to distract him.

She caught a whiff of charcoal smoke and seared meat, and wandered farther down the row, the guard at her heels. Here was a booth staffed by Tritoner women in uniform gray. They were selling strips of meat seared over a flame—chicken, she guessed, fragrant with black pepper and garlic and some green herb. The deepsiders were lined up to buy it; meat cooked over open flame must be a treat. Linnea glanced at the guard, but from his wooden expression she guessed he would not permit her to try something as risky as street food. And she had no way to pay for it anyway.

Odd, though, that she could not catch anyone's eye. The Tritoners looked deferentially away from her, with her fine clothes and her attendant; but she did not sense that it was deference with the deepsiders. They talked to each other eagerly enough, laughing and joking as they waited to be served. But Linnea might have been invisible.

Which of them was waiting for the signal she had been told to give? There was no way to tell. She studied their clothing, the tables, the commscreens for any sign of a blue flower, but there was nothing.

She wandered on along the neatly laid-out aisles, accompanied only by the guard. He served, no doubt, to keep her from veering off schedule or off course as much as to protect her. She could think of no way to get rid of him.

Watch for a blue flower.

FAINT.

She might as well start setting up the possibilities. As they passed a metal support column, she stopped and leaned against it for a moment, holding her hand to her head. The guard rumbled something solicitous.

"Dizzy for a moment," she said, waving him away. "I'm all right. Let's go on."

But he was guiding her now, in a clear direction through the crowd. They entered a side corridor, and the clamor of the main market receded. Ahead, to the right, an alcove opened off the corridor. A dozen people waited there—all Tritoners, judging from their clothes, perched on high benches or leaning against the wall. A young deepsider man sitting in back, at yet another commscreen, looked up as they came in. The white wall at the back of the alcove was painted with the familiar red cross. *Medics.* "I'm fine," she said to the guard, in irritation. Stuck away in here, she might miss her opportunity.

But here came another of the medical personnel—another deepsider, judging from the soft, loose maroon belted coverall she wore, judging by her bare feet, judging by—

The softly faded tattoo on the back of her right hand.

A blue, trumpet-shaped flower, delicately inked, pale. . . .

Linnea gave the woman—small, dark, older—one startled glance, and slid gently to the deck.

Warm fingers pressed softly against the side of her neck. Then careful hands lifted her, carried her—she felt a curtain brush past her, sensed increased warmth and quiet, felt herself being set carefully down on a padded surface. Keeping herself limp, her eyes closed, she listened as a woman's voice—the doctor's?—told the guard to wait outside. "No, *outside*—as you see, there is no other door to this room. Wait in the outer clinic, and I'll fetch you in when she needs you."

Then silence, until a warm hand brushed her forehead, settled on her shoulder. "You really do look worn-out," the woman said softly.

Linnea opened her eyes, looked up into the calm, hooded eyes of the older woman. Her hair, deep black, was partly covered by a maroon-and-black headscarf, her wide face lit only by the light from the door of this back room. "Who are you?" Linnea asked.

"Pilang is my name," the woman said. "I'm the doctor here."

"A deepsider doctor?"

Pilang chuckled. "Most certainly. We're the best, you know. Tritoners save up their complaints until we come through."

"Then I'm glad you're here," Linnea said. "I need to know—"

Pilang's hand tightened on Linnea's shoulder. "Not now. Rest." A warning. Of course—there would be monitors even here, listening ears and watching eyes.

Linnea settled back in frustration. When would she be free to ask the questions that burned in her mind? *Why am I here? Why did you call me?* She blinked at Pilang, who was turning away to a high table next to the examination bed. "Forgive me," Pilang said, turning back with her hand folded shut. "It isn't always easy to understand treatment."

Startled, uneasy, Linnea took a breath to speak, to protest, and Pilang's hand tightened still more on her shoulder. Then her other hand slid along the side of Linnea's neck—touched it with something cool and moist.

Nausea, immediate and total, wrenched Linnea. Pilang deftly tended to her, so the mess was more or less contained. When the spasms eased for a moment, Linnea could see Tereu's guard standing in the doorway, looking uncertain, outraged, and rather green.

"I'm afraid she needs emergency treatment," Pilang said. "Supplies I don't have here. Pick her up, and let's go."

Linnea saw the guard glance at the stains on her dress, saw him flinch. "I—need to keep my hands free."

"And clean," Pilang muttered, and Linnea heard the dry contempt in her voice. Then a sigh. "Hana and I will carry her. You follow if you must. Oh, *merde*—"

Another spasm of retching racked Linnea. When it was over, she opened her eyes and saw that the guard had vanished—she heard gagging sounds from outside the door. And another woman—young, with strange pale skin and white-yellow hair—had come in and was handing a wad of cloth to Pilang, who unfolded it and began to fit it to Linnea's face. A mask, some kind of mask. With a bag attached, to contain— Clammy with nausea, Linnea cut off the thought. The mask smelled faintly of some piney herb, and after a moment the sickness seemed to ease a bit.

Pilang and the other woman lifted Linnea easily in the light gee, Pilang at her shoulders and the other woman at her knees; then, with one hand, the younger woman slid a stiff stretcher under Linnea and strapped her lightly in place. The two women carried her out through the waiting area, then sharp left into a small side corridor. Through the fog of nausea and a strange increasing fuzziness, Linnea heard the voice of her guard, protesting the direction. "Her vital signs are unstable," Pilang's voice said sharply. "The emergency equipment on our ship is closer than any of your clinics. If you want her to live, you'll let us take her there."

In a queasy fog of fear, Linnea struggled to understand. A ship? No, this wasn't right, what were they doing, where were they taking her? Fear choked her, and the sickness returned. She could say nothing, think of nothing. The light headlong glide through curving corridors made the queasiness worse, much worse.

Dimness and height, the smell of oiled metal—this was a familiar kind of place, strangely easing Linnea's fear. A docking bay. She heard the guard's voice again, protesting. Then another voice, a man's, old and dry. "No need for your help, friend," the voice said. "We have her safe." Linnea heard a surprised grunt, caught a glimpse of the guard falling forward with eerie slowness, slack-limbed, his eyes rolled up until the whites showed; and Pilang turning from him with something in her hand.

Who were these people? What did they want from Linnea?

But she could no longer speak at all—her body was exhausted, her mind fuzzed into incoherence.

"Esayeh, go, get the board warm," Pilang said. "That *gorilla* had a security code, they'll be—" A yellow light in the ceiling of the bay began to flash. "Damn. Hana, help me load her. No, wait, one moment—"

Another touch on the side of Linnea's neck, a wave of some strange, chilly scent, heaviness in her chest—

Darkness.

•　　•　　•

E sayeh turned from his station to look at the Hidden
  Worlds pilot as Pilang worked to seal her into her travel
couch on the deck. The young woman was a sickly greenish
brown—what he could see of her face around the vomit
mask. Her eyes were squinched shut, and she looked flac-
cid, unpromising. He shook his head. "*This* is the one?
You're sure?"

"She's the one my cousin sent to me," Pilang said, sealing the last seam. "She gave me the sign she was told to
give. And she's definitely the one who was piloting their
ship. Cleopa says she verified that with the crew that pulled
them out—the other one was only a passenger, still sealed
up when they got in."

Esayah shook his head. "A pilot. That. She looks—
pathetic."

"You *might* want to get us out of here before they lock
down the ship," Pilang said, hurrying to strap herself in
next to Hana, who was already snug in her acceleration
cocoon. "We need to be two jumps away from here before
they come after us."

Esayeh turned back to his board, brought the engines
from standby to full. Pilang was right, as always; he was
grateful for her sense, really he was. Yet there was never
time to ask her the questions he wanted to ask, about what
she might think was wise; and later he would forget them.
He knew it. Otherspace, all his time there, the work of his
life—it had done something to his memory, fragmented it.

Or maybe he was just getting old.

Esayeh pulled the piloting leads out of their cubby and
snapped the connections into the side of his head. Once
again, after the flickering transition, he saw the status displays overlaid on the view through his port: the wide, bare,
frozen plain of Triton, dirty white with contaminated frozen nitrogen, dim-lit only by Neptune at full, almost overhead. Far away, well beyond the close-in horizon, he saw
the high, lacy plume of a geyser. So beautiful. . . .

"Go, go," Pilang's voice urged him, and he cut the cabin lights, cut loose the docking clamps with three sharp clanks, started the launch jets. Recklessly, he ran the acceleration up to nearly half a gee, feeling the strain on his heart, hearing groans of protest from the women behind him—*all but the Hidden Worlds woman, she's used to this.* Even Tritoners wouldn't follow so fast, not this ship—they'd know it was no use. The strangely regular nubbled surface of this half of Triton fell away fast, and Neptune in full phase rose higher, sharp-edged blue against black. He cut the launch jets and felt the familiar lift and freedom of zero gee. Silence echoed in his ears. Almost the moment, almost the moment—*Jump.*

A flicker of the familiar nothingness, then they were back in normal space. He knew by the stars he was thirty degrees down-orbit and a little out, more or less what he'd been aiming for. Random jump, so the Tritoners could never follow. He touched a control, and the view through the port was overlaid with points of colored light, small, numbered. Refuges, way stations, mining outposts.

Any one of them would do, for the beginning of his young guest's education—for the beginning of his chance to see what she was made of.

Whether he could trust her with his people's lives.

He chose a habitat whose name he remembered and jumped again, into nothingness—toward the beginning of his hopes.

TRITON

L ate morning. Iain sat restlessly at a table in Tereu's parlor, at one of her library commscreens, working his way down a list of histories: accounts of events in the first years after the last Line jumpship left the Earth system. He kept glancing at the chrono in the corner of the screen.

Linnea was late, of course. No more than that. Something, some person, had caught her attention; someone usually did, in a new place.

It was absurd to worry, when he knew how carefully she was being guarded. *But not by me. . . .*

He forced his eyes back to the screen, to the words there, looking for the answer he'd sought: How had humans survived here? The Tritoners in their tidy, static city did not live like people in danger of imminent attack, people who could be wiped out by one well-placed missile—so what made them safe?

Hiso and Tereu had answered all his polite questions with polite evasions. The commscreen in the suite he and Linnea had shared had no access to Tereu's library, or any other. So when he'd found the parlor empty just now, he had slipped in, activated the comm, and gone straight to the library listings.

He tapped the current file shut and moved on to the next. So far he'd found no clues in these histories, carefully preserved as they were, some of them facsimiles of handwritten records. *Account of the Noble Death of Pilot Miguel Echeverria. List of the Survivors of the Fall of Birmingham, with Notes on Their Various Escapes. Memoir for My Son, by Susana Wyeth.* But nothing covered the period relevant to his search, the time just after the Triton settlement was established.

By any logic Iain could imagine, the Cold Minds should simply have smashed what was left of the human settlements—fragile shells that they were, in the cold and vacuum of the outer system. Human pilots for Cold Minds jumpships could be bred in captivity—a horrible thought, but surely they would do it if there was no other choice. So why were there still free humans in the Earth system? Free to fight, free to plan against the Cold Minds?

Iain rubbed the bridge of his nose thoughtfully. *Just how free are the Tritoners?* He wished again for Linnea's cynical insight; she saw things through people's words that he sometimes wrongly accepted, wanting as he did to believe that everyone was honorable. . . .

The early records that had been made in this settlement only railed against the Line's betrayal of humanity, or boasted of the refugees' success in setting up bases on Triton that could support all of the remaining survivors. No mention of the Cold Minds, of plans for attack or defense. Iain thought he could sense gaps in the narratives, places where something might have been deleted, but there was no way to prove an absence. With a sigh, he turned to the next file.

At that moment, the light in the room flicked to full brightness. Iain controlled his startlement, made himself turn calmly to the door—only to see that it was not Tereu who stood there, but Hiso.

Hiso, pale with anger—or fear.

Iain got to his feet, his mouth dry, as Hiso moved to stand directly in front of him. A guard in green followed Hiso into the room, a man with pale skin and pale gray eyes who moved behind Iain, out of sight. Iain did not take his eyes off Hiso. "What is this?"

"You've succeeded in surprising me, Pilot." Hiso flashed white teeth in a snarl. "Tell me how you and Pilot Kiaho arranged her escape."

Iain stilled himself. "Arranged her *what*?"

Hands gripped Iain's arms and Hiso struck him in the face, a stinging blow. "You know about it," he growled. "I know they made contact with her yesterday."

Iain did not struggle against the man gripping his arms, made no effort to return Hiso's blow. He let the pain bring his thoughts to cold clarity, helping him push his anger away, down, kept to use later. "Linnea—has escaped?" *To where?*

Hiso's dark eyes were icy. "She's your woman. She would do nothing without your knowledge."

"If you think that," Iain said, his voice uneven, "you don't know Linnea." He worked his shoulders impatiently, and at a nod from Hiso the man released him. "Tell me what happened to her."

At the naked fear in Iain's voice, Hiso's anger seemed to diminish. "She disappeared from the marketplace," he said. "By obvious arrangement with a deepsider. One of my men, her escort, has been injured. He saw her taken aboard a deepsider jumpship, which broke free without clearance and launched."

"Did you send a ship after them?" Iain's voice shook.

"No point," Hiso said. "The pilot jumped away as soon as he was clear."

Iain looked away, thinking hard. He wished again, bitterly, that Linnea had found a way to take him with her—that she had *wanted* to take him with her. This whole journey had been her quest, her adventure; and now she had gone on, to what end he might never find out.

"You know what she sought," Hiso said, echoing Iain's thoughts. "Word of these dreams of hers, of this pilot she said called her here. He must have been a deepsider, there's no one else."

"How many deepsider pilots are there?"

"Only a few," Hiso said. "Five or six, they come and go, and it's hard to keep count of them." He shook his head. "I would have arranged a meeting with one of them, here, where she would be safe. But—"

"She isn't safe with the deepsiders?"

"No," Hiso said. "They're primitives, really—living in disorder in ancient habitats, improvised shells of old ships or hollowed-out asteroids. They seem to be dying out in some parts of the system; now and then our patrols find habitats that have been completely abandoned. Perhaps the deepsiders have become desperate. . . . And their pilots are under the command of a man without mercy or shame, a traitor to his own people—a former Tritoner, but a dishonor to our city. I would not willingly let either of you fall into his hands. Or allow him to learn more of your ship."

"And so now this man has Linnea," Iain said, bitterly.

"If it suits his convenience to return her to you," Hiso said, "he will do so. His whims are not always cruel. But if it does not suit him—" Hiso shook his head. "You will never see her again. Among the deepsiders, it's all we can do to keep rough track of the major populations. We could never find an individual they'd chosen to hide. Or who chose to stay hidden."

Iain lowered his head, took a steadying breath. "Let me go after her, then. Perhaps they'll be willing to take me to her."

"No," Hiso said flatly. "We can't spare a ship. It's a pity you cannot use Pilot Kiaho's."

"But I can." Iain raised his head and met Hiso's hard stare. "I will, if I can use it to search for her."

He saw Hiso's eyes narrow slightly, and knew that he had said too much. "If you imagine," Hiso said, "that I will let you leave Triton freely, aboard that ship, you are deeply naïve."

"I can find her," Iain said. "The sooner I go, the better the chance."

"No." Hiso's voice was sure. "You have no idea of the volume of space the deepsiders inhabit, of the number of their settlements, large and small. There are deepsider habitats in the Neptune system, the Uranus system, in the Greeks and Trojans in Jupiter orbit, in the outer fringes of the asteroid belt. They live everywhere, inside anything that will contain pressure. No one who does not know where they're hidden can find them." His eyes were cold. "You'll see her again when the deepsiders consent to it. Not before."

Iain did not speak—could not speak.

"You will remain here," Hiso said, "as Perrin Tereu's

guest, and mine. Your welfare, and your future, strongly depend on how well your assistance satisfies *me*."

Iain breathed deeply. "You've made our relative positions clear."

"It was necessary to clarify the urgency of the situation," Hiso said. "And don't imagine that you can subvert Tereu simply because she's a woman. You don't interest her at all; she is my instrument, and content to be." He smiled slightly. "Remember that. Remember who holds power here. The pilots—always the pilots. And I'm their leader."

"Then tell me how I can earn my freedom," Iain said flatly.

"I need the use of your ship," Hiso said. "Which, for the moment, only you can pilot."

Iain took a steadying breath. *"Your ship." To Hiso, Linnea is already dead.* "And in exchange?"

"If I am satisfied," Hiso said, "and if your jumpship can be adapted to my use, I will detach one of my jump pilots to take you anywhere you wish within this system. You will not, of course, be permitted to return to Triton after that."

He turned on his heel and left Iain there.

Iain touched his burning cheek where Hiso's blow had landed. Decision burned clear in his mind. For now, for Linnea's sake, he would do what Hiso required—and look for any chance, any chance at all, to escape this place and find her.

And more: Linnea's ship would never be Hiso's. Before he saw that ship in Hiso's control, with its power, its range—Iain closed his eyes.

Before that happened, he would destroy Linnea's ship—even if it meant stranding them both here forever.

TEN

DEEPSIDER WAY STATION *CLAIR DE LUNE*

Pilang coasted into Esayeh's sleeping space at the way station, caught a hand and foot in one of the tough fabric loops lining its padded walls, and swung to a swaying stop. Esayeh floated, his bare feet well wedged in work loops, hunched over his commscreen. The dim purple light he favored when he was working turned his short white hair an odd shade of lavender. "Hah," Pilang said.

Esayeh looked up—pretending surliness, as always—and she gave him a smacking kiss on the forehead to forestall his inevitable criticism. "It worked," she said. "None of your remarks."

"She's safely asleep? Because—"

"She's settled in the back room at the clinic, sacked in tight. With what I gave her, she'll sleep like a stone, and be right as sunshine in six or eight hours."

Esayeh closed his commscreen and tugged himself nearer to Pilang, then turned to match her orientation. *Unusually polite, for him.* She suppressed a smile. After a moment, he returned her kiss—politely, on the mouth—then patted her shoulder. "Well done, friend. You brought me my Hidden Worlds pilot."

"What can you do with her? Without her ship, she can't reach—"

"Kimura Hiso has her ship," Esayeh said. "But Hiso's a fool. I know him of old, knew him when he was a boy—" Pilang rolled her eyes, and Esayeh broke off. "The point is," he continued with dignity, "Hiso looks at that ship and sees the missile tubes. Weapons! Gah! Anyone can throw missiles at the Cold Minds, blow up one ship or two out of hundreds of thousands. A stupid game, and after a while they tire of it and hunt you down. But Hiso looks at that ship, and that's all he sees: the chance to destroy something he's angry at, like a child in a tantrum. So what *doesn't* he see?"

Pilang sighed. "Just tell me."

"He doesn't see the essence of it," Esayeh said. "The pilot. The human at the core, the one who wears and uses the ship. *He* can have the missiles." Esayeh grinned at her. "*I* want the pilot's mind. That gives me everything else."

"Very pretty," Pilang said, and sniffed. "And how will you win this woman pilot over to our cause? Your personal charm? Your eloquence? Your wealth?"

Esayeh turned rudely upside down. "*You* will win her over, old friend. Your people will. If this pilot heard me across thousands of light-years, and if she then had the courage to dare the journey here, *out of compassion*—then—" He let out a gusty sigh. "Then she is the key to our hopes."

Pilang kept silent awhile, absorbing that. "Strange to think of all this—ending. Generations and generations and generations."

Esayeh looked at her again, a gentle smile on his upside-down face. "Strange to think of having hope."

Pilang felt the sting of tears in her eyes and blinked

them fiercely back. "Don't you do that. You know it's too soon."

"You're right," Esayeh said. "Too soon for me to speak to her, too soon to explain. First she must begin to understand why it matters. And you will teach her that."

"What will I teach her?" Pilang asked stubbornly. "Medicine? Knitting? Vacuum cookery?"

"How we live," he said. "Who we are. Our world."

Our world. She tried, she always tried to keep her heart hard, her mind clear, but she couldn't help but treasure these slips of Esayeh's—when he described himself as a deepsider. . . . "Huh," she said, trying to sound disdainful, as she glanced at the chrono on Esayeh's commscreen. "Very interesting. But I need my sleep now. I have patients to see. The clinic list was already half-full by the time we docked. Hana's meeting me early to help set the place up, it's always a mess with the amateurs using it between our visits." She looked back at him. "You think this pilot will take such a risk? For us?"

"If she is the one we need, the one I called here," he said, "she will." He smiled, the luminous smile of a much younger man, and Pilang turned away quickly to hide the stupid tears in her eyes. Hope could be cruel, when it was wrong; and so far it had always been wrong.

This woman that Esayeh had saddled them with—she had better be worth it.

Linnea woke, dizzy and confused, in a dim space that made no sense to her sleep-blurred eyes. Zero gee—her body knew that much. She floated, still wearing yesterday's stained and rumpled dress, in a sack made of blankets that was attached to a padded bulkhead. The shape of the space made no sense, uneven and roughly curved. The only light came from a string of tiny yellow bulbs curling along the opposite wall. Every surface she could see was festooned with cloth bags and lopsided boxes and arrays of cubbyholes crammed with wrapped packages, equipment of some kind. She smelled rubbing alcohol, dust, old, dried herbs.

She pushed her hair impatiently out of her eyes and looked left and right. To the left, a dark cloth was stretched over a round opening, which had to be the door. No hatch. No floor, no sensible orientation at all, every surface crammed with loosely tethered junk. This place could not possibly ever be accelerated. So she must be in a habitat now, not a ship.

But where? If that had been a jumpship they'd taken her away in, then she could be anywhere in the Earth system. Anywhere at all. *Iain must be desperate.*

She rubbed her eyes. No time now for guilt, or worry, or fear—for this moment, at least, no one was watching her. She reached up and gripped a couple of loops above her head, then started to pull herself out of the pocket where she'd been sleeping—but a ripple of nausea stopped her. She swallowed hard, willing it away. The nausea had to be left over from whatever drug Pilang had given her yesterday; it couldn't be that *she* was spacesick, not after all these years. She clamped her lips tightly and slid free of the sleeping sack, ignoring the pulsing queasiness.

Her clothes were all wrong for zero gee. The thin silk skirt of the Triton dress kept floating up around her hips, tangling when she tried to move. And she was cold; the air was even thinner, even colder than the air in the city on Triton.

She realized that she could hear a woman's voice outside the room, beyond the barrier: a light soprano voice, singing softly and wordlessly, as if the singer was concentrating on something else.

Linnea moved carefully to the cloth covering the door and felt around the edges for a way of pulling it aside. She found a loose edge, tugged—heard a ripping sound. She stopped, appalled.

Silence. Then the woman's voice spoke from near the door. "It's supposed to sound like that. Here." A pair of pale, slender hands, one tattooed with a swirling chain of stars, slipped through the small opening Linnea had made. Then gripped the cloth and pulled. The cloth ripped loose, still anchored on one edge, and Linnea found herself floating almost nose to nose with a smiling young woman in maroon coveralls. Linnea vaguely remembered a rose-pale, fine-boned face looking down at her yesterday, wisps of white-blond hair escaping from a black cloth. This woman was the one who had helped Pilang carry her to the ship that had brought her . . . here.

Wherever *here* was.

"I'm Hana," the woman said.

Linnea nodded. "I'm Linnea."

"Welcome, Linnea," Hana said, and to Linnea's startlement, kissed her firmly on the cheek. "Hold a moment." Linnea floated obediently still while Hana deftly found and checked the pulses at her neck and wrists and ankles, shined a small light into her eyes, held a sensor against her chest while tilting her head with a listening expression. "Good enough," she said. "Any more nausea?"

"N-no," Linnea said cautiously, and swallowed hard again. "What is this place?"

Hana reached into a pocket of her coveralls, pulled out a small patch of cloth, and stuck it to the inside of Linnea's elbow. "That will get you through the leftover queasiness," she said, and as she said it Linnea realized that she already felt better. How could a drug in a skin patch work so fast? "As for questions," Hana went on, "best save them for Pilang—she knows what you need to understand. But you can help me get the clinic set up—they're lining up outside already."

Linnea only gripped the edge of the door more tightly. "Where is Pilang? When will she get here?"

"She'd be here now," Hana said, "if she was ever quite on time." She reached out and touched the fabric bunched around Linnea's hips. "Hm. That dress is silly."

"I agree," Linnea said fervently, tugging at the floating fabric. "Have you got some proper clothes I can borrow?"

"Two seconds." Hana darted to one of the storage bags tied to the wall, tugged it open, and hauled out a maroon coverall like her own. She whipped it deftly out flat and looked from it to Linnea. "The belt can be pulled tight, and you can roll up the sleeves. You're so tiny! Small as Pilang."

Linnea laughed. "I've never been called tiny before."

"That's right, you grew up in a gravity well, didn't you?" Hana's eyes were wide. "No wonder you're so short. Squashed down all the time! You must have good bones. And good lungs, breathing all that thick air. And dirt everywhere!" She jerked her head at the floating coverall. "Get changed, will you? There's a water closet in back there. You know zero-gee fixtures, right? Good. Oh, and—" Hana whipped a black cloth from a pocket, covered Linnea's hair with it, tied it at the back of her neck. "There. Can't let hair float around, it gets loose, people breathe it in. Not nice at all."

"Thank you," Linnea said diffidently, pulling at the knotted cloth to loosen it a bit.

As soon as she had changed into the coveralls—leaving her feet bare and cold, but apparently that was the way here—Linnea tugged herself into the front room of the clinic.

It, too, was disturbingly uneven, with lumpy bulkheads—walls, really, of a hard yellowish foam substance. Hana was clamping some lidded glass trays of tools onto a rack attached to one of the walls. The lights were brighter—still only chains of small yellow and orange bulbs here and there along the wall, but there were more of them. Linnea saw a standard examination lamp in among the jumble on the equipment wall. "Is this your regular clinic?"

"This?" Hana snorted. "No, this place is a way station."

"For travelers?"

"Sort of," Hana said. "When we find a small enough rock that's not tumbling too fast, in a convenient orbit, we make one of these. Hollow out part of it, seal it up inside with sprayfoam." She handed Linnea a crumpled list printed on plastic, and said, "Now, look through these trays, make sure every one has everything that's on the list. There are extras of most of these things in that cubby under the pink lights. Anything else, ask."

Linnea started to work, peering at the unfamiliar labels on the packages. "Why do you have a clinic in a way station?"

Hana was stuffing a stack of neatly folded linens into a cloth bag. "It takes a long time, hundreds and hundreds of days sometimes, to travel anywhere out here—unless you're needed somewhere so much that you can catch rides on a jumpship. So there are way stations, places to stop over and wait for a slow ship going your way, a cargo carrier or a family vessel." She grimaced. "We're off our proper circuit, thanks to Esayeh, but Pilang doesn't go to a place and not open the clinic—people count on it."

"Some people must live here a long time, waiting." Linnea said.

Hana nodded. "But that's life. Stirred around, seeing new faces. 'Here we are together, we may never meet again.'" The words sounded like a quotation.

The outer door of the clinic, a proper metal hatch, opened with a screech, and Pilang floated in, dressed for work and wearing a loose backpack. She tugged the hatch shut, then turned over neatly in place to face the room. She spotted Linnea, and her face lit up. "Better, I see."

"She's doing fine," Hana said. "She has—"

"A few questions," Linnea said.

"Not now." Pilang sighed. "Patients are waiting, too many of them." She rummaged in the backpack and pulled out two round brown rolls. "Breakfast. Eat it fast. I've had mine."

Linnea took hers, took a careful bite. The bread was chewy, filled with a sweet black bean paste. "That's good," she said. "Thank you. Pilang, I'm glad to help you here, but first—"

"First rule," Pilang said. "We don't want gossip about you. It's the only thing that travels faster than jumpships. So today you won't talk. That accent—no one's ever heard an accent like that. The less you say, the better."

"But I don't know anything about medicine," Linnea said. "How can I help?"

"Everyone can always help," Pilang said. "Records. The commscreen. You won't have to talk, just get the information stored. You *can* use a commscreen?"

Linnea considered. "Is it like the ones on Triton?"

"Maybe a little better," Pilang said. "But the interface is about the same."

The commscreen in their quarters on Triton had not been so very different from the ones Linnea had used every day for her work back home: a touch screen for input, another for display, data manipulation fairly intuitive. "Yes, I can probably use it."

Pilang flashed a smile. "Good. That will free Hana to help me with patients. Come here and let me show you what to do."

The morning passed quickly after that. The commscreen, a portable belonging to Pilang, had been clamped to a bulkhead; Pilang showed Linnea how to hook her feet through metal loops so she could use the screen without pushing herself off from the wall. Then, as patient after patient passed through the little clinic, Linnea processed them through. Each person carried, or wore on a chain, a

small data crystal embedded in the end of a clear plastic
rod the size of a finger. The first step was always to slide
the rod into a slot on the side of the commscreen. Then a
wealth of data appeared—the patient's name, age in days,
medical history, some coded information that Linnea
guessed must be genetics or ancestry; behind them was a
whole array of files marked *personal* or *library*, but these
were only ghost images, translucent—not available to the
screen she was using.

Once she had loaded a patient's information, Linnea
made notes on the case as Pilang dictated them—symptoms,
readings of vital signs, the treatment Pilang prescribed.
The words were strange, but the commscreen corrected her
spelling, she was relieved to find.

Some of the treatment was surprisingly sophisticated
for an outpost, more sophisticated than what Linnea had
seen on Triton, certainly. Much of it was medicines in
patches to be worn on the skin. And Pilang brought out a
small device that seemed to ease the pain of fractures
when she moved it over the area of the break. Perhaps it
was true that the deepsiders were better at medicine.

Though other cases puzzled her. One old woman showed
Pilang a hard, two-centimeter lump, a tumor, along the
edge of her lower jaw. Pilang studied it, sighed, then opened
a decorated metal box. She searched out one tiny jar from
the bright array inside, took a thin brush, and carefully
painted the tumor with some vivid yellow pigment from the
jar. When she was finished she blew on it until it was dry,
then kissed the woman's hand with obvious respect, and
said, "There, oldmother, that should set you up in a tenday
or two. Have it checked when the next doctor comes
through."

"Thank you, daughter," the woman said, her voice shaking with emotion, and kissed Pilang on the cheek as she
left—and Hana, too, for good measure.

Painting a tumor yellow? What use was that? Or was it

some kind of superstition? Linnea looked curiously at Hana, who was smiling but blinking back tears as she tidied away the little jar and clamped shut the lid of the enameled metal box. What had just happened? Linnea felt a wave of disorientation, loneliness—of longing for Iain that made her chest ache. His calm voice, his eyes, his wry humor—his familiar warmth. . . .

Only once did Linnea get a chance to look out into the passage outside, at the people lined up waiting. None of them looked at her—no doubt it was rude to stare. She studied them sidelong while Hana floated along the line collecting names and complaints.

Nearest to the clinic's hatch, a gray-haired woman in bright blue-green floated holding a toddler in her thin arms. The child was bundled tight in a yellow-flowered blanket, its face covered with a soft mask that held in its frequent sneezes. It wore a harness attached to the woman carrying it, which she had also clipped to one of the ubiquitous handholds. She was singing to it softly—a tune that sounded old, almost familiar, not quite.

Next to them was a girl who was obviously in the last stage of pregnancy—a girl who could not be past her middle teens—curled against the wall, chatting cheerfully with an old man whose hand was wrapped in a stained bandage. On down the line Linnea saw people of all ages—some with no obvious illness or injury, and others with a wrist or ankle in a foam brace, or a dressing covering what might be a burn, or wearing the same kind of mask as the child.

Linnea ducked back inside. Pilang was finishing with two patients at once, children in for a check, brought by an old man with a cheerful, wrinkled face and a bald pink scalp ringed by a tattooed-on crown of leaves. "Yes, yes," he was saying to Pilang. "The supplements right before they go to sleep. I remember."

"Every twenty-four hours," Pilang said. "Use the timer we gave you, or you'll lose track."

"These aren't my first children," the old man said with dignity. Then he smiled at Pilang. "But thank you. I'll use it."

When the pregnant girl's turn arrived, Pilang and Hana both greeted her with embraces and kisses, though Linnea felt almost sure they'd never seen her before. The girl seemed to warm under their welcome, and watched attentively, smiling, as Pilang measured her belly, listened carefully to the baby's heart, took a sample of her blood. "Everything's going very well," Pilang announced. "But no more travel for you until this big boy gets born, all right?"

The girl dimpled. "No, no travel."

"Won't be the first baby born in a way station. *Clair*'s a good one for that, we've a very good midwife living here, the baker's husband."

"He's given me his caller already," the girl said.

"Just so. Now, good fortune to you. Next time through, I'll hope to see you and your son both fat and healthy."

"Or on our way home, finally," the girl said, her eyes lit with shy happiness.

Before the next patient entered, Linnea said, "That one's very young, isn't she? To be having a baby all alone?"

"That's when we usually have them," Pilang said. "Before we go out to work in space, in all the rads, or start doing the really dangerous work on the farms. You try this boy, and that boy—oho, it's fun, I won't tell you it's not. And then if you're lucky, there's a child." She smiled. "I had one, a boy. Maybe you'll be as lucky."

"They told me on Triton that your numbers are decreasing," Linnea said.

Pilang gave her an odd look. "Did they, then? Well. I'd like to know who counted us, we move around so much, it's like counting a swarm of bees."

Linnea only shook her head. "Where is your son now?"

Pilang's eyes looked absent. "Grown, gone. . . . It's been a long time since I looked in the traffic files to see where he was last time he linked in. He's a fine person, but I don't know him very well." She looked at Linnea. "I was learning medicine, traveling with my teacher. But his oldmother and oldfather, they brought up two of my friends' babies, too, and they did a good job with him. I still hear from them with news sometimes."

Linnea smoothed the linens she was spreading over the examination surface. "So you never settle in one place? With one person?"

"Most do, in time," Pilang said. "Later in life, when we're safe inside—off the farms, out of the mines, not moving around anymore. Too late then for babies, most everyone's had all the rads they can handle. But people are sensible by then. It's a good time to marry." She washed her hands with a clear gel, then rubbed them briskly dry as she turned to Hana. "Call in the next one, please."

They saw many people with injuries, some old and only partly healed. Deepsiders appeared to lead dangerous lives, sheltering in fragile habitats surrounded by vacuum, surviving mostly by hard work mining metal from asteroids, or tending the sealed farms in the larger habitats. Farming seemed especially hazardous—many ways to get hurt, using powerful equipment, working under hot, bright light sources, handling the chemicals in which the plants grew.

In another moment between patients, as Linnea and Hana were bundling up some soiled linens for washing, Linnea asked Hana, "Do you have any children?"

Hana laughed. "No. I've been to too many births. Catch me messing with that! And anyway, I don't like boys."

"So you don't mind this, traveling around all the time."

Hana grinned. "It's the best life. We see everything, everywhere. Doctors have to keep moving. I'll be a doctor myself someday, when Pilang says I'm ready."

Pilang looked up from the commscreen, where she was elaborating on some of the notes Linnea had taken, and said, "Traveling's the main work we do in our guild. We have to be with our patients, get our hands on them."

"So you can diagnose them better?"

Pilang laughed. "No—so they know they'll be all right."

Linnea smiled at her. It was true: Crying babies, querulous old people, people in pain, all seemed to calm under Pilang's deft touch, listening to her warm voice.

"Next, please, Hana," Pilang said briskly.

It took nine hours to see everyone in the line, which never seemed to diminish; more people arrived over the course of the day. By the end, Linnea's belly was so empty it ached, but Pilang and Hana only set to work putting everything away. Linnea helped as much as she could, wondering when dinner would be.

As they were finishing, someone banged at the hatch. It swung open immediately after, and a child, boy or girl Linnea could not tell, popped through. "Eh, Pilang!" Linnea decided it must be a girl, maybe nine or ten. "What you have for me?" Her brown face was grubby, but her hands were clean. She wore no headcloth; her hair was shorn to black stubble, and an elaborate tattooed filigree of black leaves encircled her neck.

"Eh, Mick. The usual. Here." Pilang tugged the knotted bundle of dirty linens loose from the wall, pushed it toward Mick, who snagged it. "Come by my sleeper in an hour, I'll have some food for you. And wash your face first."

"Got it. Want to talk to you anyway." Mick looked at Linnea with lively curiosity, glanced away when she caught Linnea's eye—then shoved off expertly with her bare feet and shot through the center of the hatchway, tugging her bundle behind her.

"Now for dinner," Pilang said decisively. "Hana, go see Elga, get us some of her lemon noodles and greens, with maybe some of that salty bean curd. For four, Mick looked hungry. We'll eat in here—it's better if Lin keeps out of public space."

Hana nodded, then stopped before opening the hatch. "I forget. Elga owes us?"

Pilang frowned and tallied on her fingers. "No—no, with four dinners, we'll owe her. Ask her to come by tomorrow morning before we go—we'll work it out. I've got some odds and ends of chips in this station I can pass to her."

Hana nodded and vanished. As the hatch closed behind her, Linnea turned and faced Pilang. She said nothing, but she knew Pilang could read her expression: *It's time.*

Pilang settled against the wall facing her. "All right." She met Linnea's eyes. "Ask."

Again Linnea wished for Iain's calm, steady presence at her side. *But here I am.* "First—why did you kidnap me?"

"To get you away from Triton," Pilang said. "To get you out of Perrin Tereu's hands, and Kimura Hiso's."

"Why?"

"Because they are not your friends," Pilang said quietly.

Linnea felt a jolt of anger. "And you, who made me so sick and dragged me off against my will, you're my friend?"

"Yes," Pilang said, "I am. And so is Pilot Esayeh."

Linnea studied her, considering. *A pilot.* "A deepsider pilot? Was he the one I saw?"

"A Tritoner, once," Pilang said. "He still thinks of himself as one of them, you know, not one of us. But he's been out here with us for five thousand, six thousand days. He's a deepsider now, admit it or not. But he knows both peoples. He knows where you need to be: here with us."

"Without my ship? What use am I? What is it he wants from me?"

"He's deep," Pilang said. Her expression was somber, controlled. "His mind, it isn't always easy to understand.

He spends so much time in otherspace—he doesn't just make in-system jumps, he goes out on long circuits, gone for days." She pursed her lips. "Look, Lin. I'm no pilot. I'm no Tritoner. I never know what he's thinking, I'm just his friend. He asked me this favor, and I did it. Beyond that is his to talk about, not mine." She sighed. "There. We're square."

Linnea sighed, too. "Where's Pilot Esayeh now?"

"Working," Pilang said. "Don't think *he* wastes time waiting around stations while I see patients. No, he's off running messages to some of the remote outposts around here. Checking on them." She looked grim. "Some of those family habitats are tiny, and they don't get visited much. So—when they get into trouble, they can wait forty, fifty, a hundred days for help sometimes."

"What kind of trouble?"

"Life-support problems, supply problems," Pilang said. "Sometimes they have to lock things down, put everyone in the chiller." At Linnea's puzzled look, she said, "Cold sleep. Slow metabolism. It stretches out their oxygen, keeps them alive until someone like Esayeh finds them and calls in help."

"Can't they signal for help? I know it might take a long time to come, but—"

"There are supposed to be radio links," Pilang said. "A whole signal network. Esayeh is always lecturing people about it. But some of those people on the fringes, they don't *want* to make it easy to find them. They're afraid."

"Afraid of what?" Besides floating in the cold and dark, depending on systems that were already malfunctioning, supplies of air that might run out—

Pilang looked down, shook her head. "Out on the fringes—that's where the Cold Minds raid. If they find a habitat out there, especially if it's dark, everyone in sleep, then they go in and—harvest—the small children."

Linnea swallowed in a dry throat. "Just the children?"

"Yes." Pilang's eyes were distant, hard. "Usually the Cold Minds spiders just—let the blood out of everyone else. The ones too old to be of use for their ships." Her nostrils flared. "I saw what they leave behind, once or twice when I was on a team looking for survivors. There weren't any."

Linnea felt sick. Hiso's words about Cold Minds raids had not made this horror real to her. "I'm sorry," she said softly.

The hatch opened, and Hana coasted through, tugging a small net bag full of grease-spotted boxes that smelled of lemon, hot oil, ginger.

"Food," Pilang said dryly. "Just in time. Thank you, Hana." She caught Linnea's eye. "Dinner, then you rest some more. Here I think is best, sorry—I know it's not very comfortable. But tomorrow we'll move on. Off to *Hestia*." She smiled at Linnea. "Every deepsider's home, one time or another. Our biggest habitat. You'll like it."

"Will I be allowed to send word back to Triton from there?" Linnea asked. "To Iain. My fellow pilot. He, he's worried, I know."

Pilang looked pinched, reluctant. "Not yet. Not yet, but we'll talk to Esayeh about it just as soon as we can, is that all right?"

Linnea nodded reluctantly. *It will have to be.* With no ship, no comm, no way to escape, she was these people's prisoner until they chose to let her go.

ELEVEN

TRITON

S top right there," Iain sen Paolo said sharply to the pale, heavyset older man who knelt at the base of Linnea's piloting shell, in the glare of a string of work lights, studying the access plate to a junction of conduits. "That's sealed. Just like the others." Iain let his exhaustion and exasperation show.

"Liquid circuits again?" The tech sounded disbelieving.

"Some of them. But in any case, the pressure balance in all those conduits is critical."

The tech settled back on his heels. "Look, Pilot. If you would let me open just one of these conduits, take a few images, the schematics would make a lot more sense to the boys back at the lab. I won't pull anything. I won't *touch* anything. How can we learn—"

"There's nothing to learn," Iain said. Impatience made his voice cold—that and the tension that had been building in him over the days since Linnea's disappearance. "You could see exactly what's in there, and you'd be no closer to being able to manufacture anything like it. Our dockyards have had centuries to develop this technology, and the tools to build and maintain it. But here, you can't even make the tools to make the tools you need to start running that kind of line. Even if you could afford to build new ships. Which, from what I've seen, you can't."

The tech got lightly to his feet, picked up his case of tools. "Then I guess I'm done here, Pilot," he said, an edge in his voice.

Finally. Iain suppressed a sigh, glanced out of habit at the chrono on Linnea's main external control board. The number meant nothing. In the Hidden Worlds it would have synched to local time on docking. Here there'd been no signal; the blue-glowing numbers flicked silently past, meaningless, telling the time on some far-distant world. Iain's hunger, though, told him that it must be past time for the evening meal.

The tech lingered. "Look, Pilot. Will you at least tell First Pilot Kimura that I tried?"

Iain grimaced, then nodded. The man had only been trying to carry out his assignment. "Look," he said. "It's not my ship. And it's the only one like it in this system. We couldn't afford to risk damaging it even if that *could* help you." He moved to Linnea's board and checked it—jump engines on deep standby, all lockdown lights blue—then ran his hand across the edge of the board, shutting it down.

Kimura Hiso had made a point this morning of showing Iain commscreen images of the strong metal docking clamps that held the ship down in its bay, inside the main thermal barrier that kept out the worst of the cold, but outside the pressurized part of the station. Clamps that had been sealed in place and locked by port security. Linnea's ship was not going anywhere, not unless, by some miracle, Iain could gain access to vacuum work gear, vacuum cutting tools, and a few hours to work undetected. Which would not happen, not in this heavily monitored skyport.

The tech left, and Iain took a last look around the piloting compartment. Hiso's crew had left nothing behind; the data cables the comm tech had built on-site, to link Linnea's commscreen to a Tritoner storage device and transfer the ship's schematics, had been cleared away. Iain had worried about a monitoring device, but there was nothing he could do to prevent one from being planted.

The silence in the ship made Linnea's absence even more painfully real. Days after her disappearance, there was still no word from the deepsiders: no request for ransom, though Iain had not expected that; but also no rumor or hint of a rumor of where they might have taken her. He only knew that she'd been helpless, too sick to stand—that, after all, she had not chosen to leave, to leave him behind.

He touched her empty piloting shell, stood with his eyes closed imagining her here, again, safe at his side.

Soon.

Please, let it be soon.

Iain checked the passenger compartment, apparently untouched, and stepped through the lock to the docking tube. The hatch irised shut behind him, sealed to impervious smoothness. And the ship was safe again. Only Iain, or Linnea if—no, *when*—she returned, could open that hatch without wrecking the ship.

Back at Tereu's house, Iain paused in the doorway of the reception parlor. Hiso and Tereu stood by the hearth, in close conversation. Iain stood silent, listening to Hiso's words, the quiet ring of triumph. "—And we're on the point of successfully adapting some of our mining nukes to reload the missile tubes, after the ship's missiles are spent. We can rearm it. It's a real weapon now."

Iain strode into the room, and they both turned to face him. "What use?" His voice was rough. "What use will those missiles be? Tell me. Persuade, if you can."

Hiso looked annoyed. "Perrin Tereu and I were having a private conversation."

"Even if you can rearm Linnea's ship," Iain said, "what do you think you can do with it? What can you protect? What battle can you win? If the Cold Minds decide to finish killing humans, they could do it with a few well-placed rocks. One ship, even with a few missiles in its tubes, is not going to prevent that."

Hiso picked up a clear bulb of purple wine and sipped at it before he answered. Tereu watched, her eyes moving from Hiso's face to Iain's. "We will use it," Hiso said, "to keep our children safe. Your ship is fast, possibly faster than anything the Cold Minds have. Certainly you are a more skilled pilot—and I am sure the same could be said for Pilot Kiaho." He raised his bulb of wine in a brief, regretful toast. "Your ship and its systems can help keep us aware of Cold Minds incursions in the Neptune system. We can also use it to spy out developments in their orbital shipyards near Earth. If the number of ships under construction should suddenly increase, for example, that might be a useful warning."

"As you must have seen before they launched their invasion of the Hidden Worlds," Iain said. "Did you not?"

Hiso's smile froze a bit. "Ah. You must understand that we have never allowed *our* few pilots, *our* few ships, to approach the inner system. The Cold Minds have better jumpships than ours. We had no warning of the invasion."

"There were more frequent raids," Tereu said softly. "More children taken, for several years."

"To replace the pilots they sent off, yes, they had no choice," Hiso said. "But the raids have never been a steady attrition; some years there are many attacks, some years few."

Tereu's face was smooth, expressionless, as she listened—but her eyes, dark with meaning, met Iain's. He looked back at Hiso, who was studying them both with an odd intensity. "I have spent two days giving your work crews access to the ship," Iain said. "It can be functional tomorrow, with me as its pilot, if I am allowed to work there undisturbed for a single day. Then we can discuss when I will be free to search for Linnea."

"Which will be soon, I promise you," Hiso said earnestly. He looked at Tereu. "You've finished your wine, I see, my dear. You should go and rest awhile. I'll join you presently."

Tereu nodded silently and went out, closing the door behind her. Iain watched her go, a little startled at her docility. Or—was it fear?

Then, setting down his bulb of wine, Hiso leaned aside and touched the base of the commscreen that stood nearest the hearth. "Now she can't monitor."

Which means: Now we come to it. Iain waited.

Hiso turned away and filled a fresh bulb of wine, passed it to Iain, who took it without looking at it. "Listen to me," Hiso said. "You tell me there's no hope of rescue from the Hidden Worlds and no refuge there. I don't accept that. You tell me we are on our own, forever. But that, too, is unacceptable."

"I don't see what you or I can do about it," Iain said. "Or Linnea's ship, with or without missiles in its tubes. Your ships can't reach the Hidden Worlds; they're not set up to handle long jumps, the pilots would die."

"Which is why we need your ship's speed, its capabilities," Hiso said. "We need to change the balance of power with the Cold Minds."

"How? If you mean spying, that can be done by drones—"

"I don't mean spying," Hiso said. "I mean something much more dangerous. I didn't wish to upset Tereu, you understand—" He half shrugged.

"Go on," Iain said.

"Your ship could disable a Cold Minds vessel by detonating one of its nuclear missiles in range."

"You don't need my ship to launch a missile," Iain said.

"To move as quickly as we must, at the moment we suspect a possible raid, we need your ship," Hiso said. "Ours are too small. Too slow. You could jump in, fire, jump out, in seconds."

Iain shook his head angrily. "What use would that be? The Cold Minds own this system. They have thousands of ships, hundreds of thousands. They can build more as quickly as they need them. Disabling one or two ships means nothing." *This is insane.*

"We want to capture a living Cold Minds pilot," Hiso said.

"What," Iain said, struggling to keep the revulsion out of his voice, "*use* would that be?" *Bad memories.* He remembered Linnea's nausea that day on Nexus—she had seen the essential humanity in them at once. A humanity Iain had tried to deny, for the sake of his own peace.

"You've seen them," Hiso said.

"Yes, I've seen them." Iain took a long pull at his wine.

"And you know that they are not infested by the nanobots?"

Iain winced. "My—the Line dissected the corpse of a pilot. Its brain was—normal, by some definitions."

"We've done the same," Hiso said, "with damaged corpses left after a ship was destroyed. An infested mind can't pilot; the control structures disrupt brain function." He set down his wine. "But how do they stay uninfested, for all those years, in a ship that's crawling with nanobots?"

Iain looked at him sharply.

"That is what we intend to learn," Hiso said. "And you will help us." His dark eyes glittered. "If we knew what it is that keeps the human pilots from being infested," he said, "we might be able to adapt it to protect ourselves and our people."

"But infestation is not a risk you face," Iain said. "The Cold Minds don't come near Triton. You said so yourself."

Hiso looked patient. "Protection from infestation," he

said, "would open the prospect of capturing, and using, Cold Minds ships. Altering them for our own purposes." He looked at Iain. "And then—escaping to the Hidden Worlds."

Iain caught his breath. "You could never capture enough ships to carry every human in this system," he said. "Or train enough pilots, with the resources you have."

"Ah. Well," Hiso said, and picked up his wine again. "It would not, as you say, be possible to rescue everyone."

Now it comes. Iain looked at him. "Who, then?"

"Just—our own people," Hiso said. "Tritoners from this city and our own outposts. The true exiles, the true descendants, of Earth."

"The deepsiders are also descendants of Earth," Iain said sharply.

Hiso met Iain's look. "You don't understand. The deepsiders *chose* their exile, long before the Cold Minds rose. This is their home—space, out here in the cold." He looked Iain in the eye. "But we—we are the people your great-grandfathers left to die. This cold desolation was never our home—never *meant* to be our home. If I could correct that injustice, take even a few hundred, a few thousand, of our people to safety—relative safety—in the Hidden Worlds, that would be an achievement I would be proud to remember when I die."

"And you would abandon everyone else to the Cold Minds?" Iain did not try to hide his contempt. *He's insane. Grandiose.*

"No. No." Hiso flicked his fingers and looked across the high table at Iain, the light of the hearth a hot spark in his eyes. "Your people could return for them."

"You know we cannot," Iain said. "My people have their own war to fight. A costly one. And their own cities to defend."

"Then you will have to persuade them," Hiso said.

Iain shook his head impatiently. "This is madness. You

cannot even take the first step. And you would consign thousands of people to inescapable death."

"As your fathers did to mine," Hiso said. "Hard choices."

Iain looked away. There was no good answer to that.

"Studying one of their pilots might save hundreds, maybe thousands, of *real* humans from the same fate." Hiso looked at Iain. "It will give my people, for the first time, hope of escape. Of a future. Even with the war, the Hidden Worlds would be safer, better, than where we are."

"I have a counterproposal," Iain said. "Let Linnea return to the Hidden Worlds in her ship and come back with reinforcements. I will stay as your hostage."

"You will forgive me," Hiso said, "if I say that I do not trust you. Or your people. Or any plan of action that I do not myself control." His confidence seemed to be growing. "No. we will do this in the way I propose. You will help me to capture at least one living Cold Minds pilot. We have already begun to set up a secure, quarantined lab in a research facility over Nereid, also in Neptune orbit. If we can learn how to save ourselves, Pilot sen Paolo, we can free ourselves forever."

Iain looked away from the naked eagerness in Hiso's eyes. *No matter what else this is, it is a step toward finding Linnea.* "So I can set the ship to my own control tomorrow?"

"I will allow that," Hiso said. "Though the ship will remain under restraint until I order it freed for this mission. And you must clearly understand that Pilot Kiaho's safety, when she is returned to us, depends on your keeping your word."

Iain looked at him scornfully. "Of course I will keep my word."

Hiso's expression did not change, but there was open pleasure in his voice as he said, "I know it well."

Iain gave Hiso a cool nod and left.

• • •

L ate the next day, exhausted, Iain returned to Tereu's
  compound from his work on Linnea's ship. All day, as
always, the memory of Linnea's face and voice, and his
deep fear for her, had underlain all his thoughts—slowing
the delicate process of installing himself as the pilot of her
ship, so that its control systems would be attuned to his
mind, his reflexes.

Reluctance slowed him, too. He was erasing her, in a
way. That ached in his mind. Oh, the ship would remember
her, when she returned; but her command settings were
deeply buried now, in the core of the shipmind. The ship—
her ship—was now his.

Iain made his way down a silent, carpeted corridor toward the quarters he had shared with Linnea. She would
return. He knew she would come back to him—as soon as
she had found the answers she sought. However long that
might take, however far she might have to travel. This was
her chance—she had broken free.

Converting her ship to his own use was like closing a
door on her. He was bleakly certain that he would not see
her, would not hear her voice, for a long, long time.

He entered their dark, silent suite and turned toward the
bath without tabbing the lights on. He'd rinse off the sweat
of the day's work, eat something, then try to sleep for a few
hours before—

"Pilot sen Paolo." Tereu's voice, from the bed. "Don't
turn on the light."

Iain went still, then turned to face her, a shape in the
darkness, seated upright on the edge of the bed. "Why are
you here?" He did not trouble to make the question sound
polite.

"Hiso has given you a mission," she said.

"Yes," he said. There was no reason for Iain to lie to
Tereu; any trouble it made for Hiso was not his concern.
"You know what it is, then."

"Yes. It's something he's spoken of to me for years, a dream—your ship has brought it within his reach." She was silent for a moment, then said, "Tell me. If you succeed— what did he promise you?"

"Freedom to search for Linnea," Iain said.

"He won't free you," she said bluntly. "He'll keep you and your ship for his own purposes. He'll never let you go."

"I don't need to wait for him to let me go," Iain said calmly. "I've escaped from worse prisons than this."

"Ahh." She stood up. "Do you think his plan could work?"

"No." He regarded her, wishing he could see her expression. "I think it will prove to be a method we can't use. Those pilots have been radically altered from human norms, you know."

"I know." He heard her take a breath, let it out in a sigh. "I wanted to ask you something."

"A favor of your own?" Iain stirred, restless. "Hiso will hear this, won't he?"

"This is my own house," she said. "I know its systems, I designed them. He will never know I was here."

These twists of deception, of mutual betrayal—how he missed Linnea's clear truthfulness. "Ask, then."

She stood there, a tall, shadowy figure. She did not move toward him. "I want you to take Hiso's place," she said. "Wait, let me finish. You are the one pilot in this whole system who clearly can match his skills, and you can more than match his ship. The others would follow you gladly. You could send them out to find Linnea for you. Or, or whatever you wish—whatever you need."

"You're afraid of Hiso," Iain said harshly.

She sighed again. "I've endured Hiso for many years," she said. "He's nothing. My fear is for my people."

"Because of this plan of his?"

"Because—" She broke off. "Because of many things. You don't know him." Abruptly she stepped away from the bed, turned her back to him. He could almost see her now, outlined by the faint glow of the commscreen next to the bed. "If you were to set Hiso aside—"

"Kill him, you mean?"

"Exile would do," she said. "Exile without a jumpship, far across the system. It's done sometimes, with criminals, undesirables, they find work in deepsider mines. They don't die. But they never come home." Her voice sounded empty. "If you took Hiso's place, you would own a share of this house. You would be my formal consort, according to custom."

No. "I belong to Linnea."

Now she turned to face him, and he saw the gleam of her eyes in the near dark. "And if she's dead?"

"Living or dead," he said sharply, to hide the fear in his heart.

"You would not be required to—there would be no need for any real relationship with me," Tereu said after a moment. "You would be at my side at formal events and ceremonies, at the city games, for festivals. But in privacy you could have any—liaison you wished. If Linnea lives, and returns to you, I would not ask you to dismiss her."

"No," Iain said. "I will not consider this. I won't interfere here. If Hiso is a problem for you, you must solve it. My concern is finding Linnea."

"That's final?" Her voice was tight.

"It is final," Iain said.

"Then I have only one other thing to say," she said, and now he could hear fear in her voice. "Watch him. Watch behind yourself. He wants your ship. You are all that stands between him and taking it."

"If I were dead, he couldn't use it," Iain said. "He could not even gain access."

"He would find a way," she said. "Don't underestimate Kimura Hiso, Pilot sen Paolo. Don't trust him, or any situation he controls."

"He's dishonorable?"

"He has," Tereu said, "his own idea of honor." She laughed, a dry, bitter sound in the darkness. "For Hiso, you see, any act is honorable if it's done in the service of the only good he understands."

"Which is—"

"Human survival," she said. "The survival of our people."

"Survival *is* a good," Iain said cautiously.

"Not when there is no limit to the price one is willing to pay." She walked to the door and turned. "I won't speak of this again."

"Nor will I," Iain said, his voice quiet. "Thank you for your warning."

"I hope that it can save you," she said, her voice empty. The door closed behind her with a soft click.

Iain sank down on the bed, on the side where Linnea had slept. There was still some trace of her in the air, half a breath of her clear, clean scent.

He would keep his word to Hiso—but only to regain his ship.

And then, as soon as this task was done, he would free himself—and find Linnea.

TWELVE

As his ship emerged from the brief final jump, Iain sen Paolo gasped. Immediately before him, dark but brilliantly clear through the "eyes" of his ship, hung an immense, brown-yellow gas giant, its shadowy bulk cut by knife-edged concentric rings. The planet's shadow stretched toward him across the rings' surface, but beyond it on each side they were brilliant with sunlight. *Saturn*—the old name lingered from lessons in childhood. His ship floated deep in its penumbra; the vast planet glowed all around its edge, a vivid line of sunlight.

"Pilot," Hiso's voice said in his ear. "Stay sharp."

"Right," Iain said, deliberately avoiding the old formulas of command and response. Hiso was with Iain, of course, in Linnea's ship—linked in through the instructor's pad, but with no control linkages. Iain had carefully made certain of that.

Iain finished scanning local space, then reached for some readings, checking his position. His field of view showed a few faint objects that the shipmind had marked as moons. But among them was a yellow circle, set by his shipmind to indicate the object he'd told it to seek, swinging in orbit around the huge world. Three hundred kilometers away, it read as an irregular rock, a hundred meters long, temperature barely higher than the surrounding space.

"We're in position," Iain said.

He heard Hiso's pleased laugh. "Your ship is cold?"

"Running lights off, maneuvering jets off, ancillary systems on standby. Jump engine on standby." That last item worried Iain; it would take him several seconds to bring it back up, another second or two to jump. Plenty of time for a Cold Minds missile to cripple or destroy his ship, if he was unlucky.

"Now we wait," Hiso said. "It should be only a few minutes. My information was quite definite."

Iain kept his vision on the surrounding space. He'd seen images of Earth and its solar system since his earliest childhood. But brought close and huge, all around him, the black bareness of space in this part of the galaxy still chilled him. Utter dark, pierced by scattered stars that, when he queried, his shipmind marked with strange old names or merely a string of letters and numbers, some in an alphabet he could not read.

They were exposed, helpless, waiting in darkness for the Cold Minds. Waiting in a ship armed only with a missile whose use he had never tested, one that might or might not function as the yards had designed, that might or might not disable the Cold Minds ship. But it would certainly tell them that an enemy was here.

"That rock," Iain said. "It's a settlement?"

"Yes," Hiso said. "A deepsider way station. This one is mostly shut down—some kind of failure, or perhaps they simply ran out of oxygen. There's almost no deepsider traffic passing through the Saturn system now—the Cold

Minds have been active farther out since their invasion fleet left."

"We should help those people," Iain said.

"Not until we've achieved our objective here," Hiso said severely. "They're safe enough. Everyone left in that habitat is in cold sleep, slow metabolic storage, waiting for rescue."

"Except that it's the Cold Minds that are coming for them," Iain said. "Is that how you know they'll come here? Because these people are helpless?"

"Silence," Hiso said. "Stay alert."

Inside his piloting shell, Iain shook his head. It still didn't fit—how did Hiso know that *this* was the moment, if—

Two orange-circled readouts flicked into being, between Linnea's ship and the habitat. Numbers flickered near the circles, showing the change in vector as the ships maneuvered.

"That's them," Hiso said.

"They're not deepsiders? You're sure?"

"Deepsider jumpships? Here? Two of them at once?" Hiso snorted. "I think they have five, maybe six in all. . . . And look at those maneuvers. A deepsider pilot couldn't handle half a gee. Those are boosting at two, three gees."

Iain kept his voice level. "How did you know they would jump in at this moment?"

"Not your concern, Pilot," Hiso said. "If those deepsiders matter so much to you, this is the best way to defend them." The scorn in his voice was clear.

Iain took two careful breaths, letting his anger dissipate, then chose the detonation point for the shipmind, near enough for the electromagnetic pulse to disable the Cold Minds ships, but not so close as to damage the way station.

He flexed his mind in the unfamiliar signal to launch the missile. The ship lurched as if knocked by a hammer, and the image of the missile, circled in blue, receded in his vision, accelerating. One second, two, three—

One of the orange circles flicked out.

An instant later came the flash of detonation, sun-bright, blocked to blackness by the shipmind to protect Iain's sight.

Now the remaining unknown ship drifted, under no control, not maneuvering. "The other one jumped away," Iain said.

"And will be back in minutes, with reinforcements," Hiso said, "to search the area."

"And then to complete their mission," Iain said. "To take those people and turn them into—" He broke off.

Hiso ignored his words. "Jump back to the staging zone. We'll signal the others to go in and retrieve that thing."

"We can fight," Iain said.

"Not what they'll come back with," Hiso said. "Five ships, or ten. Those people are lost. Forget them."

Iain bit back rage. "But—"

"Jump," Hiso said. "Or our agreement is void."

A brief flick of a jump, and they floated in the shadow of one of Saturn's larger moons, surrounded by three jumpships in Hiso's command. Hiso snapped an order, and all three flicked out.

"Now home," Hiso said.

"We're leaving those people to die," Iain said.

"They might not have died," Hiso said coldly, "if you'd fired half a second sooner. Reflect on that, Pilot."

No. As Iain jumped away through a flicker of other-space to safety, he felt bitterly certain that Hiso had never had any intention of interfering with the habitat, of saving its people.

The moment Linnea's ship was locked back into its landing cradle, even before the connections to the Triton port were complete, Iain disconnected the neural leads, then shoved his shell open and stepped out. Hiso stood across the cramped piloting cabin with his back to Iain, combing his hair in the ship's selfscreen.

It took Iain a moment to master his voice. "I understand it all now," he said at last. "You knew that deepsider way station was helpless because you'd found it yourself, you or your men. And you knew when the Cold Minds would come because *you* sold those people to them."

"Only a few of them," Hiso said.

"Only the children," Iain said, anguished. "What is happening to them at this moment?"

Hiso shrugged with one shoulder. "Freedom has its price, Pilot sen Paolo."

Iain gripped Hiso by the shoulders, shoved him back against the bulkhead. The smaller man looked up at him, unperturbed.

"You made a deal," Iain said through clenched teeth. "A deal with those . . . things. Children sold for your safety—" His voice was not under his control. Years of practice, all his father's training, and he *could not* keep control.

Hiso only smiled pityingly. "We've done what's necessary to save our people. To build, to preserve all that you see in our city. Our own beloved children are safe because—"

"Because you sell deepsider children to be mutilated, to spend their lives encased in those Cold Minds ships," Iain said. "And you call yourselves human!" His voice tore his throat.

"Those children are asleep," Hiso said. "They'll never know what happened to them. They simply won't wake."

"That's a lie," Iain said. "You know as well as I do that a pilot must be conscious, must be aware. Those children will know what is happening to them. They'll remember their homes, their parents. They'll know they will never be free and human again." He took a shuddering breath. "They take out their eyes, Hiso! They neuter them. You've seen, and you can still—"

Hiso twisted out of Iain's grip, stood with clenched fists facing him across the narrow space. "My people's survival is the noble cause I am sworn to serve," he said, his voice hard. "It demands a high price—and men with the courage to pay it. When your forefathers abandoned us here, they left only hard choices, and we made them. I am ashamed of nothing."

"I won't be a part of this," Iain said.

Hiso laughed. "You already are a part of this. You've lived in our city, eaten our food, benefited from the safety that this arrangement buys for us, and for you, and for your woman Linnea. *You* are no better than any of us." He slapped the control of the ship's lock, and it irised open.

Men's voices burst in from the docking bay, shouts and excited laughter. One of Hiso's pilots leaned through the hatch, grinning. "Victory, Pilot Kimura! Our ships are safely in-system, towing the Cold Minds vessel to the study station."

"Victory!" Hiso gave the man a tight smile. "Come, let's drink to it, Abrak. Come, Pilot sen Paolo. Settle that mood with a little wine."

"No, I thank you," Iain said coldly.

"Pilot sen Paolo is sulky," Hiso said to the other man, still with the same smile. "But he'll come around, when he thinks matters through. Let's go."

As the hatch closed behind them, Iain shut his eyes and fought rage, nausea, fought to master his breathing. *Children. They are selling children, for their own safety.* After a moment, he took a long, shuddering breath, and with unsteady hands he began the familiar duties of docking and lockdown, tending to Linnea's ship.

Linnea's ship, now Hiso's weapon.

As Iain himself had become.

•   •   •

Three days later, Iain watched as Hiso's team of medtechs finished the last disconnection and prepared to lift the Cold Minds pilot from the shell where he had spent most of his life. Iain witnessed this by Hiso's command, with Hiso and the young pilot who was his attendant today. They floated above a wide window of tough plastic. Three meters below was the maimed, hairless pilot—still in his shell, which had been removed whole from the Cold Minds ship on the second day.

Medtechs in protective gear had severed the support connections with the pilot's shell one by one, replacing each with their own equipment. The tubes had been removed from the pilot's toothless, distorted mouth, from his flattened nose, all but the one through which he had to be fed. Iain had seen images on the commscreen, but they had not prepared him for what he saw now. Looking down at the pilot, who lay bathed in a bright light that he had no eyes to see, Iain felt both nausea and pity—feelings he saw reflected on the face of the young pilot beside him. Hiso's face showed only controlled eagerness.

The silver connecting leads had been removed from the pilot's empty eye sockets, and the small wounds left behind wept a little, like a parody of tears; but otherwise, the smooth, pale skin of the pilot's face conveyed no expression. Now and then a quick, rippling twitch ran across it.

Hiso nudged Iain. "You're upset," he said, eyebrows lifted.

"I still object to this," Iain said coldly. "He's a human being. A pilot. Our brother."

"That thing is no longer human," Hiso said. "And these studies might save us all." He studied Iain for a moment, then turned his head dismissively, back to the viewing window. "Living in safety in the Hidden Worlds has weakened human bloodlines, I see. I'm glad my people still have the strength we need."

The medtechs were lifting the twisted body out of its shell, the wasted limbs trailing through the cold air of the chamber below. The pilot's blank face twitched again.

Iain's view danced and shimmered through tears that would not fall. He smeared them out over his cheeks, felt them cool his skin as they dried. *My brother, I am sorry. I could have destroyed your ship, prevented this.*

I failed you.

They secured the pilot's body on a padded stretcher, the limbs tied down, even the head restrained. Below, one of the medtechs looked up at Hiso and nodded, his face expressionless behind the thick visor. "They're withdrawing the drugs," Hiso said, his voice tight with suppressed eagerness. "It should be conscious soon. As conscious as it can be."

Iain made himself look at the pilot. The skin that had been attached to the life-support machinery was wet, pink, raw-looking. As Iain watched, the pilot's blank face tightened, the forehead wrinkled. *Pain.* The drugs were trickling away, and he was in pain. Iain's hands clenched in sympathy as the pilot's hands twitched, fingers stiff, weak muscles straining against the straps that held him. Beside Iain, the young pilot's hands tightened on his hold, and he started breathing steadily, clearly fighting to control nausea.

The voice of the attending physician—the best on Triton, Hiso had assured Iain—sounded worried. "It's overreacting. I'm not sure it can handle the physiological stress. I'll have to drug it again, and I don't know how long I can sustain its functions under that treatment."

"You blinded him," Iain said, his voice rough. As Hiso turned to him in surprise, he coughed and said again, "You blinded him. You took away the only eyes he had. He doesn't know where he is. Of course he's afraid."

"We can't replace his eyes," the doctor said sharply from below. "The optic nerves are absent—atrophied or removed. We can't give him new ones."

"Give him back the eyes he had," Iain said. Hiso frowned, but Iain went on. "The leads from the ship. Reconnect them to his brain. Link them to a camera from the ship. If he can see, even a limited view, he won't be so afraid."

The doctor looked up at Hiso. "Pilot Kimura," he said, "that's several more hours of surgery to reimplant—"

"Do it," Hiso said. "The longer we can keep this thing alive, the more we can learn." He turned to Iain. "Thank you for your help."

Iain fought back nausea. "It's not you I'm helping."

"Think of it that way," Hiso said, "if it comforts you." He smiled and turned back to watch the preparations for surgery below.

The young pilot on Iain's other side flipped and shot out of the room. After a moment, hearing the sounds from the passageway outside, Iain turned away from the horror in the room below and followed him. The young man had managed to confine his retching to the refresher unit, and the system was containing it, but he floated limply beside it, looking utterly miserable.

Iain took hold beside him, pulled some absorbent paper from the dispenser by the refresher, and handed it to the young pilot. Not much more than a boy: late teens at the oldest, brown-skinned, with a close-cut cap of black hair. The boy nodded his thanks. "Forgive me. I didn't think it would—look like that."

"What did you think it would look like?" Iain kept his voice low, but he knew his anger was clear. *That's the price of what you've built here,* he wanted to say. *Of the city, the happy schoolchildren, the gardens, the concerts, everything you've shown me so proudly. That is the price.*

"I didn't expect it to look—human," the boy said, his voice unsteady.

He understands that this is wrong. The thought stood clear in Iain's mind. He said, still speaking quietly, "We don't do such things, where I live."

At that the boy lifted his chin and faced Iain. "It's not my place to question," he said. "I do my duty. I'm proud to." He stuffed the soiled paper into a vacuum outlet, wiped his hand on his tunic, and held it out to Iain. "I'm named Gareth, of family Perrin."

Iain took the hand firmly. "Sen Paolo—Iain. Is Madame Tereu a relative of yours?"

"My father's cousin," Gareth said, with a little obvious pride. "Pilot Kimura took notice of my test results after primary school, and here I am." He closed the cover on the refresher and tugged his clothing straight. "Pilot Kimura says you have a ship like no other. I would—like very much to see it someday."

"If you can get permission," Iain said, "I'll show it to you."

"Thank you, Pilot," Gareth said firmly. Then turned back toward the hatch. "I'd better get back in there. Kimura Hiso personally invited me to see this, as my cousin's representative."

Then he did you no favors. "Surely you've seen enough," Iain said. "For now."

"I'm not weak," Gareth said evenly. "I can handle this. It was just the, the shock of it."

"I know," Iain said. "I was about to throw up myself." He set his hand on Gareth's shoulder. "We could take our leave for a while, brother. What's the use of being a pilot, having your own ship, if you don't use your freedom?"

He saw the longing for escape in Gareth's face. The boy glanced back toward the observation room. Then met Iain's eyes and shook his head. "I can't. I'm attending the First Pilot."

"Then I'll hope to see you at my ship soon," Iain said. "This evening, perhaps?"

The boy looked doubtful. "Perhaps." He half bowed and turned away to return to his post.

But Iain lingered where he was, in the shadowy passageway. The vague idea forming in the back of his mind took a clearer shape. Hope. Action. *Perhaps tonight, tomorrow, I can move.*

Soon, Kimura Hiso.

THIRTEEN

DEEPSIDER HABITAT *HESTIA*

Linnea emerged from the narrow docking tube leading from Esayeh's little jumpship and looked around in awe. The docking bay formed a ring around the equator of the cylindrical habitat, and across from the docking tubes, wide windows overlooked the interior of the huge space inside. She hung back, nervous at the sheer *distance* visible through the window. She'd never seen so large a volume enclosed and under pressure in zero gee. And this place was to be her home for—how long, Pilang did not seem to know. "There's work for you there" was all she would say.

A small figure shot out of the tube past Linnea, soared across the docking bay, and swung to a stop at one edge of the window. "Eh, Lin, come and look at this!"

"Mick," Hana said reprovingly as she floated out of the tube, "city manners. Don't bump people." Pilang followed her, laughing.

The girl stuck out her tongue at Hana and turned back to the glass. "Don't need to tell me all that," she said. "I was born here in *Hestia*, you know. My mother worked in the power plant, don't know if she's still here—"

Linnea launched herself carefully past Hana and Pilang and took a place beside Mick in front of the thick glass, anchoring herself with one hand to another of the handholds that ringed the window. She breathed carefully, trying to keep her perceptions under control. If she let herself think of the view in just the wrong way, it would flick to a different orientation, becoming a pit below her. . . . She pushed the thought away and gripped more tightly. "How big is that space?" Linnea asked. "I can't tell. I can't even really *see* it, with the trees and the haze, and the light so bright."

"Everyone says that," Mick said proudly. "I grew up here, till I was three thousand days. I can tell you a lot. That's the park. Hundreds and hundreds of meters north to south, more'n two hundred across. Look at all the green. Those are real trees growing in there, did you know that? Real *Earth* trees. That stuff that looks like green smoke, those are leaves. Up close you can see. They're all different, too. One of them grows apples, wild apples, free because it's not a farm, we used to get into fights—"

"Mick," Pilang said patiently, "it's time we moved along. Did you get through to your oldfather?"

Mick's thin face fell. "I forgot to say. He's dead. Died about three hundred days ago."

"I'm so sorry," Linnea said, touching the girl's shoulder in sympathy.

Hana was having none of it. "Dead?" she said sharply. "You talked Esayeh into giving you a jumpship lift all this way, and you knew there was no one here waiting for you?"

"I," Mick said loftily, "take care of myself." She turned upside down, the lengthening stubble of her black hair making an aureole around her head against the bright light from the habitat interior. "I got a job waiting for me, in the farms, in the culture rooms, pulling the calluses apart, putting up the seedlings in little bags. Takes little hands, I still got 'em. I used to do it when I was little, see, so they'll take me back. It's a start, and you get food, and there's always someplace to sleep. So don't go floating over *me*."

Pilang joined them at the window. "Look, Mick," she said, "you know how to find me—remember, it's the Rosie and Jim Memorial Clinic at Ring Three. They can relay to me wherever I am, and they'll know to help you if you need it. So if you fall into any trouble, you call."

"Not me," Mick said. "But I'll remember." She stuck out a hand at Hana, pulled her in close, and kissed her cheek, did the same for Pilang, then Linnea. And at that moment Esayeh, the ship's pilot, emerged from the docking tube, thin and gray in his plain coveralls, smiling faintly as he looked around at what must be, for him, the sights of home.

Mick launched herself at him and kissed him as well, as he clutched at her in startlement. "Thank you," she said. "Can I call you oldfather? Because you saved my life, that way station was going to kill me, nothing ever *happens* there, I was going *insane*. 'Bye!"

Linnea watched as the girl vanished around the curve of the docking bay. When she turned to Hana, the younger woman rolled her eyes at Linnea. "Coming?"

Linnea looked at Esayeh. "Not now. I think Esayeh and I need to have a talk." He'd been evading her, evading her questions, long enough.

Hana blinked at Linnea, then looked doubtfully at Pilang, who said firmly, "I entirely agree with you, Lin."

"And then," Linnea said, "I'd like a ride back to Triton."

There was a silence, no one looking at her; then Esayeh said, "I don't know when that will be possible. When it will be safe."

Her voice sharp with disappointment, Linnea said, "You go there all the time."

"I go when Pilang has reason to," he said mildly. "The Tritoners tolerate my ship because they need our doctors.

But otherwise, I stay away from Triton. When I'm docked there, I can't even leave my ship."

"Why not?"

He shrugged. "They'd arrest me. Ancient history, but they don't forget."

Behind him, Pilang snorted derisively.

Esayeh glanced at her, then nodded at Linnea. "Look. In exchange for answering your questions, I want seven more days of your time and attention."

"For what?"

"Learning. I think you'll like it. And at the end of it—we'll see. It depends on what both of us learn."

Linnea eyed him. "Is this some kind of test?"

"An opportunity," Esayeh said, his expression serious.

"May I send a message to Triton? To Iain?"

"No," Esayeh said. "You must promise not to try that. You could endanger many innocent lives if Kimura Hiso chose to lead one of his daring expeditions to rescue you. Which he would be quite likely to do."

"And *then*," Linnea said patiently, "after seven days, you'll take me back to Triton."

"I promise you I will return you to Triton, if you choose to go, as long as it's safe," Esayeh said. "The Cold Minds stir in-system sometimes, you know."

Linnea studied him. Her increasing worry about Iain was a constant itch in the back of her mind—but the opportunity to find out more about these people and their history, a different perspective on the situation here—that could be valuable in itself. And if there was, as Esayeh hinted, something more—well, if he wanted her to spend a week under his eye, if that might lead to more answers, then she would have to try. She nodded sharply. "All right. I agree."

"Seven days," Pilang said. "Mind my words, Esayeh! I'm overdue for the loop out to Miranda as it is. Patients are waiting."

"I'll be here and ready," Esayeh said, sounding aggrieved. "When do I not come back when you need me?"

"The first time it happens," Pilang said, "will be enough for me. Watch and take care, old man." She took him by the shoulders, pulled herself to him, and kissed him on the mouth.

"I'll still be here tomorrow," Esayeh said with dignity as she floated back from him, "but I don't mind the kiss."

Pilang snorted, and she and Hana moved off, trailing their travel bags. Linnea turned back to Esayeh. "Where can we talk safely?"

He swept a wide gesture. "Anywhere."

"Really?"

"This isn't Triton. No monitors here, except for pressure and air quality and such. Well, people listen in if they can, but that's just gossip, nobody pays attention to it. . . . Come. We'll take a turn in the park. It would be a shame not to see such a wonder for yourself after coming all this way."

"All this way," Linnea said suspiciously, "means—from Triton?"

"From your home, of course," Esayeh said. "Those worlds far away. I'd like to hear about them, too. . . . Here's a lock." He swung them both into a small, chilly cubby, cranked the door on the docking-port side shut, pulled a lever. There was a hiss, and the pressure dropped slightly. Then he cranked open the inner door.

Light blazed in out of emptiness. Linnea swallowed hard, found a handhold right outside the opening, and swung around into the vast open space. She found herself facing a spongy surface completely covered with mats of a tiny-leaved creeping herb with a rich, complicated smell. She knew she ought to turn around, that Esayeh would be expecting her to admire the view, but she knew, she knew that if she thought of it just wrong—

She peered carefully over her shoulder.

Endless depths yawned below her back, and her grip on

the handhold tightened convulsively. She studied the dense green mat of herbs intently, her mind spinning. In this bright sunny light, some were silvery green, some yellow-green; and some of the tiny leaves were edged with—

"Linnea," Esayeh said wearily, "just turn around."

She closed her eyes for a moment, took a deep, shuddering breath. Then, cautiously, she turned, keeping a tight grip on the handhold. Light, space, a vast arch overhead—over there—down. But no weight, nothing holding her up—*No. Down. I am lying on a lawn. A flat lawn.* She felt Esayeh's warm hand on her shoulder, anchoring her.

"I'm sorry," she said. "I've never been in zero gee in—so much space. It's not like being in a ship." She laughed a little wildly. "In a ship, there's nowhere to *fall*."

"Look across," Esayeh's gentle voice said. "Not at the big lights, they're too bright. Past them. See the treetops?"

"Mick was talking about the trees," Linnea said. Two men holding hands scudded past, twenty meters away, out, *down*—

"Don't watch the people," Esayeh said patiently. "You'll get dizzy. I came from Triton, I know what this is like at first." He tugged loose a sprig of the herb, bruised it between finger and thumb, passed it to Linnea. "This is thyme."

Linnea looked at it in confusion, then made the connection. "Oh. We have that, too."

"Close your eyes," Esayeh said. "Focus on the scent. . . . There. Now, look out again. This is the park. This surface we're on—it's not dirt, it anchors and waters the plants, but it can't float free. This central ring is all plants and trees. North and south, toward the ends of the cylinder, look there. Maybe you can see the houses. Live here long enough, your turn comes up, you can live in the park for a while."

"Was this—" Linnea frowned. "The design's wrong. But I read stories, weren't there habitats that spun, gave some gravity?"

"Close to Earth there were," Esayeh said. "Long lost, of course, all of them."

"Destroyed?"

"Oh, yes," Esayeh said. "Broken down for metal by the Cold Minds. . . . Deepsiders don't bother with spin. Too much engineering, they say, and for what? So you can raise goats, maybe, like the Tritoners? Rabbits, chickens, they don't mind zero gee, and they taste good enough. And who wants to stick to the ground all their lives?" He swung away from the lock of the hatch. "Look. We'll pull ourselves along the surface. I promise we won't get separated from it. But I want to show you more."

Linnea let him tug her loose from her hold, and they began a slow drift along the green surface toward a distant clump of trees and buildings near one end of the huge cylinder. "What is this place? How did the deepsiders build anything so big, this far out?"

"They didn't," Esayeh said. "This was supposed to be a collection tank for helium-3 coming up from Neptune. It was never used; plans changed when the Cold Minds rose."

"So the deepsiders improvised," Linnea said. "Don't waste, don't want."

"We have a saying like that, yes." Esayeh smiled. "So deepsiders pushed this tank into a higher orbit around Neptune. The walls were double already, and we just built into them and then onto them, inside and out—workshops and sleep cubbies and food shops and machine shops and labs, everything we needed, bit by bit over the years. The docking ring was already there, we just repurposed it. When the last of us got booted off Triton, we made this our Triton, our center. The deepsider hearth. We go anywhere we want, but this is where everyone comes to live for a while, when they can. Whoops." They had drifted a little too far from the surface, and Linnea gripped his hand tightly. "That's a tree ahead," she said nervously. A tree with a round green canopy of big leaves like hands, reaching toward them it seemed. She hoped it didn't have spikes or something.

"Land with grace," Esayeh announced, and caught a branch neatly with his free hand. Of course that made Linnea, attached to his other hand, spin on around the branch, leaves whipping in her face, until she could bring herself to a stop with a desperate grip on two big bunches of twigs. A couple of small children floating past giggled, then politely looked away.

"Sorry," Esayeh said. He swept a gesture of welcome. "This, of course, is *Acer macrophyllum*. Dwarfed a bit, but the real thing."

"The tree," she said cautiously. "That's the name of this tree? Or this kind of tree?"

"The species," Esayeh said. He frowned at her. "Don't they have trees in the Hidden Worlds?"

"Not where I grew up," Linnea said.

"No trees at all!" He stared at her. "Where did you get your air?"

"The oceans," she said. "Seaweed and little tiny things, plankton. We also had fish and mud. That was about it."

Esayeh pursed his lips. "I can't promise you any mud here. Fish and seaweed—we have some of those growing in tanks."

"I don't miss them that much," Linnea said. She looked around—no one was in earshot. And there was no telling the next time that would happen, if it ever did. "Esayeh—"

She waited for him to cut her off, to put her off, but he only floated there, relaxed, looking at her with kindly patience.

So this is the time at last. She took a breath. "Esayeh, are you the one who called me here? Here to Earth?"

He did not look away. "I think . . . I did. Did you have dreams? In otherspace?"

"I saw things," she said. "Iain, the other pilot with me—" At the thought of Iain—his face, his voice, his touch—she felt a wave of longing and loss. She swallowed and went on. "Iain knew what the images were when I described them. Pictures of Earth."

"Of Earth!" He caught her by the shoulders and kissed her on both cheeks. "Exactly! Exactly! The Memorials! I knew the Line would never let them be forgotten—I knew any pilot would know what they meant."

"You were trying to reach out to other jump pilots? In otherspace?"

"Yes," he said, his eyes lit with eagerness. "I took long jumps in otherspace, out and back, for years. I reached out toward the Hidden Worlds, and I was sure, *sure* that I sensed other minds out there, other pilots transiting otherspace. Only in the Hidden Worlds would there be so many jump pilots spending so long in otherspace. Here the jumps are short, you see, just in-system. . . . But the minds I sensed were hard to touch, hard to hear—until you came. The others, they were masked, muted—but you!"

"I was different?"

"You stood out like a flame," he said. "I *knew* you were there! I sensed you out there! I spent days, weeks listening for you—when I caught you I thought of those images, I tried to make them real—"

"I thought," she said quietly, "that I was going mad. So did Iain."

"But you weren't, you see, so all is well." He beamed at her. "I'm very pleased that the information came through so clearly! I've had theories about that for a long time, about how we perceive otherspace, about whether those perceptions can be modulated, manipulated, shared—And the jump point. I was waiting, but I couldn't get near you, by bad luck Triton was in conjunction when you came through—"

"And so," she said patiently, "you kidnapped me from Triton. To bring me here. Why?"

Esayeh looked away. "I can tell you this much. You need

to understand it, anyway, before you learn more about us. I was one of Triton's leaders, years ago. I rose at last to be First Pilot, where Hiso Kimura stands now. And so Perrin Tereu became my wife—she had just ascended to the presidency, you see, after her mother's death." His voice was tight, and for a while he was silent.

Linnea waited patiently. His reluctance to continue was obvious.

"The day I took office," he said, "I entered into the secrets of the First Pilot. And I discovered that our safety was built on a foundation of—of death. Of lies. Of a bargain with demons, worse than demons." He looked at her. "With the Cold Minds."

Linnea flinched. *Impossible.*

"An old bargain," Esayeh said. She saw the memory of pain in his pale eyes. "Linnea—the reason they don't eradicate us—the only reason—is because we're their breeding stock for pilots. Tritoners are selling deepsider children to the Cold Minds."

She gathered the shreds of her breath. "How?"

"Tritoner pilots scout out deepsider habitats, find ones that are vulnerable—and the First Pilot transmits the coordinates." He looked grim.

Linnea studied him in the dappled green shade. "That's sickening," she said. "But what can I do? Without even a ship of my own?"

"You'll learn what you can do," he said. "If you're the one we need, if we can trust you—" He broke off, then said, "Seven days. Please?"

Linnea looked away. So there had never been any secret weapon, any miraculous defense against the Cold Minds; only this horror. Which meant she had failed, wasted the journey. Bitter regret crowded tight in her throat.

But she would salvage something from the journey. She would learn what she could—take that, at least, back to her people.

Resolved again, calm again, she raised her head and nodded firmly at Esayeh. "Seven days."

Sometimes during the week that followed, Linnea had the dizzy feeling that deepsiders did not themselves know what they might do next. She remembered the ordered, careful existence on Triton, with its day cycle and night cycle and perfectly regulated temperature. But the deepsiders liked edge in their lives. Or perhaps necessity had led to a custom of chaos.

A deepsider, Linnea came to understand, kept her own days and nights. Outside of the park, which had a twenty-four-hour cycle of "sunlight" and "moonlight," the passages of the deepsider city were always lit—though the light shifted almost randomly in color and intensity over the course of hours. In some stretches, the light panels had been painted in bursts of abstract color or bright pictures of people, animals, chemically blue seas, oddly perfect clouds and sky. Music drifted on the air, none of it public, leaking from private rooms and work spaces. All sorts of music, some deliriously propulsive, some thin and soft and contemplative, some austere and solemn. And people sang while they worked, or while they drank after work, sipping the fiery white whiskey from shared bulbs. No one seemed to expect silence, ever. Not even in her tiny borrowed sleeping space off Esayeh's permanent quarters did Linnea ever find it.

The temperature varied like the light, and sometimes, with a hiss and a roar, a strong breeze would swirl down the passageways, carrying scraps of leaves and other waste to be caught in the clean-screens between sections, where it would be gathered up and composted or otherwise reused.

Linnea took easily to dressing like a deepsider, the first day in clothes she borrowed from Hana and Pilang, then in some she traded for herself with the goods she earned from her work. Bread from a bakery; dried fish after her work cleaning tanks; and after a filthy day spent cleaning the grease from a centrifugal broiler, its owner gave her half the grease—which, she found, was worth more than anything else she'd earned.

Still, after the cool, floral-scented sterility of Triton, she found herself liking the smells of the habitat: steam of cooking rice, brown smell of hot oil, luscious scent of garlic and onion. Smells of people who bathed when it was convenient, which was rare in zero gee, and who washed their few clothes even more rarely. Smells of the green plants tucked in near every light panel, flowers, ripening fruit in the farms, the sharp tang of hydroponics, and the strange acrid smell of tomato leaves—a smell that meant home to her, her home back on Terranova, tiny tomatoes growing in a pot on the porch beside the front door of the little flat she shared with Iain. Again she pushed away the thought of him, her throat aching.

She worked for two days on a farm, arranged through Mick, who had indeed found her old place waiting for her. The morning of the first day, when Linnea finally found the right corridor junction, it was long past seven, the appointed time. She swung in from the tube and caught herself with a hand and a foot in the loops spaced along the walls of the cylindrical room. At first she thought she was alone, that she'd missed everyone. Then she caught movement out of the corner of her eye. There was Mick—small and thin, barefoot and barehanded in a brown denim coverall and knitted gray sweater, both mottled with chemical stains, a bright blue rag tied around her head. "Eh, Mick," Linnea said cheerfully.

"You're late, Lin," the girl said scornfully. "You still don't get around so good."

Linnea grinned. "Merciful of you to wait for me."

"Suuuure." Then Mick broke into an answering grin.

"C'mon. We're late." She held out a thin dark hand. "Want me to pull you?"

"I can manage," Linnea said, stung a bit. And regretted her words when the girl nodded, flipped neatly 180 degrees, and shot across the big shadowy space into another passageway. By the time Linnea had made it across and crawled along the wall to the right opening, she could hear Mick shouting her name derisively. "Heyah, Lin! Hey, Pilot! How'd you find your way out here, moving like that?"

By the end of the second day, Linnea could move around fast enough even for Mick—though she was still too slow at the work they were doing. Plants for the farms grew not from seeds but from cell cultures, thawed and warmed and tended until a thick callus of tangled plant tissue had formed inside the clear jars. Mick's job, and hers, was to pick out the tiny plantlets from the tangle, pinch each one into a little plastic bag covering its roots, squeeze water and nutrients into the bag from a syringe, and clip the bag into a rack under the growth lights. It was tedious, meticulous work, and, Mick had told her, important; all the tomatoes for the whole habitat came from what grew in those bags, so the next time she ate fish in red garlic sauce, she should be proud.

At the end of a ten-hour shift the first day, Linnea's fingers ached, her eyes burned, and she was soaked in sweat. This part of the farms was in the flow of the used-air intakes concentrator for this end of the habitat—hot, humid, and a little too high in CO_2 to be pleasant. She was glad of the quick rinse they were allowed in the farm refresher at end of shift—water that went right back into the hydroponics system.

Even after the rinse, she smelled of tomato leaves. The scent filled her sleeping sack that night. She dreamed of Terranova, and the pale blue pot of tomatoes sitting out on the worn bricks, and Iain coming in late, bringing her a warm handful of the grape-sized red fruits—how his

fingers had smelled of those leaves when she took his
hands later, and kissed them. . . .

The sixth day. In Esayeh's ship, Linnea hung in the darkness of normal space, far from any planet, near to danger. She could feel her heart beating hard, pure terror.

"Listen," Esayeh said, then again, "Listen."

He, too, is afraid. "Yes," she said.

"We can stay only thirty seconds. Their pickets will
spot us, and respond, within thirty-three seconds. So, we
see what there is to see, and we get out."

"I don't want to do this," she said frankly.

"I know," he said. "But until you see this—you don't
know. You don't really know."

So this was to be another part of the test. She was silent
for a while, in the darkness of Esayeh's jumpship, her eyes
on the viewscreen that would show her what he saw. "I'm
ready," she said.

Esayeh settled back in his piloting chair, the leads connecting him to the ship floating snakily in the shadowy air.
"Ready, then. Jump."

A flicker of nothingness, and—

A dark planet hung before her, almost filling her vision.
Dark gray like graphite, shining dully in the light of the
sun. Her people's true home: Earth.

But there was no home here. Her wide eyes took it
in—the brown-gray seas, the featureless gray-black of the
land, the thick, dull haze of the air. But the continents—
familiar; the seas, familiar. She closed her eyes, and bright
before them was the home of her childhood in flames. It
was the same grief.

"No human can live there now, or ever will again," Esayeh said. "Two breaths, and you would die. Now. Three
quick jumps."

Flick, flick, flick, and they were safe, hidden in deep

space far from Earth, untraceable—but Linnea's heart still beat hard. In silence, in the darkness between worlds, she floated, looking at the stars that would have been familiar if Earth had been her world—if her birthright had been hers. Those three stars close together—those were almost familiar already.

When she could speak, she turned her head, and asked, "What is it you think I can do to help you?"

Esayeh looked at her. "You are the pilot of the most powerful jumpship in the Earth system. And—you came here out of compassion. You came so far. That's why I hoped you would be willing to listen to us. To help us find a way to save our people."

"You've lived here for six hundred years," she said.

"But we won't last another ten," Esayeh said. "Since the Cold Minds' invasion of your worlds, the raids on our people have stepped up sharply. We are trying to bring everyone in to safety, but some of those families, some of the miners and asteroid prospectors, they don't want to depend on anyone else. They hide even from us, or they refuse refuge at *Hestia*. And *Hestia* is vulnerable in any case. We need—a better answer."

"I don't know one," she said flatly. "I don't know how you can be saved. Not with the Cold Minds threatening our worlds, too."

"I know," he said. "But at least in the Hidden Worlds you are far from their stronghold. Here we're helpless." He looked pale, uncertain, worried. "I had to get you away from Kimura Hiso and his plans, get you out where you can understand the truth. That is why I kidnapped you. You are the key, not your ship." He reached out and squeezed her shoulder. "Your intelligence and compassion—not your ship, not any device, no matter how powerful." He looked her in the eyes. "We cannot fight the Cold Minds with power. They *are* power."

"So you benefit, too, from the Tritoners' deal," she said

bluntly. "If it ends, the Cold Minds will smash you all, and save a few to breed in captivity—"

"We won't permit that," Esayeh said. "Nor will we let our children continue to suffer. We've been protecting them as best we can, constantly patrolling with all our jump-ships, trying to keep the isolated habitats and family ships in communication—though that's hard when they want to hide. And all the time we've been working on—a different solution." He looked at her. "But—we've always known it could not succeed without the help of your people. It demands that we trust you completely, and that you be worthy of trust. That you understand what's at stake—everything that's at stake. The Tritoners showed you the world they've made. And now you know the other half."

She nodded gravely.

"I've told you the Tritoners' greatest secret," he said. He took a deep breath. "And now I'll show you the deepsiders'. One more jump."

Darkness, at the far edge of the solar system. The sun was a star that seemed only a little brighter than the one she had learned was called Sirius. "We must be halfway to the Oort cloud," she marveled.

"Just about," Esayeh said.

"What am I looking for?" she asked.

"Wait while I switch to thermal."

Linnea blinked at what appeared on the viewscreen. Between them and the sun hung a cylinder with a complex surface glowing gray-white with the faintest hint of thermal leakage. After a moment, she noted the scale and gasped. The thing was more than eight kilometers long. "Esayeh," she said on a thread of breath, "what is that?"

"*Persephone*," he said quietly. "The deepsiders' greatest secret. And our hope of life."

"How did you build it? How did you get it here?"

"Not all the big habitats were destroyed, back when Earth fell," Esayeh said. "This one was built, essential structure and systems only, in lunar orbit. It was supposed to be called *Poseidon*—it was meant for the helium-3 project at Neptune, a long-term home for workers from Earth, with spin gravity so they could keep their bone strength and return when they liked. It was launched toward Neptune a year before Earth fell. Deepsiders modified its orbit, heading it out away from everything, into the dark. Then worked for a century to complete it, stock it. And colonize it."

"It's warm," she said. "It's inhabited now? Out here?"

"Persephone is our refuge," Esayeh said. "And more than that. Kimura Hiso and his people talk about preserving the memory of Earth? The deepsiders have done it. All the memories, not just the ones the Tritoners think are important. Long before the rise of the Cold Minds, deepsiders were already building collections of genetic material, specimen gardens stored as cell culture, animal eggs and sperm—and culturally, everything they could collect, from images of Earth to books and reference materials to records of art and architecture and music."

"Why?"

He hesitated. "They didn't want their children to forget Earth, even if they could never return there. Zero gee—the bones get weak. Deepsiders were the first permanent exiles from Earth."

She shook her head slowly. "And all that is now in this habitat?"

"In the storage levels at the ends of the cylinder, the zero-gee zones that don't spin," Esayeh said. "And there are living examples of some of the plants and animals, in the main cylinder." He smiled absently. "Have you ever seen a camel? Or a redwood tree? I have. . . . Most deepsiders don't know this place is real. It's a story children are taught, that's all. But some with skills we need are asked to spend a year or two working here, in early adulthood. Learning and tending—coming to understand what we must defend and preserve. It's half a gee at the cylinder floor, it's hard for them, but they do it." He met her eyes. "We're the ones keeping Earth alive. Not the Tritoners. Not your Line."

Linnea listened with increasing astonishment. So much that had been thought lost forever—so much of Earth— might still exist in that huge, fragile habitat alone at the edge of interstellar space. Her understanding of human history, of the universe, shifted uneasily in her mind. "Where is it headed?"

"Only farther into the dark, farther from the Cold Minds," Esayeh said. "*Persephone* has no drive of its own, and no destination. All we thought of, six centuries ago, was finding a safe place to hide."

"How much longer can it last, then?"

He looked away. "There's fusion power to warm it, and no shortage of ice out here—we find a likely chunk and bump it into a matching orbit when we can. Trace elements we bring in from sunward, and they cycle everything carefully."

"But it's not sustainable," she said. "And it's vulnerable. If the Tritoners learned of it—"

"They'd find a way to take it over," Esayeh said grimly. "That's more living space than they have ever imagined."

"And if the Cold Minds found it?"

She watched him struggle for words. Finally, he said, "That is what terrifies us. That is why I called you here." He looked at her. "Your worlds have more ships than we do. And there's much we've preserved that your worlds might want, or need. We've already begun to move the most vulnerable people to this habitat from our settlements sunside, and we need to accelerate that effort. But—there is the problem of supply."

"Is that why so many deepsiders have stayed in the system?"

"Yes," Esayeh said. "And now when we see that we must leave—we can't complete the evacuation unless we know we can be supplied, at least our minimal needs, from the Hidden Worlds."

She took a breath to protest, but he forged on. "And those same ships could begin to evacuate people to the Hidden Worlds. A few at a time, we know it will take years to move everyone—but for centuries we have waited for hope. We're a patient people."

"You ask a lot," she said slowly.

"In exchange for much of the wealth of Old Earth—genetic and cultural," Esayeh said. "Much of what your ancestors had to leave behind, that you thought was lost. Put a value on that, if you can."

She was silent for a while, then said, "I still don't see how it can happen. If there were no war, if we were safe from the Cold Minds, then perhaps we could spare some people, some ships. But as it is—" She broke off, seeing his despair. "And what about the Tritoners?" She looked him squarely in the eye. "If all the deepsiders vanish, they'll be the ones the Cold Minds raid for pilots."

Esayeh's expression tightened. "When I was a Tritoner, we used to talk about sacrifice for great causes. Perhaps they'll finally learn what it's like when the sacrifice is their own." He shook his head. "I've argued this at the Star River Meetings year after year, but I see no chance that the Consensus will ever permit the Tritoners to be told about this. The deepsiders don't trust them. And they have good reason not to."

Linnea looked down at her hands. The treasures in that habitat would be a great gift to bring to the Hidden Worlds; but still not the new weapon, the new defense they needed—that she had been sure she would find in Earth's system. She raised her head and looked at Esayeh. "I'm sorry. I don't think I will be able to persuade my own people, either."

"But you'll try," he said quietly. "I trust you to try. We'll help you regain your ship. You'll be free to go."

Linnea closed her eyes at the surge of longing. The Hidden Worlds—the chance to tell them what she and Iain had learned—

"I won't go without Iain," she said, her voice trembling.

"I wouldn't think of it," Esayeh said gently.

Tears blurred her vision. "Thank you." She blinked hard.

"Then let's go home," Esayeh said.

"Yes," she said. "Home."

Where Iain was.

FOURTEEN

TRITON
THREE DAYS EARLIER

Late in the evening, long after candlelight, Tereu stood at the commscreen in her private study signing orders, one after another: a change in calorie allocation to reflect current crop results; the proclamation of extra sweets at midday tomorrow, in honor of the birthday of the city's oldest inhabitant; a congratulatory message to the winning teams in the citywide school lacrosse tournaments.

She had wished for years that she could allow her staff to handle at least the ceremonial items—who would know? But years ago, shortly after taking over command of the Tritoner pilots, Hiso had made a great public issue of her close attachment to the daily lives of the people. He had said to the official press, and to her private council, and to every delegation of citizens how fortunate Triton was to have such a leader, in these dangerous times when the city's pilots were called to duty farther and farther from home. He knew, he said, when he jumped far away on some lonely

patrol, that at home his people were in Tereu's safe and at-
tentive care.

And thus he had trapped her even more deeply in a
tangled net of delegations and appearances and proclama-
tions, visiting newborn babies and dedicating industrial
equipment when she could be—*When I should be leading
this city.*

She glanced at the list of documents still to be dealt
with: twenty-seven more, and she was done—an hour perhaps. Then the flag on one of them caught her eye: It was
from the research station above Nereid, where Hiso's men
were supposedly studying the Cold Minds pilot. *Finally.*

But when she flicked it open, she found only a technical
report, dense columns of unrelieved text. So after three
days, she still had not even seen an image of the thing.

She read further. Apparently they had begun making
progress once they'd taken Pilot sen Paolo's suggestion:
giving the creature its "vision" back in the form of a visual
monitor it could hold and aim in its hand. That had plainly
reduced its level of panic. It could not speak, could not
convey information in any way, but it no longer needed to
be constantly drugged; its behavior could be studied, and
physiological samples could be obtained more safely. More
information, the report concluded, would be forthcoming
in two or three days. *Or ten days, or never,* Tereu thought
sourly, and pressed her right thumb on the screen to initial
the document.

She was deep in a set of proposed song selections for
the new season of the city youth chorus when she heard a
polite cough behind her. She turned, expecting Hiso, even
though he was supposed to be out on patrol until tomorrow. But instead she saw Pilot sen Paolo, neatly dressed in
dark gray as always, standing deferentially just inside the
open door. "Pilot," she said, and acknowledged his bow
with a nod. "What can I do for you? I'm afraid there's still
no word about Pilot Kiaho."

"I didn't expect any, Madame," he said, and she heard the hint of tension in his words. "I—have a request."

"I'm afraid I can't unlock your ship," she said. "I don't have the authority—it's a pilot matter."

"You should have it in Pilot Kimura's absence, Madame," Iain said. "The ship might be of use if an attack were to come."

"There will be no attack," she said. "Pilot Kimura has satisfied me on that point. Your ambush of the Cold Minds' raid will not be traced back to Triton. Your ship would have been completely unknown to them." She shrugged. "They are just as likely to suspect the deepsiders."

She saw just a flicker of anger on sen Paolo's somber face, quickly and expertly suppressed. How she wished that this man had accepted her offer of power: a man who could lead without swagger, argue without anger, inspire without fear—perhaps such a man would have been able to guide her people out of this trap.

Sen Paolo said only, "In any case, Madame, the request has nothing to do with my ship."

She eyed him. The security call button implanted in her left hand would bring instant help, and he must know or guess that that was the case. "I will listen."

"I would like to escort you out to the Nereid research station tonight," Iain said. "I think that you need to see the Cold Minds pilot for yourself."

She did not allow her expression to register her slight shock at the absence of her title. "Does First Pilot Kimura know of this expedition?"

"No," sen Paolo said, his voice hard. "Nor would he allow it if he did. He does not want you to see this."

Her heart racing, she touched her commscreen, ending surveillance of this room and wiping the record of the past five minutes. "Who is the pilot you've arranged?"

"Perrin Gareth," sen Paolo said. "Your cousin. All quite proper."

And how did you manage that? she wanted to ask him. Another part of her wanted to send sen Paolo away. Hiso loved her in his way, and certainly he loved this city—he must have a reason, perhaps a good one, to keep her away from the Cold Minds pilot.

But instead, after a moment's hesitation, she sent her security commander the code that meant she required privacy—a code that would also allow for a private absence, not to be reported to Hiso, not to be questioned. Then she locked her commscreen and turned to face sen Paolo. "What is this?"

Sen Paolo lifted his chin. "Do you know of Pilot Kimura's arrangement with the Cold Minds? Of the deepsider children?"

Her mouth went dry. "It's true that I should not know," she said. "This is a First Pilot's secret, and always has been. But—I had another husband, another First Pilot, years ago. And he told me. Hiso knows this."

"Is your first husband dead?"

She straightened with careful pride. "He went out to the deepsiders," she said. "He left Triton forever when he learned of the arrangement—he told me of it, and he left." She looked into sen Paolo's dark, angry eyes, remembering another man's anger, another man's eyes—cold light blue—looking into hers with the same accusation. Then she pushed the thought away. "How did you learn of the arrangement? Did Hiso tell you?"

"No," sen Paolo said. "It was the ambush that gave it away, when we captured the pilot. So exactly timed. And yet Hiso had claimed not to be spying on the Cold Minds' movements."

"If he let you see that much, then he wanted you to know," she said. "He wants to trap you in this as I have been trapped. He wants to make you know of it and live with the knowing." She saw in his eyes that he heard her bitter tone—but what he showed was not pity, but sternness. *No.* She would not allow him to judge her.

"In time," she said, "after you've been ashamed long enough, you start telling yourself there's no choice. You accept it." She had been terrified, at first, that Esayeh would betray Triton's crime to the deepsiders—who might then end their dealings with Triton entirely, closing off trade that her city still depended on, pulling out the doctors and technicians that Triton still needed to supplement its own.

Yet Esayeh had not done this; after he left her, there had only been silence from him, silence for years.

As she had kept her own silence.

She looked into sen Paolo's eyes and saw something else there. A flicker that might now be pity. *So he is as weak as I am,* she thought with regret. "Take me to this thing you wish me to see. I'm ready for anything."

"No." Iain's voice was remote. "No, you aren't."

The flight in her cousin Gareth's ship to the orbiting research lab was brief. Tereu was glad, though, that she'd had the thought to put on one of the antinausea patches Cleopa's physician cousin had given her last year, before her journey to inspect the research and industrial facilities on and orbiting Nereid.

Her young cousin Gareth seemed subdued into silence, which was not usually his way; so she did not make him more uncomfortable by pushing conversation on him. Nor did she offer any words to sen Paolo, who saw and understood too much. They docked, and she accepted Gareth's assistance to leave the ship. The passageway outside, lit dimly in cold blue for the night cycle, felt chilly, and she wished she had thought to bring a wrap. *Too late now.*

Gareth tugged Tereu along awkwardly, his hand on her

elbow; she kept her hands clasped tightly together, pressed against her chest, a trick she had learned to hold off the feeling of wild falling that had panicked her the first time or two in zero gee.

Sen Paolo, who of course moved easily here, waited for them at a hatch up ahead. When Tereu and Gareth reached it, Gareth guided her hands to a metal handle set into the wall. She stopped herself from rocking there like a silly balloon and glanced at sen Paolo. "Let's get this over with quickly. I want to go home."

There it was again, in sen Paolo's eyes: pity. Beside her, Gareth punched in the security code and hauled the hatch open.

Light spilled out. The compartment inside—a lock?—was small, spherical, with a huge round window of thick glass facing into the room beyond, which was filled with harsh white light. Tereu allowed herself to drift forward, curious—there was a sleeping sack in there, floating loose and empty, and a large bulb of water—

It burst from the corner of her vision and plastered itself in front of her, pressing against the other side of the glass. The shape of a man, dressed in a white coverall, silhouetted against the light.

Tereu lurched back and felt the welcome warmth of both men's arms catching her, holding her steady. Then as her eyes adapted and she saw the thing's face, she took a thin breath and let it out in a whispered scream.

It had no eyes, except for little crusted wounds. The nose had been mashed to parallel slits; the mouth drooled, shape-less and toothless. A wire led into one of the eye wounds, its other end attached to a small round object like a lens that the thing held in one hand, pressed against the glass. Aimed at her.

With a wave of revulsion, she remembered the report she had read this evening. The thing was looking at her—in the only way it could.

She took a breath. So. Sen Paolo had probably hoped for this effect—hoped for the horror, the fear that she had just shown him.

Well, that would be his last satisfaction. She drew on years of self-control—years of experience Hiso had given her that this young man could not begin to guess at. She turned herself around awkwardly to face sen Paolo, and said, almost evenly, "Did you imagine that I was not aware of this?"

"Yes," sen Paolo said. His voice was flat, sober. "I knew you were not aware of it, not in this way. Or Pilot Kimura would have paraded you out here to see it already. This is the grand opening move of his war against the Cold Minds. Surely he would want you to cut the ribbon—if he wanted you to understand it at all."

She gritted her teeth. "So what is the point of this?"

"I thought," sen Paolo said quietly, "that seeing this might remind you of who you are. Of who you *really* are."

"Seeing this monster!"

"Seeing that the policies you oversee," Iain said, "turned an innocent, healthy human child into—this."

On the other side of the glass the thing shifted its hand to look toward sen Paolo. She saw sen Paolo gather himself—saw him smile at the thing, as if it could know what that meant!

Then she shuddered. *Perhaps it does know.* Some of the children taken were as old as eight or nine. . . .

No. "Pilot sen Paolo," Tereu said coldly, "I resent this disgusting effort at emotional manipulation. Gareth, take me home."

The boy looked at her. "I'm sorry, Cousin. Not yet."

She drew her head back, affronted. "Now," she said. "Or I will speak to First Pilot Kimura, and your career will end."

"I think," the boy said carefully, "that it was going to end soon anyway."

Tereu twitched her hand, signaling for security. Gareth caught the motion and shook his head. "It won't work, Cousin."

"No help in range," Iain said. "There is only a small medical staff on duty in the night hours, and their monitoring room is on the other side of the—patient's quarters, one level up. They can't hear us."

"You're committing a crime," she said hotly.

"I'm trying to get you to listen to me," sen Paolo said. "Set aside your fear of Hiso. He can't hear you now. He can't control your actions unless you choose to allow it. All I ask is that you listen. I give you my word that you will be returned safely home tonight."

"While you and this renegade escape to the deepsiders," she spat. She saw Gareth wince.

"No," sen Paolo said. "Gareth will keep his oath to the First Pilot—he'll return and face what happens next. And I'll remain in your power. But, Madame—the ground is shifting."

She looked at the thing on the other side of the glass. "*Must* we talk here?"

"Yes," sen Paolo said. "We must."

She closed her eyes. "Then I will listen—for my people's sake."

"You're afraid for your people," sen Paolo said.

"I'm bound to them by my word of honor," she said. "And I love them." She opened her eyes and met his gaze fiercely. "Tell me what choice *you* would have made, in my people's place six centuries ago. With the Cold Minds about to crush you, about to end everything."

"I can't, of course," he said. His voice was gentle. "I never was in your place. But I've had—the opportunity to learn something about honor."

She kept her eyes on his.

"Kimura Hiso has the kind of honor my brothers of the Line held for so long," sen Paolo said. "Pledged to a proud tradition. Built on something outside himself: his ideal of your city, your people. What I have learned—" His voice actually faltered. She watched him sharply as he continued. "What I have learned is that honor like that . . . because it is external, it can be broken by forces we do not control. I—someone I love dearly taught me that the first, the most important truth to hold to is truth to oneself. Always to ask, do my actions, do my decisions reflect the man I should be?"

"You cannot tell me that Kimura Hiso is dishonorable," she said. But she heard the uncertainty in her voice. Damn—he was shaking her.

He looked straight at her. Into her. "I do tell you that. Examine yourself. Consider what was done to the human being we are looking at. Not just here, now, but at the beginning of his life, when he was sold into the Cold Minds' service. Will you say it was done in your name, and by your will?"

Out of pride, she made herself turn her head and look at the thing inside the glass. "I knew of it, and I do not repudiate it," she said firmly. "That was done to protect my people. To whom I am sworn."

His voice was careful, kind. "At any price?"

"Even my life," she said angrily.

"Even his?" Now Sen Paolo's voice shook. "I learned, through the worst—loss—of my life, that the one price you can't pay to protect what your soul treasures most is—your soul itself." He took a breath, then another, and went on. "It breaks people. As it has broken Kimura Hiso. He cannot walk away from this choice; he's paid too much of himself. You—have not, not yet."

"You don't know me at all," she said fiercely, against the sting of tears in her eyes.

"I want to help you," he said. "Has it been so long since anyone wanted to help you?"

Tears again. She turned her face away from him, blinked

hard, and looked at the thing in the cage. It had drifted away from the glass and now huddled in a far corner of the space, head down, its face mercifully hidden. And in that moment, for that moment, she saw it as human, and afraid.

As she was afraid. But to lead was to choose, even in the face of fear. She looked back at sen Paolo—be damned if he saw the tears—took a breath. And asked, "How can I free my people from this bargain?"

She saw no hint of triumph in his expression, only sober assessment of her words. "Time is short," he said. "Kimura Hiso's plan for saving the Tritoners cannot work—the Cold Minds will simply destroy you. But he has, nevertheless, set it in motion. We must end it now—by ending the bargain. Breaking it. Denying the Cold Minds their next prey."

She stared at him. "How?"

"In the end it will take all of us," he said. "My people, the people of Triton, and the deepsiders. But for now, you can make all the difference. Your cousin—" He looked at Gareth, who nodded. "In his work for the First Pilot, your cousin receives the reports of the jumpship patrols when they discover a vulnerable deepsider habitat. Gareth sets out the information for Kimura Hiso, who—passes it to the Cold Minds." He looked at Tereu. "With your permission, Madame—let him pass that same information to you as well. Then, if you wish, you can convey it to your connections among the deepsiders." There was a hard glint in his eyes. "I know that you have them."

He knows that I allowed Kiaho's kidnapping. She held herself stiffly upright. "I will do it," she said.

He bowed his head to her, the full, deep bow of respect.

"And now," she said, suddenly weary beyond belief, "Cousin, please—take me home."

FIFTEEN

DEEPSIDER HABITAT *HESTIA*

Linnea's borrowed chrono woke her early on the morning of the day Esayeh had promised to take her back to Triton. She had bathed the night before, in the steamy, soapy, noisy community refresher on this passageway, and she had gone to the laundry one passage over and carefully washed the best of her deepsider clothes. These, too, were borrowed, from Pilang—but last night Pilang had made the loan a gift: soft red trousers tight at the ankles, and a snug knitted gray shirt.

In her tiny, curtained sleep cubby, Linnea dressed carefully, listening for some sign that Esayeh was up and about in the small cluttered space beyond. In the dim light in front of a scrap of mirror, she went to work combing her hair. Just a little longer, and she could braid it—she grinned at the thought of Iain's probable reaction to that. Then she went still, with a shiver of joyful realization. *In just a few hours, I'll see him again.* She stuffed the comb into her bag, still grinning.

Last night she and Pilang and Esayeh had gone out for drinks at a pub at the far end of the park. They had drifted home late through the dim blue-white artificial moonlight in the park, Esayeh and Pilang hand in hand arguing about the words of some song, singing snatches of it back and forth. Eventually Linnea had left them behind. After all these days, she knew her way home to Esayeh's tiny quarters, to the sleep cubby he had lent to her.

But she'd never heard Esayeh come in last night at all. *His business, and Pilang's.* She tied her hair neatly into the red-and-gray scarf Pilang had brought her last night to complete the gift.

Then she unlaced the curtain cautiously and poked her head out, half-expecting to see both Pilang's and Esayeh's heads at the top of his sleep bag. But the room was empty. She turned up the string of multicolored lights surrounding the entrance door and looked around at the walls festooned with net bags of real books, wadded shirts tied in place by their sleeves, a cluster of rumpled cloth flowers, two and a half pouches of wine, a couple of archaic-looking crystal recorders, three rabbit skins tied in a bunch, and, stuffed next to Esayeh's sleeping sack, the pair of thick, insanely colorful hand-knitted socks he always put on as soon as he got home. There was no comm, of course, and Linnea saw no sign of a handwritten note.

Her heart sinking a little, she grabbed the small net bag of bright yellow tomatoes tied next to the curtain of her cubby, snagged it onto her belt, and pushed her way out into the passageway. She pulled her way quickly along toward Froyda's space, where it was usually possible to get a bulb of coffee at this hour, especially if you had some farm produce, especially tomatoes. Esayeh would surely be waiting for her there.

Only he wasn't. When Linnea poked her head through the open doorway, she found only a couple of teenagers holding hands and whispering, and a gray-haired woman reading a paper book frayed almost into fuzz; and Froyda, of course. No one else.

Linnea gave the tomatoes to Froyda, refusing coffee with polite thanks. "Have you seen Esayeh this morning?"

Froyda, a comfortably large woman whose short frizzle of blazing red hair contrasted oddly with her brown skin, shook her head. She gave Linnea a knowing smile—like everyone on this passageway she had obviously figured out that Linnea was not a deepsider, or indeed even from Triton. "You're heading out, I hear."

"I hope so," Linnea said. "Thanks. I'll be back and see you someday."

"Be glad to see you, if I happen to be here," Froyda said. Then she coughed politely into the crook of her elbow, and said, "You know, sometimes Esayeh goes down to Mechanical. He's pretty good with repairs, and they drag him in—"

Linnea smiled her thanks. "Not this time, I think." *He'd better not have done anything like that. Not today.* She launched herself back into the passageway, almost hitting an adolescent boy on air-leak patrol, who squealed and reproached her. Her next stop was Pilang's sleeping space, two passages over and one up—the space between the inner and outer tank walls was thick here, so the neighborhoods were densely woven and intertwined.

But Pilang's black cloth door was laced tight shut, and when Linnea called out for her, no one answered.

All right. The clinic next. Linnea knew she did not want to make the long trip to the docking ring only to find no one there. Someone at the clinic would at least know where Pilang was, and Pilang could point her to Esayeh.

When Linnea reached the clinic, the white-painted pressure hatch stood closed and sealed tight. She rapped on it with her knuckles. "Pilang! Hana!" But the reception comm next to the hatch stayed stubbornly silent.

A gaunt, pale, long-boned man in greasy mechanic's

coveralls, his head shaved, caught himself near her and asked kindly, "Need the doctor? There's another clinic over on Ring Seven."

"I need Pilang," Linnea said. "Shouldn't she be here?"

"They're jumping out," the man said. "Left in a hurry, I heard down by Control. Some emergency."

"Perfect," Linnea muttered. Then said to the man, "Have they launched yet? Do you know?"

"No way I could know that, sorry." He shrugged.

She looked up and down the passageway—a little wildly, maybe, because the man smiled kindly and pointed. "South, second left, first inboard, and you're in the park. Docking ring's equatorial, halfway down the park. Right on Ring Five."

Inboard. Over the years, most of the intersections had been painted to mark inboard, outboard, north, south—she'd find it. "Right. Thanks." She pushed off.

Iain, love—I'll get there somehow. I promise.

When she reached the docking-ring hatch nearest to where Esayeh always docked, she found several other people waiting to pass through, all of them medical personnel. "What's happening?" she asked.

"Some kind of rescue run," the woman nearest her said. "They're sending all the jumpships they've got, need medtechs to help. That's all I know."

"Sleepers, I heard," a tall man said, and at that moment the lock popped open. Linnea wedged herself in last, and the lock cycled, controlling the slight pressure difference between the docking bay and the park. Another *chuff* of hastily released pressure, and the four of them spilled out.

But to her dismay, she found the docking tube to Esayeh's ship sealed tight, the vacuum warning light steady red. He had already jumped away.

She gripped the handhold by the hatch, rested her forehead against her hands for a moment, trying not to swear. She could try to talk her way onto one of the other ships, but it was Esayeh who had promised to return her to Triton; she could not risk not being here when he returned. She turned to the woman she'd spoken to earlier, who was scribbling on a hand-sized commscreen held by a tall young girl in clinic scrubs. "*Allecto*, crew complete, go!" the girl called out, and turned instantly to Linnea. "That was the last spot," she said. "Sorry."

"What can I do here?" As she asked, another couple of stragglers arrived. The young girl looked them over, then told Linnea, "It's sleepers they'll be bringing in. You can all fill ice bags."

Sleepers. They were expecting people who'd been taken straight from cold sleep. She'd heard Hana mention thermal shock, the dangerous condition that could be brought on by warming people too quickly, letting their metabolic needs increase faster than the slow return of normal circulatory function.

The girl was already leading the way along the docking ring, to a hatch marked COLD STORES. "Work fast," she was saying. "We'll need a lot if we're lucky. If they get there in time."

"What do you mean, in time?" Linnea asked, as the little group swung to a halt and the girl opened the hatch.

"If they get there before the Cold Minds do," the girl said.

Fear slid chilly fingers along Linnea's spine. "They know the Cold Minds are coming? How?"

"Got word. Don't know how. Okay, look here, ice in this big bin, you fill these little bags from the locker here. Not too full, keep them flexible, they've got to bend around the patients, keep good contact with the skin. When they're done, collect them under the net on that bulkhead. We'll come get 'em as soon as the sleepers start coming in."

Linnea spent a blurred hour working, in zero gee, to

scoop small chunks of ice from the bin and get them into the bags. The full bags were slippery and hard to keep hold of, and ice kept flying loose. Linnea was shivering cold, wet through, by the time the first crew came to pick up some of the bags she and her two companions had filled.

She looked up when the medtech entered, his expression grim. She took a breath. "How did it go?"

"We got in and out, didn't see anything," the man said. "No telling how many trips we'll get to make. I've got to get this ice out there." He was stuffing full bags into a carry-sack.

Linnea bit back her question about Esayeh and got back to work. Eventually, their stores of bags ran out, and Linnea went out in search of the girl with the clipboard. The space was full of medtechs hustling limp bodies in stretcher bags stuffed with ice. A lot of them were children, eyes taped shut, limply unconscious.

Linnea turned to look the other way along the bay—and found herself almost face-to-face with Esayeh. He was crouched against a bulkhead, one arm stuck through an anchor loop, his hands wrapped tightly around a hot bulb of coffee. They were trembling. His eyes looked into nothingness.

Linnea turned herself to match his orientation. "Esayeh," she said quietly.

He looked up and saw her, but did not seem to recognize her. "Eh?"

"It's Linnea," she said. "What happened?"

"We're done," he said, teeth clenched to control his shivering. "We got twenty-four of them out."

Twenty-four out of forty. *Oh, no.* "That's it?"

"That's it." He shuddered. "Right when we were jumping out with our second load, three Cold Minds ships jumped in. Two of ours were still docked. One's back now, didn't get anyone out, had to recall the techs. I don't know—" His voice broke. "I don't know if the other ship made it."

"I'm so sorry." She set her hand on his shoulder. "Pilang's safe?"

"She went with her patients," he said. "Down to the clinic, they'll warm them there. We tried for all the children, I think maybe we got them. But the rest, some of the families—they're dead by now." He dragged the back of his hand across his eyes.

"Come on," she said quietly. "Let's get you home, get some whiskey into you. Put you to sleep."

"We tried," he said. "We really tried, Lin."

"I know," she said. "Shhh. Come along."

"We've been trying for so many years," he said brokenly. "I've been building up the patrols, trying to make sure no one was ever left like that, asleep in the dark—but we never could find them all, not in time. And this time we *knew*, we knew they were coming, we even knew when, and we still couldn't—" His face twisted, and he could not speak.

"You saved a lot of them," she said as she guided him into a new passageway.

"Not enough," he said, and sobbed.

In his quarters, as she helped Esayeh into dry, warm clothes, he told her what remained: A message had reached Pilang that morning—a message from her cousin Cleopa on Triton. It gave a time, and the name of a deepsider family vessel, a remote one exploring the thin, icy pickings at the fringes of the solar system. The only other words: *They're coming*.

"It's Tereu," Esayeh said thickly, as Linnea helped him slide into his sleeping sack. "She's the only one who could have gotten that information, the only one who could have decided to send it. I don't know why she would. Why now."

"I know why," Linnea said. "Iain's there." She dimmed the lights to a faint, warm glow, and said, "You'll be all right? Good. I'm going to go help Pilang for a while."

"I'm sorry," Esayeh said, his voice already blurred with sleep. "About your trip home."

"Time enough for all that later," she said. "Quiet now."
She changed quickly out of her sodden travel clothes into the
clean but stained set of coveralls she'd worn for her farm
work, and let herself silently out into the passageway. *I'm
sorry, Iain—I didn't make it after all.*

But it's your fault. Half-smiling, she launched herself
down the passageway toward the work that was waiting for
her.

———————

SIXTEEN

TRITON

Kimura Hiso strode into Triton Port Control at mid-morning, straight from a successful three-day patrol. Pilot Timmon's Gold Wing had verified a nice, plump target on the first day—fine work, given that there seemed to be fewer of them these days. And essential, at this delicate moment. But really, there was no reason to rejoice yet. He frowned at a young female clerk, who jumped and huddled more closely over her work. The cryptic, symbol-encoded messages Hiso had been receiving from the Cold Minds were getting both more frequent and more peremptory.

Another, more efficient, clerk handed Hiso the activity report from Nearspace Scanning. As Hiso checked it over, hiding his apprehension, he wondered again whether the Cold Minds knew anything like anger, or fear, or whether they chose their courses of action merely by calculation, like the machines they were descended from.

Soon they would be satisfied again, and all would be in train.

No doubt the Cold Minds' calculations had been upset by the mysterious new jumpship that had successfully disabled one of their ships, and by the missing pilot. . . . *Best keep them satisfied, for now.* His plans were on the move at last. The Hidden Worlds ship would be his own in a matter of days. And as for the woman who was its pilot—she and sen Paolo would make a perfect compensatory gift to the Cold Minds. A breeding pair of pilots—with that, and the whole population of deepsiders to exploit, they would hardly care that Hiso's people had escaped them at last.

Passing through his outer office, Hiso noted that Perrin Gareth's workstation was still unmanned. No doubt the boy had taken advantage of Hiso's absence to slack off on his duties. A true son of privilege, never challenged as Hiso had been in his long, upward struggle—a son of the Maintenance Guild who had gained the rare, coveted chance to prove himself as a pilot. He stalked into his inner office and sealed the door behind him.

As always, the silence and privacy of the room enfolded him, easing his taut nerves. Its richness comforted him, too, after three days in his cramped jumpship; the walls gleamed darkly, paneled in real wood, and the ancient but vibrantly colored carpet had come from Earth itself. He touched his commscreen and woke it to life, then dropped lightly into his work chair.

The message queue held nothing that looked important. But he should check for another sort of message, to see if there was confirmation of the success of the Cold Minds' raid today. Not thanks, of course, but acknowledgment of his efficiency.

He touched a blank corner of his commscreen in one precise spot, then pressed his thumb to the wordless window that appeared. The deep files faded into view and opened like flowers, showing him a carefully selected array of monitoring data. But as always he focused on the one readout for which the rest of the data were only a distraction.

The stealthed monitors in far orbit around Neptune were ostensibly for research, and they did collect data that he supposed the Scientists' Guild found some use for. But for Hiso, as First Pilot, the monitors had only one purpose: to receive, without decoding, the brief bursts of staticky communication that were his signals from the Cold Minds.

The past thirty-six hours scrolled past. A few faint contacts had registered earlier this morning; at that level they were usually noise, which was why the Cold Minds hid their signals among them. Hiso ran his finger along the range in question, then waited a moment for the data to stream in.

He slid the data file to the center of his screen, then pressed all four fingers against the icon. There was a burst of light as the commscreen recognized him, then a shimmering pool of color that resolved itself into a set of symbols. Symbols only the First Pilot knew how to read.

Hiso examined them carefully. Then again, his heart pounding.

Failure.

Interference. Modified by the symbol that meant *deepsiders.*

Explain. Modified by the symbol that meant *comply immediately.*

Hiso swore. It was bad luck, that was all, it had to be— that damned Esayeh and his defensive patrols, they found too many targets before Hiso's men did. Well, now Esayeh had gotten lucky, stumbled in just as the Cold Minds arrived.

Then Hiso noticed the time code attached to *failure.* Almost immediately after he had sent them the coordinates. They must have had a ship hovering in Neptune nearspace, probably one of their tiny scouts, waiting for his signal to give them their next target. *Can they possibly be that hungry?*

And then he saw that the symbol for *deepsiders* had two further, inner modifiers. Frowning, he unfolded them and pieced the concepts together.

Five ships.

Waiting.

Five jumpships—that was about as many as that damned traitor Esayeh could ever bring together at once. And apparently those five ships had gotten there first.

So it had been an all-out rescue operation. Which meant—

Hiso sat back and frowned. It meant that Esayeh had *known* the Cold Minds were coming. Just where. And just when.

Hiso smashed his fist against the arm of his chair.

That bitch Tereu. She's spying on me.

No longer.

Hiso strode into Tereu's dark, spice-scented bedroom, its heavy shades still closed tightly against the rising light in the park outside. She lay curled in her cocoon of quilts, and she lifted her rumpled head sleepily as he reached the side of the bed.

He tore the quilts from around her, lifted her by the shoulders, held her helpless in the air. *"What have you done?"*

She gave a terrified gasp. Then she planted her feet on Hiso's chest and launched herself away from him. She flew through the air over the rumpled bed and landed on the rug beyond. By the time Hiso had come around the bed to face her, she was on her feet and stood with her hand hovering over the call button for Security.

Hiso did not waste a glance at it. "Do you think I would not have disabled that before I came in here?"

Her hand lifted away from the button. "Tell me what's

wrong, Hiso." Her voice was steady, but he knew her: He heard the weakness, the fear.

"You degrade the office you hold," Hiso said. "You've betrayed me. Betrayed your own people."

He saw the flicker of understanding in her eyes, quickly masked—but not quickly enough. "You made me fail the Cold Minds." His voice was cold. "Fail them again. Prey has been getting scarce, did you know that? Because of Esayeh and his patrols. My men found a rich target, one that would have satisfied the Cold Minds for a hundred days at least—and they arrived to find five deepsider ships waiting. Five!"

"Did Esayeh's ships escape?" she asked steadily. "Was anyone hurt?"

"That is of no interest," Hiso said. "What matters is that now we must find another target, and at once. And if that one, too, escapes them—if they begin to conclude that we can no longer keep our side of the bargain—they will turn on *us*. On our people. Now, at the moment when all is in motion to make us free of them forever."

That penetrated, he saw. "You're mad," she said. "We're too weak to fight. And we have no escape, nowhere to go. The Cold Minds are in the Hidden Worlds, too."

"I know your old dream," he said. "To run and hide with the other cowards—with the Line, in the Hidden Worlds." He took a step closer to her, saw her shrink back slightly— *good*. "You can't imagine a fighter's solution to this. You can only imagine a woman's. Save everyone, no matter the cost to honor."

"Last night," she said intensely, "I saw that thing for myself. The—pilot you took."

Hiso went still. "Who showed you?"

Her jaw firmed. "Iain sen Paolo."

Hiso laughed. "Our enemy," he said. "A man of the Line. He has every reason to hate us. Anything he tells you is a lie."

"It sounded true to me," she said, still with the same strange calm. "Was that pilot, what you did to him, was that part of your plan? Because it's horrible, Hiso."

"It has always been horrible," Hiso said. "You saw the reality of our situation, and it broke you. When, if you had been strong for a few more days, a few more weeks, if you had been the leader I thought you were, we might all be on the way to safety and freedom."

"That is not so," Tereu said, her face still as a mask.

"I wish I had killed Esayeh, that day when he betrayed the First Pilot's secret to you," Hiso said, breathing hard. "And I should have killed *you*. Your weakness has brought us all to our deaths."

"No," Tereu said, moving slightly, and when he looked down, he saw that she was holding a weapon aimed at him. A strange one, a small white gun with a black oval opening like a mouth.

He went still. "What is that?"

"A Hidden Worlds weapon," she said. "A neural fuser. Sen Paolo gave it to me last night. He said it can cook your brain like an egg."

"You won't use it against me," Hiso said. His heart was pounding strangely. *She's a coward. Remember that. She has always been a coward.*

"To save my life, I'll use it," she said.

"But both our lives are over," he said, and with a surge of rage he was on her, gripping and twisting her slender wrist. She struggled to fire the weapon—too late. He twisted harder, and she shrieked and let him take the weapon from her.

She staggered back against the window by the head of her bed, cradling her wrist, her eyes wide. "What are you?"

"A man of honor," Hiso said.

"Honor that has destroyed you," she said.

"I," he said pridefully, "have kept our world alive for all the years of my service. I will defend it to my death."

"Do so," she said coldly. "But you will never touch me again."

"Nor will Iain sen Paolo," he said. He pulled out his comm to summon Security, to order Tereu's confinement out of communication range; but that instant the priority alarm began to flash. He touched the comm, and said, "Kimura. Report."

The voice over the comm was unsteady with poorly concealed terror. "Proximity alert from Nereid, First Pilot. From the research station. Seventeen unknown contacts, big ones, just jumped in—they ID as Cold Minds."

Hiso froze. *Then they know. They've known all along that it was I who took their pilot.*

Hiso ran.

Iain was searching a tool-storage locker in the bitter cold of the docking bay outside Linnea's jumpship, looking for the meter that would let him continue some maintenance the ship badly needed, when the bay's alert sounded its high trilling note. A light in the ceiling began to flash red, and Iain saw the status lights over every docking tube in the bay—except his own—flick from blue to yellow.

Someone in Port Control had set the jump engines to warm-up. *The pilots are going out.* Iain's heart thumped— he never forgot for a moment how close they were to the Cold Minds here. And that Linnea was out there, somewhere—vulnerable.

He closed the locker carefully and stood with his back to the docking tube, waiting. One of the first two pilots to arrive was Gareth, almost flying through the icy air—he gave Iain a frightened, half-guilty glance and vanished into the docking tube of his ship. The other pilot nodded curtly at Iain. "What is it, brother?" Iain asked.

"Ships jumped in," the man said. "A lot of them. Can

you come out with us, brother? We could use that ship of yours today."

"Locked down, sorry," Iain said, but at that moment he saw Kimura Hiso and felt himself go cold. He had never seen the man so angry.

"Pilot sen Paolo," Hiso said. "You'll ride in my ship."

There was something in Hiso's hand—Iain had to look twice to understand. The neural fuser he had given to Tereu. He wondered for a painful instant whether she was dead, whether that had killed her—then set the thought aside. "Where are you going?"

"Out," Hiso said, unsmiling. "We have visitors. You're going to meet them."

"Cold Minds—" Iain shook his head. "Hiso, we can't fight them off."

"There won't be any need to fight," Hiso said. "Get along."

When they entered the close, dim space of Hiso's ship, Hiso made Iain kneel on the deck, taped his hands together behind him, taped his ankles, then bound his hands to his feet. Trussed like an animal, Iain could not move. Hiso strapped him down against the thin acceleration padding, then started connecting himself to his ship.

A long acceleration. When silence fell, when Iain guessed that they had jumped into the orbit that would take them to the research station, Hiso turned at last to Iain. "I'm going to tell you two things before we arrive there."

Iain waited silently.

"First. I know what you did to my wife," Hiso said.

Iain sighed. "I did nothing to Perrin Tereu."

"You corrupted her," Hiso said, his voice hard. "You seduced her."

"That's not true," Iain said. "She is honest and honorable. And I'm bound, for my life, to Linnea Kiaho."

"You seduced Tereu's mind," Hiso said. "You broke her loyalty, not just to me, but to our people. She has given her body to other men before, and I forgave her. This I cannot forgive." He seemed oddly calm. "Now that I know of it, though, she's no threat. Nor are you." He touched his board lightly. "The other matter you should know is the arrangement I've made. You'll be part of it, for a while. . . ."

Iain waited.

"You'll help me finish what you helped me begin," Hiso said. He opened a pocket in his tunic and drew out a single-dose spray injector. "This is the result of our work with the Cold Minds pilot," he said. "It will reproduce the abnormal chemistry of the thing's blood, in your own."

Iain felt his heart begin to race. Surely not—

"And then," Hiso said, "we'll test whether it can protect you from the bots."

"It won't work," Iain said. His voice sounded rusty and strange.

"And won't that be sad," Hiso said. Still he did not smile. "But in time—you won't be there to know it, but in time, we'll learn how to use Cold Minds ships for ourselves. We'll adapt some larger vessels for our own use, when our people are protected from the bots and can travel in them— we can evacuate Triton. Travel to the Hidden Worlds—not as beggars and refugees, but as conquerors."

Hiso woke his board again, and through his fear Iain felt the quick, short taps of the maneuvering jets as they docked. The clamps took hold with sharp metallic raps on the hull, and Hiso disconnected the piloting leads, then pushed himself over to Iain.

"You won't do this," Iain said. "You won't have access to our ship."

"That's no longer a problem," he said. "Your woman will let me in."

"You don't know where she is." His heart was pounding.

"But she will come to me," Hiso said. "You know she will—to save her wounded lover." Carefully, he set the injector against the side of Iain's neck and triggered it.

Icy strangeness in his blood. Hiso unstrapped him, freed his hands and feet. Iain caught a glimpse of Hiso's control board, the proximity screens—saw the markers for the Cold Minds ships, hanging back, waiting—for what? "Linnea won't come," Iain said, brave words whose emptiness he was sure Hiso could hear. He did not even reply.

Hiso pulled on an isolation suit, sealed it. Behind its visor he seemed even more remote. He opened the hatch and pushed Iain through first. He had the neural fuser again, steady in his hand, but it hardly mattered. Iain was beginning to feel weak, strange, distant. The drug, whatever it was. Or grief for Linnea—for what, it now seemed, Linnea would have to endure without him.

Or plain fear of what was coming.

"I see you understand," Hiso said. "There's going to be a tragedy." Hiso's voice was remote though the filter mask. "You're going to fight valiantly to defend your brother pilot"—he almost spat the words—"from being retaken by the Cold Minds." He shoved Iain along the familiar passageway to the observation room, tapped out the code for admittance. "And you're going to be badly wounded." Before Iain could turn, resist, try to escape, he felt a hard blow against his lower back, an impact that sharpened into burning, driving agony. He grunted in pain, feeling cold air against the skin of his back, and then cried out as Hiso withdrew the knife.

Behind him, the hatch slammed shut.

Something dark, shining, floated up in front of his eyes. Small glittering blobs of blood. One splashed against the door, and he saw through the small port at its center Hiso's ironic wave of farewell. Then nothing.

Then the inner door of the lock opened.

Iain's arms and legs would not obey him. He floated, loose and limp as a corpse, out into the space the Cold Minds pilot inhabited. Brightness, painful to his eyes. . . . And a voice, not quite human, breathing high and fast in fear. There, in a corner, the Cold Minds pilot hunched in clear but voiceless terror.

Iain heard the thump as Hiso's ship boosted away from its docking cradle—and then after endless minutes the great grinding roar of one of the Cold Minds ships seizing on.

They were coming.

They were coming, and Iain had only a few fluttering rags of strength left, of thought left.

Now he heard the Cold Minds pilot crying wordlessly in its rough, cawing voice—saw it still pressed into its corner, hiding, hiding, shivering in terror as metallic *clicks* skittered along the outer hull of the station, toward the lock.

I'm afraid too, brother. . . . Iain could not shape the words to speak them.

He was so thirsty, spinning and spinning. So cold. More of the dark blobs filled his vision—how much blood could he lose before it killed him, or—

Fluttering darkness appeared at the edge of his vision, spread. *Too late,* a voice sang in his mind.

"No," he said thickly. "No. Linnea—"

Blackness.

SEVENTEEN

DEEPSIDER HABITAT *HESTIA*

Linnea floated, anchored by only her feet, in the store-room of Pilang's clinic, working to fold newly washed linens into neat packages and shelve them where they belonged. Mindless work to pass the time; she was still waiting for word of when she could hope to return to Triton, to Iain.

Someone behind her said, "Linnea." A voice she didn't know, Linnea thought, turning—but no, it was Hana. Hana with a tense expression.

"What is it?"

"Meeting," Hana said woodenly. "Pilang's office."

"Just let me finish—"

"Now, Lin." And hearing the quiet force in Hana's words, Linnea stuffed the unfolded linens under a net and followed her out.

Her heart pounding, Linnea pulled herself through the door into Pilang's inner office at the clinic. Hana followed, still with the same tense expression—and closed the hatch. Not just the privacy curtain, but the hatch itself.

And Pilang was not there. Instead, it was Esayeh waiting, his feet hooked on beside Pilang's commscreen—his face dark with an emotion Linnea could not read at all.

Linnea had to swallow hard before she could speak. "What's the—what's the news?"

Beside her, Hana looked down, avoiding Linnea's eyes, and Linnea's heart lurched. *So it's bad.*

Esayeh spoke, his voice deep, strained. "We've had word from Triton. Linnea, there was a Cold Minds attack on a Tritoner research station at Nereid. They took back a pilot Kimura Hiso had stolen from one of their ships. And—there was a fight."

Now Hana raised her eyes and looked at Linnea. "I'm sorry, Lin. Your Pilot Iain was badly hurt."

Linnea held still, made herself absorb this. Made herself think. She lifted her chin. "Tell me."

Hana swallowed hard. "Our medical contacts say there's no hope for him. Not the injury, but—" She faltered.

It was Esayeh who said it. "He was exposed to the Cold Minds. Infested. I'm sorry, Linnea."

The room seemed to go dark as the blood drained from Linnea's mind. She felt Hana's wiry arms around her, holding tight, and she tried to breathe, tried to breathe. "When did this happen?" She could feel that she was crying as she spoke, but it did not seem to matter.

"A few hours ago," Esayeh said. "They say—they say it was a massive load of bots, his blood is full of them. They left him behind, you see. A vector. You know what they do."

"Take me there," Linnea said, her voice tight with terror.

"Linnea, we can't—"

She clutched her head. "Take me to him, Esayeh. *Please.*"

"Lin, it's already too late," Esayeh said, his voice more than gentle. "They're keeping him drugged until—"

Linnea caught her breath on a sob.

Esayeh's steadiness did not change. "You understand. It's the kindest thing."

"Don't you tell me that," Linnea said fiercely. "Don't you tell me there's no hope. There must be something we can do. Hana—" She turned to the young woman. "Hana, deepsider medicine is better, I've seen that—don't you know how to save him?"

"We've never found a way to treat infestation," Hana said. "I'm sorry, Lin. I'm sorry it's such bad news." Her voice was shaking.

"You've never even tried? It must have happened many times—"

"No." Her expression was strange—compassion and fear. Fear of what?

Linnea could feel her hands trembling. "Pilang—she might be able to think of something. Where is Pilang?"

"We don't know," Hana said. "She jumped out this morning with Mick and one of the other pilots. An emergency, the dock said. She's out of reach."

Time. Time. Linnea's swirling thoughts touched on an idea, settled. *Ice.* "Could we put Iain in cold sleep? Would that slow the infestation process?"

"There's no point, Lin," Hana said. "Not when there's no cure."

"But it would give us time," Linnea said.

"For what?" Hana asked bluntly.

"For a better idea," Linnea said.

"It's cruel," Hana said. "Stretching out his death. Lin, he's in good hands, he won't suffer—"

Instantly, Linnea turned to Esayeh. "Take me to Triton. Please, Esayeh. I said I would help you. And I will. But right now I need your help."

He looked at her, considering, his old eyes mild. "If it might be of any use, I'd—"

"Thank you," she said quickly. Then turned back to Hana. "Hana, will you help me, too? Keep him alive until Pilang can come back, until we can find out if Pilang has any ideas?" The naked pleading in her voice shamed her, but this was no time to worry about pride. *He can't die. I won't let him die.*

There was a silence. Then Hana sighed. "Lin, I'll try. I doubt they'll release him to me—I don't know if they'd do that even for Pilang. But I might be able to get him cold using their equipment."

"I'll help if I can," Esayah said. "I know Perrin Tereu. If I can speak to her—"

"Let's go then," Linnea said. "Now, please now. . . ."

"Now" of course meant frantic work, because Hana had to gather the equipment needed to contain Iain's body safely, and to begin the cooling process. But finally the last bag was packed away in Esayeh's ship, Linnea and Hana were safely encased in their acceleration sacks, and Esayeh's ship dropped away from its docking cradle with a hissing *chuff* of attitude jets. Linnea tried to let the snug fabric enclosing her body calm her trembling. But tears still leaked from her eyes, tears the casing would not let her wipe away. She could see that Hana's face was turned away—the deepsider custom of granting whatever limited privacy was possible.

Iain.

She would see him again.

She would save him.

Somehow.

TRITON

During the attack and afterward, Tereu took refuge by staying out in public with two guards flanking her.

She moved from place to place, offering calming words before as many witnesses as possible. It allowed her freedom of movement, but what was more important, it made it hard for anyone to carry out whatever orders Hiso might have given for private action against her.

And, without arousing curiosity, it let her make her way in time to her real destination: the city's hospital.

Now she stood with both of her bodyguards in the nanobot-isolation ward at the city's main clinic. One of the expert physicians on staff hovered attentively at her side— DeVries was his name, she read it on the plastic badge clipped to his coat. But her attention was elsewhere: Through the thick doubled glass window she studied the sealed container where Iain sen Paolo lay.

Now that she saw him there, now that she knew it was all true, sadness left a hollow in her chest. *So much that man could have become, in time. So much hope he could have offered my people.*

She turned to DeVries. "Have you completed treatment?"

"We've done what we could do safely, Madame," the doctor said. "We don't risk surgery on the infested, especially in a case this advanced."

"Advanced? He was attacked only a few hours ago," she said.

"Yes." DeVries, a small man with neat white hands and a cap of silver hair, looked regretful. "Madame, his titer—the concentration of bots in his blood—is already very high. This was a deliberate and intense infestation. An injection of bots." He shrugged. "The Cold Minds have tried this in the past with injured personnel, hoping that we will bring the bots into the city before we are aware of the infestation. But of course we know their ways. We took Level Five precautions on the station and in retrieving the patient."

"Yet you did bring him into my city," Tereu said, allowing an edge into her voice.

"Yes, Madame." DeVries did not meet her eyes. "Those were First Pilot Kimura's direct orders. He said that it was essential to city security that this man be kept safe. Of course, that is part of his responsibilities, and I could only accede."

"But what is the point of protecting Pilot sen Paolo?" She took a breath. "He'll die very soon, will he not?"

"Yes." The doctor looked grave. "If the puncture wound in his back damaged a kidney, as I suspect, he will die within a day or two. In any case, with that titer of bots, he will meet all the criteria for euthanasia within days."

Tereu turned and looked at the container, feeling her face go pale. *So ends hope.*

The doctor shook his head. "I had looked forward to finding an opportunity to talk to him—to both of the travelers—about the state of medicine in the Hidden Worlds. Even laymen might have knowledge that could hint at possible avenues of research, help us advance." He sighed. "This is so regrettable."

"Regrettable, yes," Tereu said evenly. "Tell me. Is Pilot sen Paolo's presence in this hospital a secret?"

"No special precautions have been ordered," the doctor said.

So this is a trap. A trap for Linnea. Hiso's determination to have the Hidden Worlds ship under his control demanded Linnea's presence. He had not been able to bend Iain sen Paolo to his will. But Hiso—Hiso would be certain that no woman could resist his wishes; especially not a woman broken by grief.

Tereu's hands tightened on the handrail below the window. Linnea *would* come for Iain; Tereu knew that as surely as Hiso did. His imminent death would draw her to his side—and into Hiso's control. As Hiso intended.

Well, Tereu was not powerless. Hiso hadn't yet bothered to complete her arrest, no doubt thinking her too weak to act on her own behalf. Or anyone else's.

That will cost him. Tereu turned away and sent a coded summons to her chief of security.

The long arrival process on Triton barely registered with Linnea—only the time it cost to descend from orbit, the precious minutes wasted waiting for port security to clear them. But they were cleared, and promptly. Esayeh's look of perplexity at that barely brushed the surface of Linnea's perception. *Iain. Oh, God, hurry, hurry. . . .* Hana packed her medical bag with methodical care, flicking one glance at Linnea. "Should I give you something to keep you calm?"

Linnea realized she was crying again. She wiped her face and shook her head without speaking. No drugs. She needed all her focus, all her intelligence for this.

And all her courage. Because Iain might already be dead.

Still, she was unprepared for what awaited her and Hana when they left the dimness of the skyport tunnel and entered the city square outside. It was empty and silent, the shops shuttered. And Perrin Tereu stood there waiting for them, her expression severe, accompanied by at least a dozen of her green-clad guards.

Linnea approached Tereu slowly, dread choking her throat. When the moment for speech came, she had no words. Hana saw it; Hana spoke for her. "Madame," she said, and ducked her head in an imitation of a bow. "We understand that Pilot sen Paolo is being treated for his injuries in your city. My friend Lin and I would like to see him. Can you arrange it?"

This violated several different kinds of protocol, Linnea knew, but to her surprise and gratitude, Tereu did not appear to notice. "I can arrange it," she said to Hana with a gracious smile. Then she stepped forward and laid a hand on Linnea's arm, with what seemed to be genuine sympathy. "I expected you to come," she said. "I'll escort you there—to avoid any possibility of delay. Come." She indicated one of the silent utility carts that were sometimes used in the corridors.

As they climbed in behind the driver, Linnea saw Tereu glance at Hana, who was settling a bag of medical supplies in the long, deep cargo bin at the rear of the cart. "A doctor, isn't she, Linnea? Do you know—is there some deepsider treatment for infestation?"

"I hope there will be," Linnea said, and closed her eyes as the cart started off.

You have to let me see him," Linnea repeated raggedly. "I'm his next of kin." She stood, flanked by Hana and Tereu, in the outer area of the isolation ward. So far they had not been able to persuade this man to allow them any farther. A single hospital security man stood facing Tereu's men, and a distressed-looking nurse, a tall, capable-looking woman, stood at the doctor's side.

The walls of the waiting area had been painted a delicate, calming blue that made Linnea want to scream. "Please. I have a right to see him and decide on his treatment."

"There won't be any treatment, Miss," the doctor said. "Surgery would endanger my staff, and for nothing. I'm sorry to be blunt, but there is no hope for that man."

Tereu faced him, standing very straight. "Dr. DeVries," she said firmly, "you cannot ethically make any decisions about this man's care without the permission of Kiaho Linnea. After all, she is his wife."

Linnea's heart thumped in startlement, but she kept her gaze on the doctor, who only looked more angry. "I apologize, Madame," he said, "but our procedures require proof of relationship."

Tereu did not look at Linnea. "*I* am satisfied that it is

true," she said. "Do you care to challenge my word? Pilot sen Paolo told me himself that it was so."

Linnea glanced at Tereu, then looked back at the doctor, whose shoulders sagged in defeat. "Of course I must accept that, Madame." He seemed to gather himself, then turned to Linnea with an expression of remote but practiced compassion. "Miss, er—"

"Pilot Kiaho," Tereu said.

The doctor's eyes widened slightly. Then he seemed to shake himself, to reassume his role. "I must warn you that there is little hope. We have stabilized Pilot sen Paolo's condition with respect to the injury. He'd lost a great deal of blood, which we have replaced. But the bots are multiplying by the moment, and soon the change in viscosity will begin to impair his circulation, perhaps causing a flurry of small strokes. Then emboli will—"

"I know what happens," Linnea said. "I know how they die. I've seen it." She swallowed hard. "Please. Take us to him."

Down a long, cold corridor, and through a lock to slightly lower pressure. And cold—the isolation ward was a cold place. All the windows leading to patient rooms were dark—all but one. It hovered and swam in her vision, a rectangle of harsh white light. She moved toward it, as if drifting, as if drawn, knowing that Iain's sealed container was just on the other side of the thick glass.

But when she reached the window, she could see only the long silvery box. She could make out nothing through the thick protective plastic film that sealed him in. The inside was filmed with silvery condensation from his breath, his sweat; his body was only a shadow. She looked up at the doctor. "Let us in there, please."

"Impossible," the doctor said.

Hana's calm voice took over. "Is that container adequately sealed?

"Level Five," the doctor said. "But as a matter of

procedure, we still maintain complete isolation. Do you have any idea what it would mean if those nanobots got loose in the city?"

"Yes," Linnea said evenly. "I do."

"We have an idea for a possible treatment," Hana said. "It begins with cooling, physical and metabolic. It's our thought that this might slow the process enough to gain us the time we need to"—her voice faltered a little—"proceed with treatment."

"There is no treatment," the doctor snapped. "Miss, are you even a physician?"

"In training," Hana said steadily. "Please. We can hardly do your patient any more damage than he's already suffered."

Tereu spoke. "It is my personal request that you allow this, Doctor."

He gave her a challenging glare this time, then a curt nod. "The container is sealed, but protocol calls for full hazard suits." He waved a hand at the hovering nurse, who turned away, opened a storage closet, and pulled out two of the suits. Linnea's hands were shaking so hard that Hana had to help her with the gloves and seals.

After an odd, blurred interval, she realized she was standing in the room with Iain. With Iain's container. Hana had gone straight to the commscreen and called up Iain's chart. But Linnea moved forward slowly and looked down at him through the thick plastic film. "Ohhhh," she said, a slow, sad exhalation. Now she could see his face and body, blurred but unquestionably his. Iain's eyes were closed, and an oxygen tube trailed across his upper lip. He was naked; his left side, toward Linnea, had been smeared with some kind of yellow surgical antiseptic, and partly bound in bandages. It had been clumsily done—by people in isolation suits, of course. People who had not really wanted to touch him.

She set her gloved hand on the film above him. It

was stretched taut in its metal frame, and the surface was concave—the pressure inside where he lay would be lower, of course, so any leaks would be inward, not outward. She wished, with a yearning that was pain with every breath, that she could touch him. Against her will she spoke to him. "I'm sorry—" Her voice broke. "I'm so sorry, love. . . ."

And Iain's eyes flicked open.

She gasped, and he looked up toward her, blindly—no, he could see her shadow above him. But he was still afraid. He couldn't see her. He didn't know her.

Linnea tore off the visored hood of the suit, ignoring a shout of protest from DeVries. She saw Iain's eyes widen— then saw the black despair in his face, the depth of his grief and terror. She leaned close over him. His mouth worked, voiceless. With an effort she made herself see his words, understand them.

Kill me.

He was crying, and one of his hands came up, pressed against the plastic under hers. Just barely through the thick film, through her plastic glove, she felt the pressure of his palm against hers. She ripped off the glove, and then she could feel—she was almost sure she could feel the warmth of his fingers. Maybe for the last time.

He tried again to speak. *Kill me. Please. You promised.*

And she had; they had promised each other this, long ago. But only if there was no hope; and there was still a shred.

She shook her head. "You'll be all right," she said in an odd light voice.

The doctor touched her shoulder. "It would really be better if—"

And the little stunrod she had been concealing was in her hands. "I need you to release this man to our care."

The doctor flicked a glance at the small black rod, puzzled, then back to her eyes. "You cannot possibly expect me to allow this man out of isolation. You cannot possibly care for him, even with this—medtech to help. He'll be dead within hours."

"No," she said. "We'll save him." The odd strength spread from her voice to her body, spread and filled her. "You must allow this. It will please Perrin Tereu. If you want, I'll use this." She shifted the rod a little in her hand. "It knocks you out. It hurts, and it gives you a terrible headache, but then you'd have an excuse for why you couldn't stop us." She saw Tereu through the window, watching intently; when Linnea looked at her, she nodded once.

The doctor's hands went up in supplication. "No need for that. I am more than delighted to allow Madame Tereu to bear full responsibility for this. *Full* responsibility to First Pilot Kimura." He and Tereu exchanged hard glances.

Linnea looked down at Iain through the plastic, but his eyes had lost the sharpness of attention; he seemed to be staring into a horror he could not escape. "Hang on, love," she said bleakly. "The ride will be wild for a while. But soon you'll sleep. And soon—" She broke off. She had nothing else to promise him.

Hana had already stripped off her own hazard suit and gone to work, injecting a drug into the IV line snaking into the container. "He'll sleep now," she said. "He'll start to slow down. We'll start cooling him at the ship, as soon as I can get the central line in. Let's go." She set the oxygen tank and the IV reservoir on top of the container, checked that all the lines were clear, then nodded at Linnea.

"Please consider what you're risking," the doctor said in a hard voice. "You can't save this man. You can only endanger yourselves."

"We have considered it," Hana said flatly, and slid the inner door of the lock shut in his face.

Another cart ride, this time with Iain's container filling the cargo bin, and Tereu in front with the guard. Long, slow, dreamlike progress, eerily smooth in the noiseless cart; but at last they reached the tunnel to the skyport.

And Tereu touched Linnea's arm. "Your ship," she said. "I've ordered it unlocked from its launch cradle. Pod 34 in the patrol sector. I don't know how soon Hiso will notice and seal it up again." Her face was pale but resolute. "This may be your last chance to steal it back from Hiso."

Linnea could not think about that now. She nodded at Hana, and they lifted Iain's container out of the cart. "Let's get Iain to Esayeh's ship," she said. "Then we'll see."

"Esayeh!" Tereu's expression was perplexed. "Esayeh is your pilot?" They were already moving, but Tereu kept up, trailed now by only two of her guards. The skyport tunnels were still empty of other people, evidently by an order Tereu had called ahead. They traced the maze, following the glowing signs to the branch corridor that led to Esayeh's ship.

Dread filled Linnea as they came around the last long curve of the corridor. But the docking tube display still showed Esayeh's ship in place. The tube's hatch opened as they neared it, and Esayeh stepped out, his eyes on Tereu. "It's been a long time," he said, in his mild old voice.

"Esayeh," Tereu muttered. She had gone rigid. Linnea and Hana pushed past her with Iain's container and carried it into the docking tube.

In the ship, they strapped it down, then, her decision firm in her mind, Linnea turned to Hana. "Thank you," she said, her voice shaking. "Now, Hana, please—get Iain safely home to *Hestia*, to Pilang. She ought to be back by now. She'll know what to do."

Hana looked shaken. "You aren't coming?"

"I'll follow in my own ship."

"You'll follow," Hana said intently. "That's a promise, right, Lin?"

"A promise," Linnea said. "To you and to Iain." She

leaned forward and kissed Hana's cheek. "Good fortune." Then she turned and climbed back through the docking tube. Tereu and Esayeh stood close together, absorbed in a conversation Linnea could not linger to hear. She only nodded as she rushed past them.

By the time she reached the patrol sector of the port, she was running, leaning far forward to keep her traction and to keep close to the ground. No one had interfered with her progress or even questioned her—so Tereu had been able to prepare the way even here.

Almost to the corridor leading to her ship, almost safe home. In the dimly lit corridor she did not see the man who stepped out in front of her until it was too late.

They both went down, tumbling slowly end over end, but his hold on her did not loosen. They settled to the floor at last. "Let me go," she hissed, twisting around to face him.

"No," he said, smiling down at her.

It was Hiso.

Linnea convulsed beneath him in raw panic. Being held down, being restrained—the shivering echo of her terror, years before in Rafael's control, overwhelmed her.

"Stop that," Hiso said sharply.

And she saw what he had in his hand: a neural fuser. She froze, breathing high and thin. *Iain's. It must be.* She took a shaking breath. "If you use that on me," she said, "you lose that ship. Iain's d-dead—and there's no one else to g-give it to you."

He snorted contemptuously, then released her and rolled to his feet, still holding the fuser at the ready.

She stood up slowly and faced him.

"This is an interesting weapon," he said with a bright smile. "From what I've been told, I can do you a great deal of damage without killing you, if I shoot you in the foot. Or the hand."

She could not repress a shudder at the thought. But

more persuasive still was the cold-eyed, dark-skinned man who appeared from the corridor behind Hiso, obviously as ordered, and took Linnea's right elbow in a strong grip, one that promised pain if she struggled.

She kept her face expressionless. *It's over anyway.* Esayeh must have gotten Iain and Hana safely away by now. Nothing mattered now—nothing but watching for a chance, if there still was one, to get into her ship alone.

And so, of course, they held her in a small room in the port security office for hours, while she thought with increasing fear of what might be happening to Iain. Without her there, how hard would they try to save him? Without her there, would Hana's mercy move her to give him what she was sure he needed most—to give him death?

Tired into numbness at last, she fell asleep on the cold floor for an hour or two, woke to find herself being dragged to her feet by one of the guards. "First Pilot needs you," he said.

And there was Hiso. "Pilot Kiaho," he said genially. "That was expertly done, and I give you full credit for the effort. But you went to a great deal of trouble to rescue a dead man. I saw his test results."

"I saw them, too," she said, shivering with cold and exhaustion and sinking fear.

"Matters are moving very quickly," Hiso said. "Raids and incursions everywhere. My ship is inadequate. I require yours." He stretched out a hand in a gesture of invitation. "Shall we go and arrange it?"

Under the guard's persuasion, Linnea started forward, Hiso close at her right side, the fuser firmly gripped in his right hand. Out of reach.

But still—they were moving toward her ship. Her heart raced, but it did not outrace her thoughts. "It can't be done, you know," she said. "You can't have my ship. When its interface probes enter your brain, they'll interfere with the wires you've got implanted there. That will damage the probes—damage my ship." She bared her teeth. "And also your brain. Not that it concerns me."

"That is a risk I will have to take," Hiso said airily. "And a small one, I feel confident. This is something I have considered and researched for days now. That ship is the final weapon I need to proceed with my plan to save my people." He glanced over at her. "Since your departure, by the way, sen Paolo reconfigured the ship for his own use. So don't think of escaping in it; it won't respond to you. And in any case, it is locked down, held tight. If you tried to launch, you would tear it apart."

Linnea looked down in feigned despair, to hide a brightening flicker of hope. Hiso did not know, then, that once a ship had been equilibrated with a pilot, it would recognize her again on a moment's notice, and adapt itself to her; the laborious fitting of ship to pilot, system to nerve, was necessary only at the beginning. She made herself sigh. "I thought he might do that."

"He was never blind to opportunity," Hiso said. "As my wife might tell you if she ever wishes to be honest."

Linnea heard his words, pushed the thought away. They were passing through a long, cold passageway, gray plastic and gray metal, leading out to the satellite port where she knew her ship was docked. She was deeply conscious of the profound, killing cold just on the other side of the tunnel walls, and under the floor. Their breath made puffs of vapor. This world was no place for humans to live.

Again grief stabbed through her at the thought of Iain. She should never have brought them here; if she had not, Iain would be safe at home on Terranova, in the warm sun of Port Marie. Maybe they would be walking down by the waterfront, looking out over the smooth blue bay. . . .

They entered the bay where her ship was docked. With a parody of courtliness, Hiso waved her into the tube whose other end was sealed to her ship's side. Then fell in close behind her.

She knew the neural fuser was still in his hand—and she wished, not for the first time, that she knew how to fight by any means beyond blind instinct. When she got to the ship, within reach, she would be one step closer to escape. To the chance of it. Then she would act.

They reached the ship, and as the lights in the little bay flicked up, she felt the fuser's black mouth pressing against her left shoulder blade. "If you shoot me there, I'll die," she said coldly. "My heart will stop."

"I'll risk it," Hiso said. "Now. Admit me to my ship." She heard the caressing note in his voice, the ugly note she still sometimes heard in nightmares of Rafael. Triumph and power, a silk wrapping over the steel of cruelty. The fuser pressed more tightly to her back, and she turned her head and looked at him. "Take it away," she said, "or I won't do this. I've got nothing left to live for anyway. Not if Iain is dead."

She saw the little flicker of satisfaction and amusement in his eyes, felt the weapon's pressure lift away from her back as the pain in her heart eased, just a bit. *If Iain really were dead, if they'd caught Esayeh's ship, Hiso would have taunted me with that now.*

And at that instant the tall, dark guard behind Hiso struck him down.

She gaped at them both, stepped back against the cold metal of her ship's hatch, expecting the guard to attack her next. But instead he half bowed. "That was a gift from Madame Perrin Tereu," he said. "According to orders. She said to tell you, you have a good man." He bent and picked up Hiso.

"Thank you," she faltered.

"My city's duty is first to Madame Tereu," the man said. "The First Pilot has been known to forget that."

Linnea nodded numbly and slapped her palm against the identification pad by the hatch. It dilated, and her ship welcomed her—the familiar scent of metal and plastic, the faint familiar hum of a jump engine on standby. As the hatch closed behind her she was already opening her piloting shell.

She touched it carefully, letting the ship know that she had returned, that she would be piloting. Around her in the semidarkness, the boards woke to life. She had very little time, she knew that; that blow would certainly not have killed Hiso, and he would order her stopped as soon as he could.

At least, on so short a jump, there was no need to bother with the elaborate life-support connections. She climbed into the shell clothed, settled back, felt the familiar sensation of her ship shifting to accommodate her body in a comfortable acceleration couch. Then the cold tingle she knew so well, as the neural connection leads touched her temples; the faintly dizzying sensation as they made their way into her brain, to the programmed sites.

Then the shell vanished, the ship vanished, and its eyes were hers. She made the gesture that brought the launch engine to life, checked the ship's cradle—nothing was restraining it. One with the ship, she rose into the black sky. *Iain, I'm coming.*

High overhead she saw the cold green glow of Neptune at first quarter, burning bright, sharp-edged against blackness as her ship climbed from the frigid crystalline plain. Frozen ammonia, nitrogen snow. The moon's precise horizon receded quickly, curved; the universe beyond it was empty.

She thought about the warmth of human places, crowded and smelly and familiar no matter where they were—bubbles of life, tiny and fragile, in cold and dark that went on without end. But it was that way everywhere, every life a bit of warmth and brightness between two darks. . . .

She clung to stubborn hope—making herself believe that time reached on ahead to a future of free air and blue skies for all these people—a future that children alive today might see instead of being sacrificed to the Tritoners' bitter bargain.

Linnea guided her ship toward the dark. She feared that she was about to face the end of her hopes—the clear bitter point from which there could be no returning. When she would know the exact proportion of her happiness and Iain's that she had wasted with her fears and her pride.

When it was too late.

She wondered if there was any chance, any at all, that she would sleep again in Iain's warm arms. Anywhere this side of death.

EIGHTEEN

HESTIA

Hana floated beside Iain's cold-sleep container in near despair. Over the past hours, Linnea's fear for him had become her own. She would, in any case, do everything she could to save a patient. But no one had ever been cured of an infestation once it had become established. Pilang was called in on those cases sometimes, on Triton—but only because everyone knew that deepsiders had the gentlest, surest poisons.

Hana looked again at the commscreen linked to Iain's container, at the number burning red in one corner: the bot count in Iain's blood. It had not changed in the last hour. But he was very sick; irreversible damage to his organ systems, to the structures of his brain, might already have begun.

The cold sleep was helping, Hana thought, and the attending doctor at the clinic, an old man named Raymon, agreed. Cold sleep might even have stopped the invasive process entirely; it was too early for blood assays to tell them that. But Iain could not stay in stasis forever. There were troubling signs that his kidney had indeed been damaged by the stab wound. And eventually, even in cold sleep, that would have its deadly effect.

And where was Pilang? Still she had not returned; still no message came.

Linnea had not arrived from Triton. Not yet. She was tough and determined, Hana knew, and she would find a way if there was one. *But on Triton, if Kimura Hiso wants to keep you, he keeps you.* So Tereu had said. And Hana could believe it.

And that was another problem: Tereu. The Tritoners would assume she had left against her will—they would never imagine that she had boarded willingly, willingly put herself into the hands of old mad Esayeh. Old mad Esayeh whom she, the First Citizen of Triton, evidently knew of old. . . . So strange. Hana had settled Tereu into a sleep sack in the staff room here, after giving her a drug patch to handle her adaptive nausea. Further measures would have to wait until Tereu decided what she was doing here. And until someone else had time to deal with the matter.

Hana's fingers clenched tight on the handhold above Iain's cold-sleep container. *Where the hell is Pilang?*

She floated out to the front office, where Pilang kept her commscreen, and looked around, again, for any sign of a message. Even on paper. Slips of paper were stuck everywhere on the walls, reminders of appointments and therapeutic levels of drugs and cryptic notes from Pilang to herself, but nothing new. At that moment the air system sighed again, drawing loose material toward the catch screen in the center of one wall.

That slip of paper there—

Hana dove and snatched it, then hooked on next to the grating and smoothed the paper out over her palm.

Hana. Message from my cousin says attack due day

202 0032 UT fam vessel Soj Tr. 6 people, Mick and I off to get. Set up cold.

Hana's heard beat hard and slow. That date and time—she looked at the chrono again. Less than two hours from now. Pilang and Mick had left before Esayeh and Linnea and Hana had all jumped to Triton. . . .

So they should have been back hours ago.

Hana dove into the passage, pulled herself along to the cubby where she'd stowed Tereu. "Ey! Wake up!"

Tereu blinked at her sleepily in the dimness.

"Did you pass word of an attack to Cleopa? An attack now, tonight?"

Tereu rubbed her face. "I—there hasn't been any new alert. No news of one, I haven't had a chance to—"

Her voice faded as Hana dove back up the corridor, woke her commscreen with trembling hands, coded a call to Docking Control. "Is Pilang's ship back? She was out with Drojo, I think. Emergency run."

The young girl at the panel shook her head, bewildered. "No word, no word yet."

"Any other ships?"

The girl looked down at a commscreen Hana couldn't see. "One just docked, no ID, but standing orders from Esayeh say let that one in whenever it comes—"

"A new ship?" Hana said. "Put the pilot on with me."

"She's gone through alread—no, she's locking down now. A moment, Hana.".

Hana waited, breathing hard, then shaming tears of relief flooded her eyes when Linnea appeared in the screen, tense and disheveled but alive. "Lin," Hana said, her voice thin and strange, "Pilang's in a trap. A Tritoner trap. She went out to pick up some cold sleepers, she thought she knew when the Cold Minds were coming, she should be back by now—"

Hana saw Linnea's eyes widen. "I need a jump point."

"Control will set you one. Control, I need you to send Lin to family vessel *Sojourner Truth*. Orbit should be on file." She gripped the handholds beside the commscreen and tried to keep her voice steady. "Less than twenty-five minutes, Lin. If the attack time is right."

"Right. Out now." And Linnea was gone.

OUTER ASTEROIDS
DEEPSIDER FAMILY VESSEL *SOJOURNER TRUTH*

Linnea locked down her ship with trembling hands, her eyes on the orange-circled unknowns that had just appeared in the display over the board. They seemed to be hanging back. Had they seen her approach? Were they only waiting for her to leave her ship to make their move? Or were they ignoring her, waiting for some other signal?

It didn't matter. The jumpship Pilang had arrived on was still sealed to the lock next to Linnea's, on the shadowy side of the bulky old ship. Someone long ago had painted a pattern of stars on the outside of the battered cylindrical vessel, a shape like a bent-handled cup.

Now the ship was dark, silent. Fearing ambush, Linnea had not signaled—a good thing, she knew with a shudder. The Cold Minds were early.

But no matter. Pilang was somewhere in that ship. And Mick, too.

One thing at a time. *Find them. Then worry about getting them out.*

Linnea pulled on her thermal suit and sealed the front seam, feeling the heating unit buzz to life. Pilang would surely have jogged the ship's life support, but it would be very cold in there still. *Please, both of you, be safe.*

Dark inside the way station, and so cold the air hurt her lungs. Linnea turned on her headlamp and pulled her way along the metal passageways, batting aside floating detritus, watching the shifting shadows. "Pilang!" Her voice echoed back to her. "Pilang! Are you here?"

Then, tailing on the last of the echo—a reply? Linnea clung to the wall, called again, cocked her head and listened.

Faint, distant. "Lin! Here!"

That way. Linnea launched herself along the passage, still calling, following Pilang's voice through the twists of the passage, past the black doorways of empty compartments to the center of the ship. Long before she reached it she saw the faint light from the compartment where, she guessed, Pilang was working to wake the sleepers.

Linnea swung through the hatch, stopped herself, and looked around at the dim space. Pilang did not turn; she was bent over the stiff, dead-looking body of a toddler. "Lin," she said in brief acknowledgment. "We had trouble finding the sleep cases, Drojo's off warming the engines, we'll be off in a moment—"

They both heard the clank of docking grips letting go, felt the big ship lurch as a small one jumped away. Pilang looked grim. "Or, Drojo decided you could be the one to lift us home. . . ."

Linnea saw Mick hanging anxiously in the dimness outside the circle of light where Pilang was working. "Pilang," she said, "they're here. They're already here. It's too late, we've got to go—"

"I'm taking the children," Pilang said. "There are only three, they'll fit in one passenger shell. The Cold Minds won't be interested in the adults, but we have to take the children." Mick floated up beside her, holding a thermal blanket; she turned a pale, frightened face to Linnea.

"No time," Linnea said fiercely. "I said, they're here already. Bring the children cold, or leave them. If we don't leave now we'll—" Her head went up sharply, and she broke off, hearing the sudden hollow roar of jets from a ship touching the *Truth*. "They're docking." *We're dead.*

But Pilang was stuffing the child back into the cold-sleep bag. "We'll hide. Mick, take this one, I'll get the other two. Lin, close that hatch over there, the parents are still in there, maybe they won't find them. . . ."

How do we hide from thermal sensors? Three of us, and three bodies? Linnea looked around, her mind racing. Cargo. Storage. Everything the family that ran the ship wanted to keep safe . . .

Food. "Freezers! There's got to be a big freezer in a ship that goes this far out, runs this slow." Linnea looked around the big, shadowy space, a confusion of storage cubbies, hatches, dark control boards. A child's toy, a black-and-white stuffed bear, floated past her face, and she jumped. The light from her headlamp made the shadows leap wildly. She felt Mick grab her arm. "Lin—"

There. A big hatch with a temperature readout, soft green, saying *–19.9.*

At the same moment they all heard the thin screech of metal being cut. "They're coming in," Linnea said. "Hurry!"

"In there?" Mick squeaked, as Linnea pulled open the refrigeration unit.

But Linnea saw Pilang suddenly half smile. *She understands.* "Yes, Mick, in there. Quick now." At that moment, they all felt a faint breeze, heard a distant hiss of atmosphere. Linnea saw Pilang's eyes widen. *They're in.* No one said anything.

They pulled themselves into the unit, which was the size of a small room, and Linnea sealed the hatch behind them. The space was crammed with white bags and boxes with scribbled labels. While Pilang and Mick tucked the three small bagged bodies behind a storage rack, then anchored a couple of crates to hide them, Linnea drew her knife and began to slash at the bags. In a moment, Pilang was doing the same. Lumps of frozen food floated out. "Mick. Help us scatter these. Fill the air. Quick." She moved to the next bag.

Soon the chamber was a cloud of frozen bits of food—peas and beans and chunks of potato and squash. "Good enough," Linnea said. "Now get down in back, behind anything cold you can find. Then—quiet as can be. Don't move. Don't move *ever*. Mick, with me."

In moments she was huddled down behind a crate marked "FISH 500g×128," with Mick under her arm, saw that Pilang was also safely hidden, switched off her headlamp. Mick was crying with fear, but voicelessly. Linnea breathed in a tear, fought a sneeze, wiped the girl's face with her left hand. "Shh," she said. "Hush now. It will be all right." Carefully she wrapped her arms around the girl. Her knife was still in her right hand; she held it carefully—next to the side of Mick's neck. *They won't get her. Whatever happens, they won't get her.* "You'll be safe," she breathed. "Quiet now."

The girl's shuddering subsided, and they waited. Through the fabric of the station, Linnea could feel the faint vibration of—*something*—moving. It steadily increased. A rapping, clattering sound—something crawling along the metal walls.

Faint blue light filtered through the small round port in the door, illuminating the cloud of floating frozen food above their hiding place. The Cold Minds had found the cargo hold, where they knew the cold sleepers would be—the safest part of the ship. Linnea closed her eyes, thinking with aching pity of the three people still helpless out there. *Too late, we were too late—*

The clattering came closer. Linnea could hear hatches opening, closing, all along the walls of the chamber. Searching, they were searching—

The door of their refuge creaked open. Harsh light played around, illuminating the mess in the air from the

side, tiny lumps of food in half-phase, swirling slowly
in the bitter air.

Clatter. Closer now. Inside the cooler. Linnea's arms
tightened around Mick, her grip on the knife tightened. If
the light found them, one quick slashing cut, and Mick
would be safe, Mick would never be one of their pilots. . . .

The light stabbed, turned, the clattering sidled along
the metal walls—

Gone. The hatch's spring swung it closed. Linnea
squeezed Mick, putting all the warning into it that she
could. *Wait. Wait. Don't move yet, don't speak.*

Almost an hour passed, and there was only darkness
outside, only silence; but Linnea knew, as Pilang must, that
this was not time enough to be sure. They waited. After an
endless time, they felt a bump and shudder, then a brief
sketchy roar of jets against the skin of the ship. Mick
stirred in her sleep in Linnea's arms. Then utter silence fell
again.

Finally, Pilang spoke in a low voice. "That's it, I think."

"It must be," Linnea said, shifting her aching limbs.
Only the faint light from the internal temperature readout
oriented her in the utter darkness, but she was afraid—
truly afraid—to turn on her headlamp. *Too close.*

"Lin," Pilang said quietly, "please keep Mick with you
for a moment." The thin beam of a tiny wristlight lanced
out, and Pilang found the hatch, opened it, and passed
through. She was gone only a few moments and returned;
in the faint reflected light Linnea saw her face—grim
and pale. "They found the parents," she said. "Dead. I closed
the hatch on, on where they are, but—Mick, listen, there's a
little blood out there. Just—close your eyes, okay? Lin will
pull you."

Obediently, Mick closed her eyes and put both hands
over her face. Linnea switched on her headlamp and made
her way, hauling Mick through the floating food debris to
the front of the freezer. Behind her, she heard the thump of

heavy crates bumping together as Pilang cleared them aside to recover the unconscious bodies of the three small children. Linnea pressed the handle and shoved the hatch aside, then floated through, Mick in tow.

It was, as she'd expected, more than a little blood. It stirred idly on the cold drifts of air, a constellation of droplets that seemed to twinkle in the light of her headlamp as they danced and jiggled. She kept her head down, her mouth tight shut, and when they'd reached the hatch to the ship's main passageway, she closed it behind them with a wash of relief. "Mick, hang on here, okay? I have to go back in there and help Pilang gather her medkit."

"That's my job," the girl said.

"Not this time," Linnea said, and at the grim note in her voice, the girl offered no more arguments.

Together, the three of them got Pilang's equipment and the three children to Linnea's ship—Pilang had simply bagged all three in a big cargo net, with frozen goods packed in around them to keep them cool. Pilang and Linnea were splashed with drops of blood. "Put the children into the passenger shell," Linnea said. "Then find something to hang on to. I promise I'll barely boost."

The slow acceleration out to a safe jump distance was agonizing. Sealed in her shell, she could not even speak to Pilang; a few quick words had been all she'd been able to give her about Iain's condition, about Linnea's hopes that Pilang might be able to save him. And Pilang had gone very quiet after that. Ominously quiet.

But she didn't say it was impossible.

Linnea counted the seconds down raggedly, watching the chrono with her inner eye, watching the space all around—empty, still empty—*Now.*

Weary, sad, aching with dread of what she might soon have to face, Linnea jumped for *Hestia.*

NINETEEN

DEEPSIDER HABITAT *HESTIA*

When Linnea docked her ship at *Hestia* at last, medtech teams were waiting to take the three rescued children off for the care they needed. But Linnea, Mick, and Pilang needed about as much care, or so the doctor in charge of the teams told Pilang, frowning. "How long has it been since any of you slept?" he demanded. "You did good work, Pilang. Don't follow it up with bad. You've got more sense than that. Go and rest." He looked over at Linnea, who was holding Mick. "All three of you. Rest and a bath, eh?" And he was gone, launching himself briskly after the last of his stretcher teams.

Pilang had commed the clinic first thing and learned that Iain was stable; and now she insisted firmly that there was no use in going to look at his cold-sleep container—no, Linnea would not be able to see his face, he was sealed up, didn't she understand that? "Let go and rest, Lin," Pilang said gently. "You've done what you can for now. You've done miracles."

The sympathy broke through what was left of Linnea's strength, and she could not speak for a while. "I only need one more," she said at last, blinking back tears. She saw Pilang's mouth tighten. Then the older woman sighed, reached out, and caressed Linnea's cheek. "We'll see, eh? After we've both had some sleep. I don't want to see you for ten hours, hear me?"

Linnea looked away. "I'll try."

Pilang, obviously not convinced, trailed along with Linnea as far as Esayeh's quarters, which were still empty. She helped Linnea strip off the sweaty, stained coveralls she had been wearing for so long and climb into the sleep sack in her old cubby, then dimmed the lights to a faint amber glow and left her there.

Linnea had had no intention of sleeping, but a dark, towering wave of sleep overwhelmed her almost instantly. But she slept lightly and strangely, coursing along just under the surface, her mind swirling with sharp-edged and vivid dreams. Terror and joy in waves; and always, beneath it all, ran the deep dragging tide of dread.

A long time later she jerked awake. Stillness all around her; she glanced at the chrono. Four hours, only. But her buzzing, nervous alertness warned her that she would not sleep again, not soon.

Good. Time to go see Iain. To get as near to him as she could, and make them tell her *everything* about his condition.

She slid out of the bag into the chilly air, found her last clean clothes, and dressed hastily. Two minutes later she was soaring along the passageway, past glowing curtained doorways, spills of herbs and food plants under flickering fluorescent lights, here the sound of someone playing a reedy wind instrument, there an argument in some other language. The brown smell of baking onions. She took a shortcut through the park, in night cycle at the moment, the blue "moonlight" making deep shadows under the trees. Far off she heard a group of women laughing, and nearer a couple making love.

The intensive-care clinic never closed, so she swung her way into the little waiting room, expecting to find a few people, friends or family members of patients, and the hovering medtech who processed records and doubled as a receptionist of sorts. But the room was empty.

Linnea did not bother with the tautly curtained door; she pulled herself through the window usually manned by the medtech, and on down the passageway beyond, following the bright painted signs pointing to COLD ROOM.

She arrived to find light spilling from the door, and an intent murmur of voices. She pulled herself to a stop before swinging into sight, then peered around the corner—and froze in shock.

Pilang was there. And Hana. And two other techs. And—Iain's container lay open, clamped to a rack around which they were all huddled. It was open. An infested patient, open to the air.

Iain. She saw him, lying stiffly strapped in place, clearly still in cold sleep. But they had pulled him out of his capsule, turned him over—Pilang was leaning over the purple, ragged stab wound in his back just under the rib cage. She was painting something into the wound. Something black, from a jar Hana held for her. Through her shock and terror, Linnea made out a few words—"Let them work their way well in." Pilang's voice, tired but satisfied. "We'll get a good image in a couple of hours."

Linnea found that she had pulled her way through the door, that she was clinging to a handhold just inside. And she saw Hana look up and gasp, saw Pilang jerk around to face her.

"He's infested," Linnea said in a thin voice. "You can't—it's not safe—" Then, with a wild glance at the jar in Hana's hand, she cried, "What *are* you? What are you people?"

"Get her out now," Pilang said flatly. "She's not safe in here."

"What are you doing to Iain?" Linnea started forward, but two of the medtechs she did not know caught her, pushed her back into the passageway. One of them held one of the ubiquitous medication patches, and he reached out with it for Linnea's neck. She twisted away, twisted away—but firm hands caught her and held her. The patch touched her neck, and the world spun away into darkness.

She drifted awake, soon after or long after, to find herself tied into a patient's cot. She began to struggle to reach the ties and free herself, knowing it was hopeless, and a moment later Pilang appeared in the doorway. Linnea shrank back against the firm support of the cot. "Don't come near me," she said in a thin voice.

"Lin—"

"You're infested," she said. "You're—them. Part of the Cold Minds."

Pilang did not move closer, but her calm expression did not change. "Lin, I am as human as you are. And the Cold Minds have never touched me. They never will."

"But you were right there with Iain, all of you—" She broke off. "Is he cured?"

She saw her answer in the sadness in Pilang's eyes, before she spoke. "No. He's not cured. We were setting up for a test to determine whether his kidney is injured. Maybe to correct it."

"They said surgery wasn't safe," Linnea said. "On Triton."

"It *wasn't* safe—on Triton," Pilang said. "Lin, there are some things you don't understand. And you have to understand them, because you need a treatment, now, right away, and I want you to give free consent."

"Wait," Linnea said. "Treatment?"

Pilang sighed. "Lin, we—the deepsiders—we can't be infested by the Cold Minds. That's why they want us for their pilots. Those ships—their bots are everywhere inside. Someone who wasn't immune would last only a few weeks as a pilot in one. They get infested, they lose their piloting ability, they die."

"How?" Linnea took a shaking breath. "How have you done this?"

"We infest ourselves," Pilang said evenly. "With bots we control, that are dormant unless they detect Cold Minds nanobots. Then they bloom out in our bloodstreams and destroy them."

Linnea was silent for a while, absorbing this. "Bots . . . that you control," she said slowly. "How?"

"Nanobots were deepsider technology from the start," Pilang said. "We'd been using them for a hundred years for our own applications, for manufacturing, for medicine. Where we lived, if they got away from us, we had vacuum, radiation, everything we needed to control them right there; energy and resources aren't unlimited out here, so they can't run wild. We controlled them. We still do. But— eventually someone got greedy. Brought the technology to Earth, without our knowledge—stole it for one of their own industrial processes. And"—she looked sad—"in time, they broke loose."

Linnea stared at her. "You're telling me that your people—the deepsiders—*you* made the Cold Minds."

She saw Pilang wince at that. After a moment, the older woman shook her head. "My people," she said steadily, "*fight* the Cold Minds. We die fighting them." But the grief was clear in her eyes. "But, Lin. This is what I need to tell you. You walked in when you shouldn't have, last night. You may have been exposed. I need—" She sighed and rubbed her eyes. "I need to inoculate you."

Linnea felt herself go rigid with fear. "You mean—with bots."

"With our own nano. Harmless nano." Pilang looked her in the eye. "Look, you've already had them in you for short times—that's how our drug patches work so fast, the nanobots carry the drug straight to the target. Then they destroy themselves."

"But these would stay in me forever," Linnea said.

"It is safe," Pilang said firmly. "They're dormant in your bones unless needed. They can't even be detected in your blood except during an infestation."

Linnea's breath caught, and she looked toward the door. "Could this—Pilang, could your nano save Iain?"

"No, Lin. I'm sorry." Pilang looked grim. "It would be as little use as giving someone an immunization for a disease when they're in the last stages of dying from it."

"If you gave him a lot of your nano at once—"

"The metals and toxins from all the dead bots would only kill him faster."

Linnea looked at Pilang, her mind racing. "All right. Give me the bots. Then—let's think of what you haven't thought of."

Linnea sat fighting nausea while a medtech carefully painted a patch of black on the inside of her left elbow. As she watched, the black faded, leaving a residual yellow like a bruise. *They're burrowing in.* She felt a sudden chill, felt her face break out in a sweat. The tech got a bag over her mouth in time. As she retched she thought, *Now it's happened to me, too, Iain.*

Clinic hours were over, and Pilang had finished her rounds. When Linnea's stomach had settled, she made her way a little unsteadily to Pilang's office. As she came in, she saw that Esayeh and Hana were there as well. Esayeh looked up at her and shook his head slowly. "Dear God, Lin." Then he filled a little bulb full of the fiery clear whiskey of the deepsiders, squeezing it from a half-full pouch hooked to the bulkhead beside him, and handed it to Linnea. "You could use this."

She took a sip, held it in her mouth—sweet and mild,

deceptive—then swallowed. Fire all the way down. "Oh," she said with her eyes closed. "Oh, that's—good."

"No more for a bit," Pilang said dryly. She coughed. "It's time to consider our problem. The infested patient."

"Iain," Linnea said stubbornly. "He's still Iain. Use his name."

Pilang flung up her hands. "All right. Look, Lin. Here's the outline. Iain's blood is full of bots. And we can't filter them out without filtering out his blood cells, too."

Linnea looked at her. "Can you separate the cells from the bots somehow?"

"No," Pilang said. "We don't have the tech to do it fast enough when he's warm, to keep up with the bots' growth rate, the damage they do."

"But in the cold—"

Pilang shook her head. "No, Lin. I'm sorry. We can't do sorts in the cold—the blood is too viscous. And if we warm him even a little, the bots take over and—there won't be anything left to do but kill him."

"Can you—" Linnea shook her head, thinking hard. "Just drain out all his blood and replace it?"

"A complete replacement would kill him in his weakened state," Pilang said. "Even if it didn't, the blood would just be reinfested from the surrounding tissues."

"But at a lower titer," Hana said with a frown. "After a few cycles, it might be low enough for our own nano lines to handle what was left."

"But by then, Iain would be dead," Esayeh said. "Right, Pilang?"

"He'd be dead—" But Pilang's eyes were distant. "Unless—"

The little room was silent, all eyes on Pilang.

"We could keep him cold," she said slowly. "Run a line with his blood out of the cold, warm it, do a sort—low volume, we can handle that—cool it, and run it back in."

Hana scratched her head. "Constant slow filtration."

Pilang nodded. "His whole blood volume, running through enough times to bring his level down to where our bots can handle the rest."

"That would take days," Hana said.

"We've got days," Linnea said, her heart thumping. "Don't we?"

Pilang reached out and squeezed Linnea's hand. "Okay, then. Esayeh, just you get me a snap of that whiskey, and Hana, get on the comm and see if you can track down Gunter, he's the one who knows the sorter inside and out." She took the bulb Esayeh silently handed her, drained it, coughed once, and said in a raw voice, "We'll have to move Iain to Gunter's lab, I don't think he can get all the pieces here at once—"

The next days passed slowly for Linnea. She spent as much time as the irascible Gunter would permit hovering in his lab, watching the slow trickle of blood out of Iain's container, into Gunter's jealously tended and obviously patched-together sorter, then back into the container and into Iain. Day by day Iain's bot count slowly sank; day by day his condition remained steady. Sometimes she let herself imagine that he was almost saved; sometimes she woke at night in terror, sure that he had died, that the long, unnatural process had led to organ failure, cardiac arrest, any one of half a dozen possible disasters Pilang had laid out for her at the start.

Tereu was a comfort to Linnea in the times when Gunter forbade her the lab. Linnea occupied herself with showing the Tritoner woman the sights of *Hestia*. She kept, reluctantly, the promise Esayeh and Pilang together had extracted from her the first day: She did not tell Tereu the truth of what was being done to Iain, or of what had been done for her. "It's an edged gift," Pilang told Linnea one night in Esayeh's quarters, where the three of them were sharing a sack of tea. "If Tritoner children were immune to the bots, they'd be prey for the Cold Minds, too."

"Shouldn't the Tritoners have a choice?" Linnea demanded. "Why should you decide this for them?"

Esayeh sighed. "Look, Lin. I know those people, I was one of them. They like order, uniformity, efficiency. Zones and plans and grand civic games and ceremonies. They like what they know." He sipped at his tea. "They don't want to be deepsiders. They don't want to hand themselves over to the unknown, let something they can't control into their bodies. They don't, they can't trust us. And with reason."

"With reason," Linnea echoed. "After all, you're going to leave them behind. When you all vanish into your ark."

"*Tchah*, Lin, we don't talk about that here," Pilang said.

Linnea frowned. "I still think it's a decision you have no right to make for them."

"We have paid," Pilang said with slow anger, "more than enough for our freedom. They have earned, more than earned, their fate."

"Their pilots made a bad bargain, centuries ago," Linnea said. "And so none of their people deserve any mercy."

"Lin, we can't save everyone," Esayeh said, his voice tired.

"Not if you don't try," Linnea said.

"You saw that ship," Pilang said. "Talk to me about mercy after you talk to those children about their parents' death."

"Hard choices," Esayeh said.

"Ah." Linnea felt a flare of anger. " 'Hard choices,' yes. I've heard that a lot over the years. And do you know what I've noticed? Often 'hard choices' is code for something else. Code for 'an easy choice I'm ashamed of making.' " She caught her breath, then looked up again. "I'm sorry."

"We're all under strain, until Iain is better," Pilang said evenly.

"No," Esayeh said—and something in the tone of his voice made Pilang turn to him, her eyes wide. "No, Pilang. Lin is right."

Pilang gripped his arm. "Esayeh—"

"She's right." He rolled his bulb of tea between his fingers, his old face lined with sadness. "I was—those were words I was taught years ago. When I came to the first and last position of power I have ever held, and learned about the bargain with the Cold Minds. When I first had to try to—find a way to live with it." He looked very old. " 'Hard choices.' "

"Let's see if Iain lives," Pilang said. "Then we'll look at those hard choices, eh, old man?" She looked so weary, so deeply sad, that Linnea wanted to cry.

She closed her eyes, tipped her head back, let herself float.

Please, Iain.

Please live.

TWENTY

TRITON

Kimura Hiso reached out, almost without willing it, and picked up, again, the printed image of the guard who had betrayed him, who had struck him down and permitted the woman pilot to escape. The man deserved what had been done to him; yet sometimes, sometimes Hiso could not help but think about how far things had fallen, how far, far down from the nobility he remembered from his boyhood. . . .

He held the flat image in nerveless fingers, trying to wake his courage with self-contempt. The guard had allowed the woman pilot to steal the ship that should have been Hiso's. The ship that should have been his, now, for the fight that was so clearly coming.

And so, and so it had been . . . necessary, to do what he had ordered done.

Hiso made himself look, one last time. The harshly lit image showed a gray-white pavement of water ice, blackness beyond, just outside one of the main city locks, marred by an odd arrangement of chunks frosted white. They made up the barely recognizable outline of a human corpse. The man had been pushed out, suitless, to freeze instantly, to fall and shatter. He could have felt nothing after the first instant of absolute cold. The effect was for others. . . .

Hiso clenched his jaw and fed the image into the cycler next to his worktable. It had been another hard and necessary act. Another act of courage.

He pressed his clenched fists against the smooth wood of the tabletop. *Courage.* It was too bad there had been time for nothing worse. If Hiso ever got his hands on Tereu, he would think of something.

The incursions were getting worse—sightings on all the long scanners, those that still functioned. The scanners were going off-line, one by one—were being destroyed, that was clear, just as it was clear that the Cold Minds were closing in on the Neptune system. Scouting it, for what action Hiso did not dare to speculate. The hideous vulnerability of his city, always real, did not bear thinking about. If they came, if they wished to kill, his city would die.

And it might be possible, for a weakling like Tereu, to argue that it was his fault. Hiso had thought the Cold Minds would not recognize the Hidden Worlds ship; instead, it was increasingly clear that they had known it for what it was, recognized its source—and assumed, when they saw one ship, that a stronger force would follow. They clearly intended to crush their potential enemies in the Earth system in advance of that illusory attack.

Which meant everything was coming to an end. Unless he, Kimura Hiso, could follow the example of his great predecessor six hundred years ago—and make a new bargain with the Cold Minds—

He leaned his head on his fists. Not possible. His position was too weak. Tereu had seen to that. He had nothing, nothing to give them. Nothing of enough value that they would spare his world—for a little longer, until he could find some escape, some solution. There had to be one.

He took a shuddering breath. He was a man of Triton, a pilot—he would die well, if it came to that. But until then he would think, plan, bargain as he had been taught to do by the example of his predecessors.

He had the end of a thread in his hand. He would follow it, and hope. He touched his comm. "Have Perrin Gareth brought to the interrogation room."

A few minutes later, he stood in the shadows of the cold little room, studying his former aide, Tereu's young cousin. Gareth was clamped into a metal chair, held firmly by wrists and ankles. His red prison coverall was too large, sized for a man who had finished growing; the loose cuffs at wrists and ankles hid the bruises Hiso knew were there, from the beating that he had ordered. The beating, for passing secure pilot information to his cousin Perrin Tereu, was only the beginning of Gareth's punishment. He would have shared the fate of the guard this morning but for his family connections. Tereu was still popular within the city; her name was still something to reckon with. And so Perrin Gareth lived.

Hiso studied the boy, letting the silence stretch. Gareth's thin face was unmarked by bruises or cuts—Hiso had ordered that no blows be given above the neck, unwilling to risk damaging the delicate piloting implants in the boy's brain. Gareth might still be of some use as a pilot, if only as a sacrifice in a hopeless action. And it seemed all too likely that there would be a hopeless action soon.

Unless this worked.

"Tell me what you know," Hiso said mildly, "about your cousin Tereu."

"I know less than you do," Gareth said, his voice low and steady. "I've never lived in her household."

"Tell me what she did with the information you gave her," Hiso said.

"I don't know," Gareth said. His hands clutched the arms of the chair.

"Who did she give it to?"

"I don't know." The boy's expression did not change. He was afraid, yes, but he was fighting it. Hiso had to respect that. But he also had to break it, if he could.

"I know your cousin," Hiso said. "She has certain people who are loyal to her, certain members of her staff. She doesn't change. I believe that you have some idea of how she passed the information to the deepsiders. You're clever, you observe things—or I would never have taken you on, family connection or no."

"For all I know, she sent it by radio," Gareth said.

"A transmission would have been intercepted," Hiso said. "A coded transmission would have been logged—I would have been told of it. No, it must have been passed personally, face-to-face or as a note. Surely someone strikes you as likely. Someone who might have links of their own to the deepsiders."

"I don't know anything about it," the boy said again. But Hiso caught the tiny hesitation before the answer. The boy was being brave, clinging to silence.

Which meant he had something to tell.

Hiso touched the comm. "Dr. DeVries," he said briefly.

When the physician was brought in, his white cap of hair disarranged slightly from his confinement, Hiso smiled at him. "As we arranged," he said, "I require you to make this boy willing to answer questions."

The physician glanced at Gareth, who was regarding him palely. Then DeVries looked away, not at Hiso, not at the boy, and Hiso knew he had already decided to cooperate. Only a few formal objections remained. "You cannot ask me for this," DeVries said.

"You will be freed, safe and well, when everything is finished," Hiso said. "I want only to be assured of your cooperation. That you regret your actions in regard to my prisoner and Perrin Tereu. That in future you will be a reliable citizen of Triton."

"I can't drug a man against his will. My oath—"

"You have a difficult choice to make," Hiso said softly. "And I can allow you no time to consider it." *This will not, I think, be the last prisoner you help me with.* One name would lead to another. And what took threats to accomplish this time, a reward would accomplish the next. The downward path was an easy one, for the weak.

DeVries gave Hiso another frightened glance. Then turned and opened his medkit.

Hiso smiled. A thread, still; but he had hold of it now. And who knew where it might lead?

DEEPSIDER HABITAT *HESTIA*

Early morning. Linnea scrubbed her face, hard, with a rough rag that she had soaked in cold water and then squeezed nearly dry inside the drain sack. Another night she hadn't slept well; but no wonder. There could not be much longer to wait: soon, maybe even today, Pilang would have to pronounce Iain cleared of bots, would have to wake him. The bleak fear of the past few days would end.

Linnea ran the rag over her arms and chest and shivered in the cold, in Esayeh's little kitchen cubby, then stuffed the rag into a clamp near the bag that covered the tap. Hastily, she grabbed her warmest coverall and slid into it. Even sealed, it still felt cold against her skin at first; she went on shivering.

Esayeh spoke behind her. "You could go to the baths, you know. It's warmer there."

She took hold of the wall and turned to look at him. "When did you come in?"

"An hour ago. Been out on an emergency run." Then at

her startled look, he snorted, and said, "I got *here* just a minute ago."

"Hah." Linnea floated to her sleep cubby, found her comb in her bag, and started working it through her hair. "How is it out there?"

"More and more sightings," Esayeh said. "More ghosts, more shadows. Lin, I don't like it. They're stirring like a kicked beehive."

"Or trying to panic us." Linnea tucked the comb away and deftly tied a cloth over her hair. "There's nothing we can do. Isn't that what you say?" The old familiar fear had waked again: nightmares of Freija, nightmares of Nexus, nightmares of her nightmares through all those months and years. *Nothing to be done about it.* "There's no way to fight," she muttered.

"I know that, Lin," Esayeh said. "We live in a metal bubble. My pilots are evacuating as many of our people as they can, four or five runs a day each. They can't do more, what with having to break every jump into two or three to be sure they aren't traced somehow. And you know our ships—all the runs we can do, that totals up to maybe a hundred people a day. It will take fifteen days, twenty days, to get the last of us off *Hestia*. And meanwhile—they'll be watching. They can't track our ships to—where they're going. But they'll see something is up."

"The Cold Minds?"

"The Tritoners." Esayeh ran his fingers through his short hair. "Soon as this place goes silent, they'll start making guesses."

"The Tritoners have problems of their own," Linnea said flatly. "*They* have nowhere else to go."

"You haven't—said anything to Tereu," Esayeh said. It was more than half a question.

"I've kept my word," Linnea said shortly. She had said nothing to Tereu about *Persephone*, about the possibility of escape or refuge. Or about the immunity to infestation the deepsiders had been concealing for so long. The unspoken truths stuck in her throat sometimes, made her feel sick.

There were innocents on Triton, too. Waiting helplessly, without hope, for what the Cold Minds might choose to do with them. She had seen it before, on Freija; she was afraid she was about to see it again.

"I'm sending Tereu back to Triton," Esayeh said abruptly.

"No," Linnea said in a low voice. "Please, Esayeh—Hiso will arrest her."

"She wants to go, Lin," Esayeh said. "It's her home. They're her people. She wants to be with them at the end."

Linnea looked down. She knew she had to respect Tereu's choice. Still—"I wish we could stop her."

"We have no right to stop her," Esayeh said. "There is a division between Tereu and me. Between the Tritoners and our people. I know you have these notions, Lin, but it can't be healed. Let her go the way of her people. And you and I will go the way of ours."

"Let me be the one to take her back," Linnea said.

"No," Esayeh said flatly. "I don't want them to know your ship is here. And"—he looked away—"word came today from Triton. Kimura Hiso is arresting deepsiders. I don't want anyone getting into his reach who knows about *Persephone*."

"I wouldn't tell him," Linnea said.

Esayeh snorted. "He'd get it out of you. For his cause. For his people. . . . No. I told Tereu I would send her over in a freighter, as soon as I can spare one. And that will be the end of it."

"She was your wife once," Linnea said unsteadily.

"It doesn't matter, Lin," Esayeh said, his old eyes distant. "It can't."

Linnea closed her eyes. She knew, too well, that Esayeh was the product of a society that could not afford mercy.

She had learned, years ago and far away, how life in constant terror could make humans less than human.

And yet she had known some who transcended that. She had thought Esayeh might be another. "I'm sorry," she said quietly.

"It's not your worry, Lin," Esayeh said. "You've got troubles of your own."

Linnea looked up at him sharply.

He nodded. "Iain's finally clean, Lin. Pilang said to say, it's today. They're waking him."

Linnea's breath caught. "When?"

"Soon as you can get there."

But she was already out the door.

L innea shot through the door into the cold room and swung to a halt on the opposite wall. "I'm here," she said tensely to Pilang, who was waiting with Hana in the corner near the cold-sleep container that held Iain. Linnea pushed off and floated toward them. "How soon can we get started?"

"Now listen," Pilang said, straightening and catching Linnea by the arm, halting her so that her own momentum turned her to face the older woman. "You have to understand, Lin. We do not know how he'll be when he wakes."

"He's clean of the bots," Linnea said fiercely. "Esayeh told me you said so." She twisted away. "Please!"

"But, Lin—" Pilang roughly seized her, turned her so they were face-to-face. "Lin, listen to me! No one has ever been put in the cold with an infestation. No one. We know it slowed the bots. We know they're gone now—our nano cleaned out the remnants, and the trace metal levels are down to undetectable."

"That's good news," Linnea said raggedly. "Right?"

"Yes," Pilang said, patience clear in her voice. "But you should be ready for there to be—damage."

Linnea looked past Pilang to the hatch of Iain's cold-sleep compartment. "Then let's find out. Now. Please. I can't stand it." He throat closed, and she could not say more.

"You should go wait with Mick," Pilang said, caressing Linnea's cheek. "Really, Lin. This takes time. And he'll look—alarming, at first."

"I want to know everything you know," Linnea said, her voice low but steady. "Right when you know it."

Pilang looked hard into Linnea's eyes. Then nodded and touched a control on the bulkhead. The lights in the room burned more brightly, and Pilang turned to the hatch of Iain's compartment, the only one lit with a status display. "Lin, unwrap the thermal blanket—the packet next to my kit. We'll start slowly—just collecting his own heat." As Linnea shook out the silvery padded blanket, Pilang stuck a sheaf of drug patches to the bulkhead, where they would be in easy reach. Then looked over at Hana. "Ready?"

The younger woman nodded, looking past Pilang at Linnea. Her expression was serious, worried. Pilang opened the clamps along the rim of the hatch, swung it open. Cold mist puffed out. Pilang reached into the dark space with both hands, worked blindly but deftly, then tugged.

Iain slid out of the container all at once, in a folded lump. His sallow, naked body looked too small to be his—folded, compressed, pressed tight. As Linnea had expected, his eyes were taped shut. Linnea's fingers itched to remove the tape, to see his beloved face clearly again. But it was not time.

Carefully, Pilang and Hana arranged him along the stretcher. Pilang straightened his arms and legs with gentle hands, then felt the pulse in his neck, wrists, ankles, her eyes abstracted. "Good," she muttered, and a little of the singing tension in Linnea melted.

As if sensing that, Pilang looked at her sharply. "His heart hasn't accelerated yet. That's the dangerous part,

when that happens. If you ever happen to pray, pray now."
She reached out and took the blanket Linnea was still
holding in nerveless hands, and arranged it over Iain's body.
"We'll move him down to the monitoring ward. We have
cardiac equipment there. Then—we wait."

"I'll stay with him," Linnea said firmly.

He did not know where he was. Fierce heat beat in his
hands and feet. His heart felt swollen, squashed inside his chest, beating sullenly stroke after stroke.

Blackness filled his mind. There was something terrible, something he almost remembered—

The voices—

The whispering in his mind, he remembered it
beginning—remembered the fear—

He listened. The sigh of an air system, indistinct voices
in another compartment somewhere. Human voices. They
were real, outside him. The whispering . . . was gone.

But not the fear. He could not open his eyes.

He tried to protest—his throat made a rusty sound. His
hands moved, but clumsily, as if cased in thick gloves; he
tried to brush whatever it was away from his eyes, but
he could not direct his movements at all.

A woman's voice spoke, familiar, half-familiar. "*Ssst.*
Hold still, Iain." Tugging, pulling—then someone held his
head still, and a warm ointment slopped onto his closed
eyelids. Soft fingers rubbed it in, then rubbed away the ex-
cess. "Open slowly. We've got the lights down low. That
and the gel will make it hard to see."

He opened his eyes. Yellow light, lancing, and blurred
ovals of faces. Tears flooded his eyes, and he blinked. He
tried to speak again, made only a cawing sound, ragged as
a crow.

Strong, warm hands took his shoulders.

Hands he knew.

A beloved voice said, "Iain." Then again, brokenly—
"Iain, you're safe."

He closed his eyes then, and pulled himself closer to
her. Her warm arms enfolded him, and he breathed in,
breathed in her scent. Clean soap, and the spice of her skin,
the scent of her dearness that never changed.

Linnea.

Linnea, love.

"Stay," he muttered.

Her arms tightened around him. "Always," she said.
And no more words were needed. He was home. Safe, enfolded, he let himself drift again into sleep.

Linnea held Iain close and looked up at Pilang. "He's all
right," she whispered. She was afraid to make it a question.

Pilang, floating within reach, looked down at them both.
Unshed tears shone in her eyes. "Just hold him quietly for a
while," she said softly. "He'll sleep on and off all day. Call
one of us in when he wakes—we'll check his vitals, make
sure he's oriented. . . . It looks good, Lin. So far." She was
working with Hana's help to spread a soft, stretchy blanket
over them both, anchored on three sides. It gave a comforting feeling of pressure, holding them both against the padded bulkhead. "You sleep, too, if you can. I—think it's
going to be all right. We'll examine him more carefully in
a few hours, when he wakes again. But I don't see any danger signs, not yet."

And that would have to do. Linnea knew she would not
sleep, even after Hana, smiling gently, dimmed the lights
and went out, closing the dark curtain behind her.

He'd almost died. Almost. And there might still be some
lingering damage, some injury he would bear forever. Her
mind shied away from the possibilities Pilang had listed for
her days ago.

It didn't matter. Whatever they had to face, in whatever time they had left—Her arms tightened around him.

Whatever is left, we'll share it.

She would not waste another day, another night that they might have spent together. No matter what came now, no matter if the Cold Minds swatted this habitat into nothing. If they fought, they would fight together. If they died . . .

They would die together.

Calm now, sure of the only thing that mattered, Linnea slept.

E sayeh floated with his head and shoulders inside the routing cabinet for the commscreens in Docking Control. A good thing he'd never carried out his plan to upgrade them to an integrated system—they were still crudely wired together much as they had been long ago, when the deepsiders' ancestors labored to repurpose the big helium-3 tank into a habitat.

"Pilot," a young voice said doubtfully, "are you sure this will work?"

"No," Esayeh said. He backed out with care and closed the cover, snapping it into place.

A young woman with a sunburst tattooed on one cheek floated beside him, looking at him with a sad expression. "I still think we can man all three control rooms," she said. "And that we should. I want to stay."

"No," Esayeh said again. "Niamne, this place isn't safe."

"You said yourself. The Cold Minds want this habitat to last—they need us, they need a stock of humans, and this place will hold thousands. They won't attack it."

"But they'll capture it," Esayeh said. "They've got weapons. Anyone left here will be their captive, to use for their purposes. And that won't be you." He touched the main screen awake and saw with satisfaction that it now carried feeds from all three traffic-control stations. He could manage traffic for the whole habitat from here, at least once it thinned out some.

"But you won't tell me where you're sending me," Niamne said, and he heard in her voice how young she was.

"I can't," he said gently. He pointed at the hatch. "Go. Now. Make sure all the young ones go with you—mind that! I'm holding you responsible for the count."

"But there's too much to do. You need my help." He heard how close she was to tears.

"You've been a good second," he said. "I've been proud to work with you." He made himself frown fiercely at her. "Don't ruin it all by falling apart now. Tell Drojo I want you, and Frith, and Jack, you three, on the next jumpship out. Not one of the cargo ships, a jumpship."

"What's the hurry?"

Esayeh hesitated. "Where you're going—They'll need control for incoming jumpships. More than they're used to handling. You can man the scanning screens there."

"I wish you'd tell me what this is about," she said.

He found himself smiling at the grimly stubborn expression on her young face. "It will be the best surprise ever," he said. "A gift from your grandmothers going back twenty generations."

"I'll see you there, then," she said doubtfully.

He felt an odd lifting in his chest, a feeling of freedom. When everyone he loved was safe, he could rest.

Soon. He smiled. "Right. Now go."

Still scowling, still suspicious, she turned and pulled herself out through the hatch.

He turned back to the monitors with a frown. He hoped she had not had time to see what was on the scans. Incoming radio traffic from the last ilmenite freighter to appear in-system had said that the Cold Minds were closing in. Big ships jumping in, continuing to jump in, and the scans bore that out. Converging on Triton.

The Cold Minds were going to smash Triton. That much was clear. And then—they would come for his people. To secure their supply of human pilots.

But his people would be gone. Esayeh took hold of the loops of metal on both sides of the local-space summary screen and took a deep breath, then another.

Then he hit the general evacuation alarm.

L innea was watching Iain sip from a pouch of egg broth in Pilang's office, waiting for discharge, when the strange, cold whoop of the alarm began. Iain looked up sharply. Linnea was already moving to the door when the curtain was torn aside and Pilang shot in. "Lin. Get Iain to your ship. Get off *now*."

"What's—"

"Evacuation." Pilang began stuffing extra supplies into her medical kit. "And we won't be back. The Cold Minds are moving in. It's big."

"You come with us, then," Linnea said.

"Can't. I'm surgeon for the evacuation team in this section." Pilang pulled the data crystal from her commscreen, tucked it into a pocket of her work shirt. "Freighters are coming in, rerouting here, we called them all. They dumped their ore out-orbit to make room for people."

"But freighters—they're slow, and they can't jump," Iain said.

"They can move pretty fast with a light load, just people," Pilang said. "They can get us out of the Neptune system. Lin, hand me that hand scanner. . . . They can scatter us in so many directions the Cold Minds can't possibly follow us all. Then we'll pick up the passengers in jumpships as fast as we can. It's the best we can do." She shook her head and sealed her bag, slung onto her back. "Go, now. They have medical facilities at . . . the other end. Iain will be all right for as long as the jump takes." And she was gone.

Linnea looked at Iain. "So they're abandoning this place," she said numbly. "Their home."

"It can't be defended," Iain said, his voice quiet.

"I know," she said. "It's just—so much to lose."

Iain pushed the soup pouch under a storage net, useless neatness probably. She saw again the fine tremor that still remained in his hands. "They'll save the people," Iain said. "That's what matters."

Time to get it out into the open. "What about Triton?"

"Triton?" Iain said. She heard the note of anger in his voice. "You can't expect the deepsiders to worry about Triton."

"Can't I?" Linnea said.

He swung and faced her. In the background the alarm continued its monotonous whoop, and Linnea heard voices—other people who'd come to the clinic to collect supplies, no doubt; and they should be getting to Linnea's ship.

But not until Iain understood what she had to do now.

She looked him in the eye, took a long breath. "Iain, I am not going where Pilang told me to go. Not yet. I have to go to Triton. I'm the only one who can tell them, who *will* tell them where, and how, they can escape this disaster."

"Whatever it is, it's not your secret to tell," Iain said. "You gave your word. You wouldn't even tell me."

"Yes," she said. "I kept to my word. My honor. But—" The words came hard. "But, Iain—by breaking my word, I have a chance to save ten thousand people. To save Triton." She looked at him. "Would you hold back? Should I?"

He did not answer, but she saw the deep relief in his eyes.

"All right," Linnea said, feeling certainty gathering. "Let's go. I need Tereu. And I know just where to find her."

TWENTY-ONE

TRITON

Linnea guided her ship down toward the surface of Triton, toward the waiting docking cradle that would draw it inside the thermal barrier. She'd been given clearance to land as soon as she was able to make Triton Ground believe that she had Perrin Tereu aboard, alive and well. Throughout the last maneuvers, Iain lay strapped onto the instructor's pad, minimally linked in to the ship, silent. Tereu occupied the passenger shell, unlinked but strapped in safely.

Linnea managed the careful, low-acceleration landing—wasteful of fuel, but necessary for Tereu's safety. Her body chemistry and her bones were adapted to Triton's feeble pull. Linnea knew that many more months in zero gee would have an effect even on herself and Iain, one that might complicate their return to the Hidden Worlds. If they returned.

No. When.

"Pilot Kiaho," Triton Control was saying as her ship

settled into its cradle. "You and all passengers will remain aboard until we can verify your passenger's identity."

Linnea pushed her shell open and stepped out, unsteady on her feet after so many days in free fall. Iain was already sitting up, stripping off the ship's leads. "I wish," he muttered, "that you would ever, once, be patient. You could have been safe—"

"And we would never have come here," Linnea said rebelliously. She lifted her chin and faced him. "You caused this, you know," she said. "All of this. You talked Tereu into passing information to the deepsiders. Didn't you see that this would happen?"

"I couldn't let the raids continue," Iain said. He looked grim. "You wouldn't have, either."

"No," she said shortly. "I saw one, Iain."

"Ah. I'm sorry." He touched her shoulder, then rose lightly to his feet and turned toward Tereu, who was just sitting up in her shell. She looked ashen after what would, to her, have been battering acceleration. But she said nothing. She took Iain's arm with a grateful nod and stepped down from the shell.

Tereu had put on, again, the Tritoner dress she'd been wearing when she escaped. There had been no way of properly cleaning it, as it could not simply be washed in water, so she looked rumpled and a little sweat-stained. But to Linnea's eyes, she also seemed to have regained much of her former authority. Perhaps it was the gravity. Perhaps it was being home.

The port inspector arrived, and Linnea permitted him aboard, as she must. There was no question of the outcome. Tereu drew herself to her full height as the inspector entered the aft compartment, and the man practically wilted. "Madame," he said in a strained voice. "A, a pleasure and an honor as always, and even more so to see you safe and . . . well."

"Where is First Pilot Kimura Hiso?" Tereu's voice was steady, with the calm weight of accustomed authority.

"The First Pilot is out on patrol, Madame," the man said. He was tall and thin, but face-to-face with Tereu, with his pale face and eyes and hair, he seemed to be fading into the background. "All ships have been out for two days now. The emergency—"

"Did the First Pilot leave any orders regarding me?"

The man swallowed hard. "The—the patrol hierarchy may know. I have not received any direct orders through my own commander."

"Then I and my guests are free to go," Tereu said. "Thank you, Inspector. I shall remember your helpfulness in future."

The man looked doubtful, almost afraid, but settled for muttering, "Madame."

Tereu swept past him, and Iain and Linnea followed. Though Iain's strength seemed to have returned quickly, Linnea doubted it would last long; she guessed that he needed days, weeks of rest to recover from his ordeal. Not that he would admit to it. He walked at her side, watchful, a hand in the pocket of his tunic.

By Tereu's choice, they went first to her city offices, which were more public and thus safer than her residence; and Linnea was struck by the sense of relief that washed from all those they encountered on the way, even in the corridors. Tereu's own staff crowded into the outer room when Tereu arrived, followed not just by Iain and Linnea but by several city guardsmen, who had resumed their duty of protecting her the moment they saw her pass. It was as if Triton had been in the grip of a sickness, and Tereu had come to cure it. Linnea saw one young assistant hanging back in the shadows, weeping for sheer relief.

Tereu's deputy emerged from her office while Tereu was accepting the congratulations of the staff. She was a sallow, sturdily built young woman who looked strained almost beyond bearing. "Madame!" She hurried forward and gripped Tereu's arms. "Madame, thank God!"

"Merike," Tereu said. "How is my city?"

"The citizens are afraid, Madame," she said. "We need to get word of your return onto the comm system. Nothing would help more at this moment."

"Do that," Tereu said. "And say I will address them all in one hour."

Merike looked tense. "You have news?"

"So I am told," Tereu said cryptically, and waved Linnea and Iain into her office. "Leave us undisturbed until I call you in."

As the door closed on the three of them, Iain felt a sinking sense of worry. The strain and tension of the attack had obviously taken their toll on the whole city. How would the people react? *Could* they react, even to save themselves?

Tereu remained standing, facing Linnea and Iain. "So. Linnea. Tell me of this matter you could never seem to speak of on *Hestia*."

Carefully, clearly, Linnea outlined what she had come to say. That there was a refuge, a habitat, at the rim of the system to which the deepsiders were fleeing. That Linnea knew where it was and could give the jump point to the Tritoner pilots. Iain could sense her watchful tension, but he could see no doubt in her.

"So we could find refuge there?" Tereu shook her head in clear disbelief. "The deepsiders would allow this?"

"Soon it won't matter," Linnea said. "There are no longer two human peoples in this system, whether you see it yet or not, whether the deepsiders accept it yet or not."

"And they don't," Tereu said flatly. "I was there on *Hes-*

tia. I saw them and heard them, when they knew who I was and where I came from. They would leave us to die. I have no doubt that that was their intention."

"That—may be true," Linnea said. "That's why I'm here. To make it impossible."

"But what can we do?" Tereu had sunk into her work chair, sat there now with her hands folded tight before her. Behind her, a commscreen showed a view outside the city, Neptune high above the horizon in a sharp black sky, its bluish light faintly coloring the bleak bitter surface of the moon. "How can we get to this refuge? And why should the deepsiders allow us to stay?"

"You have three times as many ships as the deepsiders do," Linnea said. "Do as they did from *Hestia.* Fill them with people, send them out in all directions. Then when they're out-system, we'll start the rescue operation while the Cold Minds are otherwise occupied."

"Occupied with what?" Tereu looked pale.

"Destroying your city," Iain said gently. "I'm sorry."

At Tereu's look of shock, Linnea spoke. "They *will* destroy it. That's their intention. Remove the human foothold in this system. They don't care if your people die drifting in space. They may follow some of your ships, destroy them, too—but if you stay here, you will all die."

"I know that," Tereu said. She kept her eyes on her clenched hands. "One more question. Why did you return? Why are you helping us? When you know—" She raised her head and looked hard at Iain. "You must know what we, what Hiso, did to your worlds."

Iain saw dawning disbelief in Linnea's eyes, but he only nodded. "He told them where to find us. The other secret, wasn't it, that the First Pilot keeps?"

Tereu nodded stiffly.

"I thought it was so." Iain felt Linnea move close to his side, but he did not touch her.

"He thought you would respond to the attack by coming here in force," Tereu said. "When it didn't happen, from one year to the next—"

"He thought we were stronger than we are," Iain said. "There's nothing to be done about it. Nothing but to try to survive this." Now he could sense that Linnea was calmer. "Madame," he said, "save your people. Call your ships home."

Tereu closed her eyes for a moment. Then slapped the comm control. "Merike. Contact the patrol fleet. Tell them the First Citizen orders them home."

"Hiso," Linnea said. "Can you trust him?"

"We must hope so." Tereu looked stern. "That is the risk you took when you made me this offer. The risk we all take when I accept it."

Iain looked away, slid a hand into the pocket of his tunic. Felt the neural fuser waiting there, unknown to Linnea, to anyone.

Not so much risk, perhaps. Though he had wondered, from the moment he had seen this necessity coming, whether Linnea would understand the need for it. And whether, for all her anger at Hiso, Tereu would let Iain survive the act.

HESTIA

Esayeh floated in the dimness of his control room in the docking ring, struggling against his own tiredness. One or two other older men, former pilots, had agreed to help cover the shifts, now that the young people had been evacuated—but first, they had family to see to safety. And Esayeh understood. One was an oldfather, and the other had a husband in poor health. Esayeh himself had been deeply relieved to see Mick's name, and Hana's, on the last ship's list of passengers when it departed. But getting the others safe was taking too long. He was so tired. . . .

The evacuation was proceeding with all the orderliness Esayeh had come to expect from deepsiders—which was, of course, almost none. But they hadn't panicked. Not yet.

Though their fear was growing—he could feel it. He could see it. He blinked wearily at his commscreen, which showed a line of people moving slowly into the docking tube of the latest ore freighter to arrive. On the comm, when they docked two hours ago, its captain had been as angry and frightened as all of them at the prospect of boosting out of Neptune orbit, heading out into the dark almost at random, to await either the Cold Minds—or a vaguely promised rescue. . . . Frightened as they were, though, most of the habitat dwellers in the line clutched bags of food, blankets—what they would need to keep themselves alive, though certainly not comfortable, for the days they would wait for rescue. Deepsiders might not be predictable, but they had sense.

The opposite of his own people. Esayeh glanced at the nearspace status board, which was updating sluggishly now with so many of the deepsider remote monitors gone missing—as well as many of the Tritoner probes whose transmissions Esayeh had taught the deepsiders to intercept. Yet so far the Cold Minds had done little more than scout the edges of the system. As if they were waiting for something.

Waiting for news.

Esayeh shook his head to clear it. At least Lin had gotten off, and the other pilot, in that fine new ship of hers. Now that was going to be an asset for them all—why, that ship would boost ten people at once, or twelve, do the work of two or three of his little ships. He hoped Lin would get the wounded pilot settled on *Persephone*, in the hospital there if he needed it, and come back here, where she was needed, to start helping with rescue runs from the ships that were safely out of the system. A day or so, maybe, would be all the time she would possibly need. He would be glad to see her. . . .

Somebody was tugging at him, turning him in the air. He had gone to sleep again. He blinked blearily and saw Pilang hanging there upside down to him. He rotated and saw that her expression was haggard, strained. "I thought you'd never wake up," she said. "You get someone else in here to cover this station now, or I won't be responsible for what happens, you understand?"

He looked past her at the commscreen. The freighter had finished loading its full cargo of forty-eight passengers; their names, with their datalinks, stood in a neat list down the right-hand edge of the screen. As he watched, the light over the hatch on the inner end of the docking tube flickered from green to red, and he sensed through the fabric of the habitat the heavy docking clamps disengaging. Radio silence meant that was all the departure notification he would get. "Godspeed," he muttered, then turned to Pilang. "Give me some more of that patch you put on me yesterday," he said. He could hear how thick his voice sounded, and knew she could, too.

She shook her head stubbornly. "You've had enough, old man. Done enough. There's no freighter due for eight hours. You go get a sleep sack in the layover barracks, or I stop helping you at all."

For a moment the prospect of sleep pulled at him, and he sighed heavily, dizzy with longing. But as he reached out to lock down his board, he saw the urgent pulse of the message light. He touched it, and the message flicked onto the commscreen.

He blinked at it in puzzlement. It was a code, but a code he knew well. A recall order—for every Tritoner ship. Even the patrols. *Return to port.* Now?

Then he saw the authorization code at the end of the order. One he knew well.

Tereu.

Tereu, who was supposed to be here on *Hestia*, waiting for the trip home he would arrange when he could.

Which meant she had found another way home. And the only possible ship was—

"Oh, no," Esayeh breathed, and called up the departure logs. Lin's ship had launched twelve hours ago—with three aboard. Three, not two. Jumped as soon as it reached range. But not, it seemed, to *Persephone*.

Lin was on Triton.

Lin knew where *Persephone* was.

He swung to face Pilang. "I need those drugs," he said. "Now. And I need to get to my ship."

"You can't just—"

"Lin is on Triton," he said raggedly. "In a few hours, Kimura Hiso will land there. He'll arrest her. Find out all she knows. And Kimura Hiso is in communication with the Cold Minds."

He saw horror wake in Pilang's eyes. Then she turned away and opened her medkit.

I ain watched, out of pickup range, as Tereu spoke to her people. Linnea stood beside him, expressionless, her hand in his as they listened. There was no turning back now, not for Tereu, not for any of them. Tereu had told her people the truth, the long secret of the Tritoner pilots, and why the bargain must now be repudiated.

"We will not surrender one more child, even a deepsider's child, to the control of those machines," Tereu was saying. She was speaking without notes. "I have chosen for you. Maybe not wisely, but the only choice I saw. We will all be refugees now. A fleeing people. And yet I can offer hope. I can say no more than that: There is hope, more than we ever had here even in the best of our years in our beloved city." Her voice had become unsteady. She looked hard into the pickup. "Trust me. Trust in my love for you. And get ready to board your ships."

Now she did glance down at a datapad. "Assignment

lists will be distributed to neighborhood newsboards. Families with children will receive priority. The rest of us will follow soon after. I know that my pride in you—" Her voice broke, and she waited a moment. "I know that pride is well placed. I know that you will show me, again, that Tritoners face even great fear with calm, and order, and respect for law." She held up her right hand, and her voice steadied. "The oath I made you thousands of days ago binds me now: to protect your lives and our city with all my strength and will, to the last ounce of my blood. Well, you are our city now—the people of Triton. And I will lead you to the stars."

TWENTY-TWO

Esayeh landed at Triton port without clearance; there were no patrol ships to stop him, and he ignored the frantic queries from Control. As he expected, they ordered him to stay in his ship. He considered asking to speak to Tereu; considered trying to send a message, through her, to Pilang. The worst of his regrets was that he had not been able to tell Pilang how long, and how deeply, he had always loved her.

He settled into his piloting chair, waved the cabin lights down, and called up some music. *The* music—his beloved Bach. The endless trove of recordings on *Persephone*, transferred to his ship, had been his companion on many long, lonely jumps over the years, and though his ambition had been to hear all of Bach, somehow he never had. Because there were some he returned to, again and again. He closed his eyes, and his breath caught as the first notes of the massed voices washed over him. In a language long dead, a cry for mercy—a cry that he had never thought would be answered again.

And now, perhaps, against all hope, it had.

But it did not seem to matter, now. He settled back in his chair and gave himself to the music: an intensely human construct, and a noble one, called into existence by a sense of the nearness of God. *Standing on the brink of the infinite*. Whether judgment or reward ever came, for Esayeh or for anyone he loved—whether or not he ever knew it—for now it seemed not so trivial a thing, to have been human. Not so worthless a thing, to have been alive.

He waited, peacefully, for what he knew was coming.

The demand for entry came within the hour. Esayeh silenced the music, rose, and undogged the hatch.

Kimura Hiso stood there, smiling at him. "Suarez Esayeh," he said.

"Not my name any longer." Esayeh studied him. Had he hurt Lin? Or did he not yet know what she could tell him? "Ask my family. They'll tell you."

"Oh, they've forgotten you were ever part of them, I'm sure," Hiso said. "But now it is time for your city to reclaim you, even if your family will not."

Esayeh only looked at him. Kimura Hiso had always talked too much. Sometimes over the years Esayeh had wondered whether Tereu had found Hiso as hard to bear as he did.

"Link in again," Hiso said. "You're going to take me somewhere."

Esayeh shook his head, the weariness coming back as the drugs Pilang had given him wore off. She had warned him that that was truly the last dose, that his heart might not survive another. And she had watched him go, with that look of worry he had so often seen on her face. Because of him.

"You're going to take me," Hiso said, "to *Persephone*."

Esayeh felt the lurch of fear in his chest, making his heart stammer. "I don't know what that is," he said.

"I have known that name for thousands of days," Hiso said. "Just not what it was, or where. Only that it was important—the man who said the name died soon after, without saying anything more."

Esayeh lifted his chin. "The deepsiders don't tell me everything," he said. "They remember where I was born."

"You are their lead pilot," Hiso said. "Don't toy with me. And now I know, from the Hidden Worlds pilot, the woman, that there exists a refuge to which she has persuaded Tereu to lead my people—abandoning their city. Which I will not permit." He smiled. "I intend to give the Cold Minds a much more important gift. And a reason to spare my city."

"You'd trust the Cold Minds to keep a bargain like that?" Esayeh let all his contempt show.

"They kept the last one for centuries," Hiso said. "Now. Take me there. I need the jump point. Then I won't trouble you any further."

"I don't know where it is," Esayeh said.

"Linnea Kiaho would tell me otherwise, I think," Hiso said. "If I asked her. But you'll do this for a better reason than that. You'll do this to save Perrin Tereu."

He looked sharply at Esayeh then, but Esayeh only waited.

Hiso's eyes narrowed. "I give you my word that, if you provide me with this information, Perrin Tereu will live on. In prison, but unharmed."

Esayeh looked down at his hands—then moved to his piloting chair and began snapping the leads into the side of his skull.

Hiso turned and waved the guards off the ship, then sealed the hatch. He turned and faced Esayeh, and in his hand was a knife. It looked wickedly sharp. Esayeh had

always hated knives. . . . "If you go anywhere but the place
I have named," Hiso said, "you die. I can pilot your ship
well enough to return to Triton from anywhere in this system. And as soon as I return, Perrin Tereu and Linnea Kiaho will die. I need the jump point. When I return, safely,
with that, you will be freed, and the women will be safe."

Esayeh felt fairly sure that he knew what kind of freedom Hiso was talking about; but it no longer mattered. Let
him indulge in the kind of honor that put fine words above
mercy, used them to justify cruelty. Hiso finished strap-
ping himself into his acceleration cocoon and gave the order that freed Esayeh's ship to launch.

The music, Esayeh's music, filled his mind as he rose
from the surface of Triton. And as he jumped.

There it was, his dream for so long: *Persephone*. Dark,
immense. From this distance, at this scale, he could see no
signs of ships arriving; yet he knew they must be there. The
rescue of the human race was beginning. The first part.
Manning the lifeboat. He smiled. "Pilot," he said, "have you
the mark?"

"Yes," Hiso breathed. "Oh, yes. They will like this. They
will like it very much."

"They," Esayeh said wearily, "can't *like* anything. Are
you ready to go home?"

"Ready," Hiso said.

"Good," Esayeh said, and jumped.

He heard Hiso's cry of fright, or rage, when he saw the
viewscreen; Esayeh's vision, enhanced by his ship, saw
more than that. The vast dark limb of a world, nightside, a
tracery of pale blue light, far too near below them. And he
saw the Cold Minds picket ships already beginning to
close in.

Earth. He had always wanted to go there.

"Welcome home," he said to Hiso, urged his ship forward, and tore out his piloting leads. A little blood came
with them, but it didn't matter anymore. In his second mo-

tion, gripping the arms of his chair, he raised both feet
above the piloting board, smashed them down. The surface
shattered, bits of metal and plastic scattered everywhere.
His bare feet, soft deepsider feet, were bleeding. He smashed
the board a second time, for good measure. Hiso would
never pilot this ship anywhere.

Esayeh grinned as he saw the first flicker of fire along
the skin of his ship, clear on the viewscreen. He raised his
hands toward the light. And smiled as the other man's fingers gripped his hair; smiled as he died. Then the light
took them both.

TWENTY-THREE

PERSEPHONE

On their first night of rest since the last shipload of refugees came in, Linnea lay side by side with Iain in the soft, fresh grass of the hills outside *Persephone*'s largest town. Linnea was tired, but in a good way. *Persephone* had been kind to them. The five thousand former deepsiders who had been living there all along had expected their own people, but not Tereu's—ten thousand more, but not twenty. As a complete outsider, Linnea had already been called in to mediate more than once. Iain had escaped that, though not other kinds of attention; the town's hospital had reluctantly released him only today. His condition, as a survivor of infestation, still fascinated the Tritoners who had begun to join the hospital staff. Even though none of them need fear infestation again, once they had accepted the deepsider treatments. . . .

She rolled onto her side, still awkward in the half gee, and propped her head on her arm so she could look down at Iain. Faint golden light from overhead shone in his eyes.

The other side of the interior of the habitat, more than a kilometer away, glimmered with lights, as did the moving lifts at each end, rising toward the axis and zero gee; she'd learned that if she watched carefully, she could see them move. But for now she only smiled down at Iain. "Glad to be free again?"

"Free but pinned flat," he growled. "Even when you aren't crushing me down. I liked eight percent better."

"So what will you think of full gee at home?" She smiled again at the thought. They *were* going home. No other ship could make the necessary jump; no other ship could carry this news. Pilang, and now it seemed Hana, would come with them; Pilang's grief over Esayeh had not prevented her from seeing the need for someone expert in the deepsider nano to present the idea in the Hidden Worlds. It was going to be a long fight to get them to accept it.

Iain yawned. "By the time we get to Terranova, I'll have forgotten even half gee again."

"It won't be so rough this time," Linnea said. "We know where we're going. And how far it is."

"And how long an argument we're going to face when we get there," Iain said.

Linnea turned onto her back again and studied the pattern of lights across the sky from them. That dark patch was a lake, she was fairly sure she remembered that much from daytime. She wondered if there were fish in it. Probably. "Our people will want this place," she said. "What's in it. We lost so much, leaving so fast. This is like—like finding a living piece of Earth."

"Almost," Iain said. He turned his head and looked toward the lights on the end cap, where a lift was rising toward the hub.

Linnea had ridden that lift the day before, to see Pilang and Hana—and catch a glimpse of Mick. Most of the deepsiders were still living in the hub, or in the end caps, which did not rotate. "The deepsiders are crowded in those hubs."

"I've heard," Iain said. "Do you think, once they start moving into the Hidden Worlds, that they'll ever learn to live groundside?"

"I think they'd feel even more crowded there," Linnea said. "Held down, held in. . . . Anyway, why should they move groundside? We've got whole systems where we're only using one world. Plenty of room for them to live where they like. How they like."

"If we win," Iain said somberly.

"If we don't lose," Linnea said. "That's about the most we can hope for." She turned to face him. "I wish Esayeh had lived to see his people safe."

Iain looked at her. "He made them safe. He died for the deepsiders."

"Not just for them." Linnea looked up at the lights again, to hold the tears back. "He knew what I was going to do. He could have used the time he had to stop me. But instead he put himself between us and Hiso."

"I know," Iain said quietly. "He saved Triton, too."

Linnea rested her head on his shoulder, and they lay quietly for a while. Then she said, slowly, "Do you regret this? If we hadn't come, we'd still be at home, and maybe the deepsiders and Tritoners would still be where they've always been."

"With the raids, and the fear," Iain said. "No. That was already ending. It had to end. Though it took a man from two worlds to see it."

"And a woman from no world at all to help him," Linnea said.

He caressed her cheek, kissed her gently. "That's always been your gift. To hear what no one else will hear."

She sighed. "I wish we could have saved him."

"Hiso would only have killed you instead," Iain said, his voice deep with anger.

"It's a price I'd have paid," she said. "Ending those raids mattered to me. It still does."

"And you did," Iain said. "Twice now you've helped patch together two halves of humanity—"

"By wrecking all their peace," she said glumly. "And you helped."

"So," he said, "let's go home and wreck our own people's peace again. Maybe in the end we'll be strong enough to win the war."

"Or at least to outlast it," she said. "Yes. Let's go home."

She lay there beside him in the cool, prickling grass, hearing the wind in the trees behind them, and faint music from the town over the hill. A home, built when the old one was lost. Made in necessity, in fear and danger. And yet it was no less a home for the people there because the human race had never been born to such a place. They made it theirs, as her own people had made the Hidden Worlds theirs: by building their lives there. By finding love there. And always, by holding on to hope.

She slid her hand into Iain's and felt his fingers tighten around hers. He had taught her hope, once; and she had taught him the same. And, always, love. The home she'd thought lost—maybe she'd been wrong to think to find it on any one world. Maybe parts of it were everywhere—in the people, and the places, she loved.

And, always, the stars. The stars—and Iain by her side.

ABOUT THE AUTHOR

Kristin Landon lives in Oregon with her husband, a daughter, two occasionally present college-age sons, and a spaniel puppy. In addition to her writing, she works as a freelance copy editor of a wide range of nonfiction and technical books. Visit her website at www.kristinlandon.com.